THERE WAS NOTHING
BUT NOTHINGNESS...

The grayness of hyperspace enclosed Jeff. Now there was no ship to keep him safely in a bubble of normal space. There was only Norby's protective shield, which was invisible, so that Jeff felt utterly lost, surrounded by opaque gray.

Nothing was up, nothing was down, nothing was here, nothing was there—and how long would the nothingness last? Jeff didn't know how long it took Norby to refuel in hyperspace, for the robot had done it alone before. Inside this nothingness beyond nothingness, was it possible to tell how much time was passing? Or did time pass? Jeff had no answers.

A feeling of panic engulfed him when he began to wonder if the meager supply of oxygen trapped inside Norby's personal field would last. He realized that he was panting anxiously, using up the oxygen supply that much more quickly...

JANET AND ISAAC ASIMOV

NORBY: ROBOT FOR HIRE

ACE SCIENCE FICTION BOOKS
NEW YORK

Norby: Robot for Hire has been
previously published as two titles,
Norby and the Lost Princess
and *Norby and the Invaders.*

This Ace Science Fiction book contains
the complete text of the two original
hardcover editions. It has been reset
in a typeface designed for easy
reading and was printed from
new film.

NORBY: ROBOT FOR HIRE

An Ace Science Fiction Book/published by arrangement with
Walker and Company

PRINTING HISTORY
Walker and Company editions published 1985
Ace Science Fiction edition/February 1987

ISBN: 0–441–58635–X

Ace Science Fiction Books are published by
The Berkley Publishing Group,
200 Madison Avenue, New York, New York 10016.
PRINTED IN THE UNITED STATES OF AMERICA

NORBY AND THE LOST PRINCESS

To our favorite other worlds:
Lake Mohonk Mountain House,
Bermuda,
and—most fantastic of all—
the island of Manhattan

1

A New Mission

It was peaceful, for the moment, in the apartment of the Wells brothers. Outside, Manhattan taxis on antigrav were not honking much. Inside, Norby, the Wells's robot, was silently repairing the kitchen computer—once again.

Norby's small metal barrel of a body hovered above the floor, held up by his personal mini-antigrav. His telescoping legs were fully retracted, his double-palmed hands were busy making adjustments, and his rear pair of eyes were firmly shut.

His owner, Jefferson Wells, was quietly studying at the kitchen table. He was fourteen and tall for his age. Sometimes he felt much older because he so often had to cope with problems caused by a mixed-up robot and an adventurous older brother.

Jeff's brother, Fargo, was in the living room about to shatter the peace and make concentration impossible.

Bim! Bam! Boom!

Norby spun once on his axis, and all four of his eyes opened wide. The dome of his built-in hat slammed down as his half face retracted into his barrel. Then it popped up and his eyes glared at Jeff from under the brim of his hat.

"Jeff! Tell Fargo his drumming vibrates my microcircuits!"

Bim, boom, bam, bam, thud . . . "Oh blast, I hit the center again," said Fargo from the living room. Boom, bim, rumble, rumble, bam . . .

When Fargo's penetrating tenor voice began to harmonize with the deep tones of kettledrums, Jeff picked up his ear plugs. He was about to insert them when, over the din of Fargo's drums and Norby's grumbling, he heard the phone ring. He jumped up to switch on the kitchen extension. The imposing face that filled the screen was all too familiar.

Admiral Boris Yobo, while not beautiful like Helen of Troy, looked as if he could launch more ships, and he had. "Cadet!" barked the head of Space Command, "what is that horrible noise?"

"Fargo's composing a tenor tympani concerto with orchestra as a hedge against our not winning the group singing contest. . . ."

"Shut the door! I can't make out what you're saying!"

When it was a little quieter in the kitchen, Jeff looked apprehensively at the large face in the holoscreen. After all, the Admiral had final say about the Space Academy and about Jeff's scholarship there. He was also the confidential employer of a twenty-four-year-old secret agent named Farley Gordon (Fargo) Wells. Jeff was relieved, therefore, to see a broad smile reach the velvet black of Yobo's high cheekbones.

Unfortunately the smile promptly disappeared. "What? Spending your vacations on a singing contest? A waste of time!"

"Yes, sir. You're right, sir," said Jeff.

"You're *more* than right, Admiral," put in Norby. "I disapprove of singing; especially when I'm not allowed to join in."

"You sing off key," said Jeff.

"Whether off key or on key, singing is irrelevant to the realities of the situation," rumbled the Admiral. "I'm thinking about our last joint mission, the one to the planet of the dragons—"

"Jamya," said Jeff, who liked dragons as long as they were small and civilized.

"—and I have a new mission for you and Fargo—"

"And me!" shouted Norby. "They can't do without me! They can't even get beyond the Solar System without me!"

"Yes, yes. You go wherever Jeff goes. That's understood," said the Admiral. "Norby, I want you to take Fargo and Jeff on a search for a group of humans who may have been taken from Earth during the Ice Age. Find out if those mysterious aliens, the Others, left any data on the planet Jamya that might reveal *where* those lost humans were taken."

"But Admiral," said Jeff, "You can't ask us to do that on our vacation. Fargo's got his heart set on winning the big Federation singing contest. Even if Norby can make the *Hopeful* work on his hyperdrive again, we wouldn't have time to go on a search. And besides the contest, I have to be back in the Academy in a week."

"This is more important than contests *or* your Academy studies, Jeff. Federation scientists aren't getting anywhere in cracking the secret of antigrav that is miniaturized like Norby's. We have the Jamyn antigrav collar you gave to my lab, but we still haven't figured out how it works. And since mini-antigrav seems to be the key to Norby's ability to travel in hyperspace, the Federation needs it or we Terrans will remain confined to our own Solar System, deprived of interstellar exploration."

"I wish I could tell you how I travel in hyperspace," said Norby, "but I don't know. I'm sorry I can't be of more help, Admiral."

"Humph!" said the Admiral. "Sometimes I'm sorry I've kept your secrets. Nobody knows about Norby's hyperdrive but the three of us and Fargo, and that cop he associates with. Nobody else knows that most of Norby is an alien device from the planet Jamya, manufactured by those enormous Jamyn robots who were made by the Others. We owe it to the Federation to find . . ."

"But Admiral," Jeff interrupted, "not even the Jamyn robots know how to make Norby's special abilities again. The old Terran spacer, MacGillicuddy, must have accidentally created them when he found Norby's alien parts on one of our asteroids."

"That's what I'm getting at," said the Admiral. "The Others certainly had hyperdrive, and if we can't catch up with them to find out how they did—or do it, then we must track down anybody who had contact with the Others. Therefore, Cadet, go find those lost humans!"

Jeff realized that the living room was quiet. Was Fargo listening?

"But did the Others actually visit Earth?" asked Jeff, stalling.

"Certainly," said the Admiral. "Your All-Purpose-Pet, Oola, is proof of that. She was bio-engineered from Ice Age cave bears and saber-tooth tigers or something. Fortunately she was made smaller. And you told me that the Jamyn robots have a legend about Oola's ancestors and some human beings from Earth who were removed by the Others and taken someplace else."

Jeff looked around. "Where *is* Oola, Norby?"

"Under the bed in the bedroom. Or in it, with her head under the pillow," Norby answered. "She's not fond of tympani. I wouldn't be surprised if she grows her leather shell around her and hibernates."

At the sound of a slight hiss, Jeff looked up to see Fargo's handsome face poking around the door. Fargo put his finger to his lips; he was not within range of sight from the screen.

"Cadet, are you paying attention to me?" asked Yobo, scowling. "I repeat—I want you to find those missing human beings. Aside from everything else, they may have been enslaved and, considering my African ancestry, I have a particular dislike for the notion of slavery. Got it?"

"Yes, sir."

"That's all, then, Wells. You have your orders."

"Yes, sir."

When the screen was safely blank, Jeff sighed. "Why am I always sent off on strange ventures when I've planned to do something else?"

"We'll do both," said Fargo, drumming his fingers against the wall. "We'll zip out to look for lost humans and zip back for the contest. No trouble at all."

Jeff ran his fingers through his curly brown hair in exasperation. His brother could never resist an adventure and never imagined that he'd run into any trouble.

"Fargo, how can we zip out and back when we don't know where they are?"

"*I* will find out," said Norby, who could never resist sounding important. "While you and Fargo are outfitting the *Hopeful*, *I* will zip out to Jamya and search the main computer's memory banks for any data about the lost human beings."

"And meanwhile," said Jeff plaintively, "you haven't even fixed the kitchen computer for our dinner tonight."

"I have too. Hold out that bowl. Perfectly tossed salad on its way!"

Jeff leaped forward with the salad bowl just in time to get heavily seasoned greens full in the face. "You've tossed the salad in the wrong direction, Norby! The funnel has to point down, not up!"

Fargo had disappeared—he always did when there was something to be cleaned up—but as Jeff picked lettuce from his hair, a small green animal resembling a cat trotted into the kitchen and patted him on the leg.

"Wowrr?"

"It's all yours, Oola," said Jeff. "Eat away."

Although bio-engineered from carnivores, Oola was a vegetarian and particularly enjoyed salad, even on the floor. As she went from leaf to leaf munching, the cause of the mess—Norby—telescoped his legs outward as he sank to a standing position between two clumps of lettuce.

"It was only a small mistake, Jeff," Norby said contritely, "but I'm making a large apology. I'll go at once to Jamya before anything else spills." With that, he withdrew the whole way into his barrel, elevated on his antigrav, and suddenly vanished.

Norby's disappearing act always unnerved Jeff. Hyperspace is the basic fabric of the universe and exists everywhere, so one can move into it from any point at all. But the resulting disappearance from normal space is disconcerting to observers.

During dinner Oola burped ominously while Jeff picked at his food.

"Don't worry," said Fargo. "Oola's just a little under the weather from eating a two-man portion of salad."

"It's not Oola I'm worried about, it's Norby. I forgot to tell him to hurry back. Maybe he's mad because I yelled at him. Maybe he'll want to stay on Jamya with the robots there."

"Norby is part Terran and will be back," Fargo said firmly.

"If he doesn't, we can't go and get him."

"Not until Yobo's scientists invent hyperdrive, I'm afraid."

"Erp," said Oola, and decided to give a lot of salad back to the floor.

"This time," said Jeff, "*you* clean it up, Fargo. The housekeeping robot is working only spottily since Norby adjusted the circuits."

"All right," said Fargo, "but let's leave Oola home. We'll get a cat-sitter."

"We can't. Anybody who comes to feed her will find out that if you think about any animal long enough, Oola is likely to change into that animal's form. And who would believe in a vegetarian cat? The zoo officials will pick her up and we'll never see her again."

"Then we'll have to watch her tendency to overeat," Fargo said, as he reluctantly got to work.

The next day, although Norby had still not appeared, Fargo and Jeff kept reassuring one another that he would return any minute. And they proceeded to ready the *Hopeful*, which (by special permission of the city under pressure from the Admiral), was parked on the roof of their apartment building.

Just as Jeff had put in the last of the supplies, the door to the roof opened, and Fargo's cop emerged. Manhattan Police Lieutenant Albany Jones—blonde, beautiful, and incredibly brave— was exactly Fargo's age. (Worse luck, thought Jeff, who liked her a lot in a bashful way.)

"Hi, Albany," shouted Fargo, "Come aboard. Jeff, did I remember to tell you that I invited Albany to come with us? Actually, we need a soprano, but Albany's contralto will just have to substitute."

"Thanks a lot. It's so thrilling to be a substitute," said Albany. She carried her suitcase into the *Hopeful*. "Where's Oola?"

"Still in the apartment, recovering from indigestion," said Jeff. "I'm glad you're coming, Albany. You're the only one who can keep Fargo in line, and I've got to get back in a week."

"Don't listen to Young Man Gloom, Albany," Fargo said airily. "We'll be back long before that, in time for the singing contest."

"And just where is it that we're going?" asked Albany.

"Nowhere, unless Norby shows up," muttered Jeff.

"Come into the control room and I'll explain," said Fargo.

Jeff, shaking his head, stepped to the roof door and promptly collided with Admiral Yobo in his full dress uniform, medals dangling on his huge chest and a large suitcase in his hand. "Well, Cadet," he boomed, "is that robot back yet? We've got to get on with it."

"But Admiral—"

"I decided to join the crew. Since you and Fargo are orphans, you need someone older and wiser—"

"But Fargo's supposed to be my guardian, Admiral."

"I think that makes my point, Cadet," said Yobo.

"Yes, sir. You are very welcome, Admiral. Albany Jones is coming with us, too."

"Ah," said Yobo, smiling broadly. "Then there will be at least two sane persons aboard. And I've brought some interesting music we can practice during the mission. I've thought it over and decided to join your group for the singing contest. You need a bass."

"That's true," said Jeff. "I'm a baritone now, but my voice still cracks now and then. You'll be a useful addition, Admiral."

They entered the *Hopeful* and Yobo, staring at a dim corner of the control room said, "What have you got there? Oversized turtles?"

"My tympani," said Fargo. "I haven't set them up yet, but when I do, I'll tune them to your bass voice, Admiral. Perhaps my tympani-tenor masterpiece should be turned into a quartet."

Without warning, the control room grew more crowded still as a metal barrel and a small green dragon appeared in the middle of it. Jeff gave a cry of relief.

"I'm back," said Norby. "Mission accomplished. I found coordinates for a planet where the lost humans are supposed to be. All I have to do is feed the coordinates into the *Hopeful*'s computer and we'll be off."

"But why have you brought Zargl?" asked Fargo. "She's welcome, of course, but—"

"I'm not going with you," the little dragon said, spreading her leathery green wings and flying (with the assistance of her Jamyn antigrav collar) to Yobo's big shoulder. Switching to the Jamyn language because Terran Basic was still hard for her, she said, "I asked Norby if I might stay in your apartment while you're gone so that I can practice your difficult language by watching your holoTV."

"Do you have your mother's permission?" Jeff asked in Jamyn.

"She does," said Norby. "Zi wants Zargl to be able to speak Terran Basic perfectly."

"I wish I could understand what you're all saying," said Albany.

"You will," said Fargo. "Zargl, give Albany a little nip."

Surprised but stalwart, Albany stood firm when Zargl flew to her shoulder and gave the back of her neck a slight nip.

"There," said Jeff. "In a short while, you'll begin to understand the Jamyn language, Albany. The rest of us were nipped when we visited Jamya. A dragon bite makes you able to talk telepathically to anyone else who's been bitten, if you touch them while you're doing it. And the dragons have a way of teaching Jamyn quickly through telepathy. Zargl, take Albany down to the living room and teach her while we get ready."

Fargo said, "And have Albany teach you how to feed Oola, because I think we ought to leave her behind with you."

"Okay," said Zargl in passable Terran Basic. "I'll send Albany back up when she's ready, and I'll say goodbye now. Have a good time, Admiral."

"Thank you, Zargl."

"And Jeff," added Zargl, "don't let Fargo get into trouble."

"That's been said to me all my life," said Jeff.

2

The Planet, Izz

"A wandering minstrel I, a thing of shreds and patches, of ballads, songs and—"

"Fargo," said Admiral Yobo, putting down his sheet music and massaging his bald head, "I do not believe Gilbert and Sullivan intended for that tenor aria to be accompanied by nothing but kettledrums, especially when we're all tense from watching Norby make three passes at those planetary coordinates and getting each one wrong."

Albany yawned. "I never realized what it would be like to be stuck in hyperspace. I'm tired of looking at that peculiar gray in the viewscreen."

"Maybe I'd have found the planet by now," Norby said peevishly, "if I'd been allowed to relax my emotive circuits by singing too."

"You're still as off key as ever," Fargo said as he fondled a drumstick. "You put *our* singing off. Way off."

"That's just your opinion. I think my electronic voice is very beautiful. Anyway, with that quartet you tried, and that awful tympani-tenor concerto, you have some nerve telling me that *I'm* off key."

Before Fargo could continue the argument, Jeff said quickly, "Let's all be silent while Norby tries for the coordinates one more time. Remember that this hyperspace jump is difficult because the coordinates are just numbers from the data bank of the Jamyn computer. We don't know anything more about the planet we're trying to reach."

Albany brushed back her long hair and said, "There's one thing that bothers me. Shouldn't we discuss what we're going to do when and if we get to this alien planet? All we seem to do is practice for the contest. Surely this mission is a *little* more important."

"Um," said the Admiral, who had gotten them all on a mission only to absorb himself in music.

"What's to discuss?" said Fargo, who hated advance planning.

"A great deal," she said. "The human beings we're looking for are likely to believe they're the only humans in the Universe. Unless the Others told them about their origins, these humans will think they originated on the planet they're on now instead of on Earth. They may consider us alien, and be unfriendly. Shouldn't we try to learn more about them before we land?"

"Right on, Lieutenant," said Yobo. "We should have Norby bring the *Hopeful* just far enough away from their planet so we'll be unobserved but still able to tune into their broadcasts, if they have that technology by now."

"The Jamyn dragons have the technology," said Jeff, "because the Others gave it to them. So I imagine that the lost humans have it too."

"I wish you'd all stop talking," said Norby, waving his arms. "Noise, noise, noise. Just leave me to myself and let me try again."

Everyone became silent, including Norby. He put his hands back on the control panel and seemed to freeze for a moment. Suddenly the ship was no longer enclosed by the gray of hyperspace.

"Ah," said Yobo with satisfaction.

"Wow!" said Jeff. "Look at that!"

They all crowded to the main viewscreen. In it was a beautiful planet, wreathed in clouds that parted to show patches of blue.

"I told you I could do it," said Norby.

"You sure did," said Jeff. "From what we can see, it may be a little like Jamya. One big land mass in the ocean, and—"

"Look!" they all shouted simultaneously.

"Spomes!" said Jeff. "All around us!"

Space-homes, or "spomes," had been in use as artificial orbital space settlements for many years back home. It was clear that these displaced human beings had them, too.

"I've got something on radio—no—holoTV," cried Norby. "These humans are technologically advanced."

Jeff turned up the sound and they all studied the screen.

The voice and face on the screen seemed human indeed. The language was a strangely accented Jamyn with many new words. A loose—very loose—translation was something like this: "And now for an update on the news. King Fizzwell has announced that due to the tragic loss of the pioneer interstellar ship, he will not throw out the first gweig at the opening game of the gwo-gwo season this afternoon—"

"What's he wearing?" asked Albany. "It looks like a night-shirt."

The announcer was clothed in a shimmering garment that fell loosely from his shoulders, very much like an old-fashioned nightshirt. His hair was braided around his head and his beard was braided, too, with a clip at the end.

"Find us another news broadcast," said Yobo. "If these people have interstellar travel, then they're way ahead of the Federation."

"They used the term 'pioneer' ship," said Fargo. "That may mean 'first'—or even 'only'."

"Here's another broadcast," said Norby.

Another face and voice appeared, this one female and of a different hue and shape of eye from the first, indicating that the Others had selected human specimens from different parts of the Earth. "The last broadcast from the missing ship, *Challenger*, has now been released to the general public. Since the broadcast is of sound only, we will now show Princess Rinda's favorite portrait of herself."

The announcer's face was replaced by that of a beautiful girl with unbraided coils of scarlet hair piled on her head, surmounted by a wedge-shaped hat so jeweled that it was obviously a crown. Her shimmering nightshirt was overlaid by fantastic capes trimmed with jewels. Her cool, aristocratic face was a little fuzzy, as if the painter's eyes had been filled with reverent tears while he painted.

"Hello, everybody," said a lilting soprano voice. "This is Princess Rinda, speaking from a newly discovered planet I have named 'Melodia.' Captain Erig wants me to tell you that it's an Izz-type planet—that means we can breathe the air—but it's not anywhere near as beautiful as Izz, of course. The Captain says she thinks the coordinates for this planet must have been accidentally programmed into the ship's computer, and would the Court Scientist please determine how this could have happened?

"Oh—what? Oh, yes, I'm also supposed to tell you that this broadcast is being sent by tape-packet jetted beyond the planet's weird electronic field, which seems to prevent Izztio broadcasts from the planet's surface, so you can only hear; you can't see. This is a shame because I'd like you to be able to see the natives, who are very friendly, and who really appreciate my voice. Oh—yes. The fruit and vegetables are edible, too.

"I'm just thrilled to be the first to discover a new planet, and now I have to sign off because we're going to a concert that will take place around a lovely tree in a sort of courtyard. I expect that I'll be requested to sing. The library robot can't make any sense of the native language, but it doesn't matter because they get their ideas across. This will be a great place for tourists from Izz, and—yes, Captain Erig, I'm almost finished—we'll be leaving for home in a few days. And now I'll sign off and go to the concert. Love to—"

The sound broke off abruptly and the announcer's face came back on the screen. "There is no hint of real danger in that broadcast except for the mention of a strange electronic field that deactivates the usual form of communication. Still, the sound was broken off suddenly, and it has been two weeks since that broadcast was received. Because there have been no further communications, there is great alarm at Court, and the Court Scientist says he is working on another interstellar ship to send on a retrieval mission.

"The planet Izz and its satellite colonies have been plunged into deep concern for our beloved Princess. Proper contemplation of the Infinite will take place before the start of the gwo-gwo game, accompanied by the Izz National Anthem."

As the music started, the portrait of Princess Rinda came back on the screen.

Fargo said, "A stunner, isn't she?"

"I am not amused," said Albany. "She's beautiful, probably rich, undoubtedly spoiled and thoroughly rotten to live with. On top of that their National Anthem is excessively boring."

"Rich?" said Fargo. "Now there's a thought. Did you notice her jewels? All we have to do is rescue her and the Izz royal family no doubt will shower us with rewards."

"That would help provide funds for the Federation's scientists to discover hyperdrive," said Yobo thoughtfully. "Or we might ask for the Izzian system of hyperdrive, directly, as our reward."

"Wait," said Norby. "Listen!"

Another newscaster, wearing a plainer nightshirt that shimmered only slightly came on and said, "Attention! It has just been announced that our space patrol has discovered an unknown ship in orbit around Izz. This may have something to do with our lost Princess. Patrol ships are closing in on the unknown ship with gravity grapples—"

"Norby," said Yobo, "take us into hyperspace at once."

"Too late," said Norby. "Whatever those gravity grapples are, they already have a tight grip on the *Hopeful*'s engine. We're being drawn toward the planet—see those little cruisers ahead? They're pulling us."

Fargo went back to his drums and tuned them carefully. Then he began humming softly a rather pleasant version of the Izz National Anthem, accompanying himself by light tapping on the drums.

"Aren't you even a little bit worried?" asked Jeff.

"Not at all," said Fargo. "We, you see, have the goods—the only working interstellar ship in the vicinity—"

"Only because you've got a robot whose hyperdrive makes it work," said Norby.

"Correct, my little metal barrel," said Fargo. "But they don't know that, do they? We have something to sell—a rescue mission. This won't be just an Adventure—it will also be a business venture."

Once on the planet, Jeff wondered if Fargo's optimism had been justified. The welcoming committee, if that was what it was, wore shimmering nightshirts that seemed as stiffly formal as uniforms. Perhaps they *were* uniforms. And the committee members didn't look friendly, either.

"Shall I open the airlock?" asked Norby, after a bumpy landing on what looked like lavender moss. They were in a town square bordered by odd buildings. A strange looking edifice at the far side could only be the Royal Palace, judging from the lavish gardens in its front yard.

"Certainly," said Fargo. "How else are we going to sell ourselves as rescuers of the fair Princess?"

"Don't think you get to keep her after the rescue," said Albany.

"And the decision on opening the airlock is mine to make," said the Admiral. "I am the senior officer present—"

"Interlopers!" shouted a voice in Izzian, through the loudspeaker system of the *Hopeful*. "We are the planetary police. We have control of your ship. Emerge at once! You are under arrest in the name of Queen Tizz and King Fizzwell."

"Arrests are my department," said Albany, serenely, tightening the belt of her dress uniform. "Once we get out *I'll* handle it."

Fargo said, "All right, Lieutenant Jones, my love. It's your party if you want it."

As usual, Jeff was the only one who seemed deeply concerned over their plight. He wondered whether the Izzians would thaw out if the Terrans sang their contest songs. How do you make friends with long-lost relatives—human beings who don't know the Earth exists?

When they had all emerged from the airlock and were standing at attention—Albany in front—Fargo said, "Look at that palace again. Doesn't that look like gold paint?"

"Not paint," rumbled Yobo. "Sheets of yellow metal—and if that's gold—"

"It *is* gold," said Norby. "The ship's scanners figured that out. Didn't I tell you?"

"You did not," Yobo said grimly.

"Sorry. There's lots of gold all over the place. Even the holsters holding the weapons of the police are gold."

"Weapons?" Jeff saw that what he had thought were decorative sets of straps on each of the Izzian police were indeed holsters containing weapons. Each police officer wore a gold helmet, too.

Fargo said, "We'll be rich. If we walk off with a few of those helmets—"

"Silence," rapped out the female leader of the police—in Izzian, of course. Her hair stuck out from under her helmet in tiny pigtails. "Communication in code is against the law. You are also breaking the law in the way you wear your hair. Unbraided hair is a royal prerogative." She pointed to Yobo, "And shaving the hair is *no one's* prerogative."

Albany took a step forward, coming to a halt with a loud click of heels and a snappy salute.

"Greetings," she said in passable Jamyn, which resembled Izzian sufficiently to be comprehensible. "I am—" she searched for a suitable Jamyn word "—an unbraided lieutenant representing the armed forces of Manhattan. We have come to speak to Their Majesties about the Princess Rinda."

The police chief looked astonished. "Are you from the planet Melodia? We were not given to understand that the Melodians were Izzoid in appearance."

"We are not Izzoid," said Albany frostily. "We are as Izzian as you are, but of another tribe, a lost Izzian tribe from another planet in another part of the Galaxy, far away."

"That's impossible," said the Izzian police chief. "We are the only Izzians. You are under arrest for additional infractions—spacing without a license, arriving under false pretenses, impersonating unbraided Izzians, carrying contraband goods—"

"What contraband goods?" Albany asked scornfully.

"In that barrel," said the Izzian police person, pointing to Norby. Norby was, of course, entirely closed up and in Jeff's arms—the standard way of hiding his robotic nature.

"Seize them," commanded the Izzian police chief, and her underlings surrounded the Terrans. They drew out chains that were golden but, under the circumstances, ugly. They had strange but serviceable locks.

"Handcuffs," muttered Yobo. "How humiliating."

"Stop, stop!" A gravelly voice cried out from the direction of the palace. "In the name of Queen Tizz—and King Fizzwell, of course—I insist that you stop arresting these people!" The man leaped over a bed of orange flowers and headed straight for the Izzian chief of police.

He was very tall and very thin, with pale yellow hair in a long pigtail. His thin yellow beard hung limply beneath his chin in two braids. On his oddly short nightshirt was a gold medallion containing a bright red gem and, emerging from under the stiff gown was a pair of baggy pants that fitted inside his pointed shoes. He was followed by a robot, more human-looking than ordinary Terran work-robots, but just as blank-faced.

"What is he?" whispered Fargo, "the palace clown? Why does he have a robot?"

"I don't know," said Jeff, "but have you noticed that the gardeners are robots?"

The Izzian police chief, who was almost as tall as the newcomer, looked at him with an obvious lack of friendliness. "Do you have written permission from the Queen, Scientist Einkan?"

"*Court* Scientist Einkan," said the Izzian with the pants. "In this emergency, I need none. I have brought one of my robots to help escort these strangers to the palace."

"Without written orders from the Queen, I cannot release these dangerous criminals."

"Stupid!" hissed Einkan. "These are obviously Izzians, and they come here with a hyperdrive ship. *My* new hyperdrive ship is not yet ready. We need *this* ship to rescue the Princess, and we need *these* Izzians to pilot that ship. If you impede this mission, Officer Luka, you are endangering the Princess's life. The Queen will be *displeased*."

The emphasis on the last word made it sound deadly, and Officer Luka blinked. "Very well. Take them to the Queen, but witness that I have released them reluctantly, without written permission."

Einkan strode up to Albany. "You are in charge, of course?"

Albany stifled a grin. "Of course."

"Permit me to introduce myself. I am Einkan, Court Scientist, and I will escort you to the Queen." He smiled and took Albany's arm.

Officer Luka and her police stepped aside, and the Terran expeditionary force followed Einkan and Albany. Fargo frowned and looked annoyed as Einkan drew Albany close to himself. Fargo moved forward to listen.

Einkan said, "Luka's a good police person, but we do not get along. I was one of her early husbands and it was no good. I was much too dominant for her tastes. You are very beautiful, my dear . . . what did you say your name was?"

"I didn't. I'm Albany Jones. Lieutenant Albany Jones."

"Albany. A romantic name. Do you disapprove of a strong strain of dominance in a male?"

Albany unwrapped Einkan's arm as it ventured around her waist. "What I disapprove of are males who do not answer my questions. First, I would like to know how many interstellar ships you have."

"Only the one, the *Challenger* that, alas, our beloved Princess insisted on accompanying during its maiden voyage. I invented the hyperdrive for the ship, but I have not yet put together another engine for the next ship. How could I know that the Princess—and the *Challenger*— would not return?"

"How indeed?" said Albany. "Then it will be necessary for you to take our ship and find the Princess?"

"Indubitably."

Yobo intervened angrily, "Do you think we will permit that?"

Einkan looked back at Yobo, who was his same height but twice as wide. "How did you get permission to do without hair on your head, sir?"

"Do *without?*" roared Yobo. "Do you think I shave my head?"

"How else would you not have hair?" said Einkan, skirting a bed of flowers in shades of pink.

"Admiral," said Jeff, switching to Terran Basic. "These humans may have descended from people lacking genes for baldness."

"That is their loss, Cadet. Baldness is cleaner and more impressive."

Jeff said, "Yes, sir." He turned to the Izzian robot walking stolidly at his side. "Do you help the Court Scientist in his laboratory?" he asked.

"I do what I am told."

"How do you feel about that?"

"I do not feel. I serve."

"Did you help invent the hyperdrive engine?"

"I helped install it."

"Did you watch the Court Scientist invent it?''

"I do not watch. I serve."

The robot walked away into a small doorway off to the side of the broad marble steps leading to the double front doors of the Palace. Einkan headed that way, too.

"Just a minute," said Yobo. "Why are we not going up the front steps? Is this the way visiting dignitaries are treated?"

"We must first have a conference on hyperdrive in my laboratory," said Einkan. "You know, of course, how to work a hyperdrive engine, beautiful Lieutenant Jones."

"Umm," said Albany, who didn't really know.

"Good," said Einkan. "You and I will confer while these others wait. Then you and I will go to rescue the Princess, while these others stay behind."

"That will be impossible," said Albany. "My colleagues are all essential to the running of the ship."

Einkan looked disappointed. "Are you sure? Oh, that's too bad."

A disembodied voice suddenly assailed their eardrums.

"Einkan, you numbskull. How dare you take matters into your own hands? Bring those strangers to the throne room at once or I will send you to the Courtyard of Guilt to be immersed for several days in the Pool of Plurf!"

Einkan sighed. "Yes, your Queenness."

3

A Question of Rescue

The matter of the Queen's disembodied voice did not long remain a mystery, for along the walls of the Royal Palace were decorative gold trumpets that were clearly loud-speakers.

Einkan and the Terrans, with Jeff still holding Norby, marched up the wide front palace steps to the huge front door, where purple-nightshirted robots stood stolidly on each side. The gold-panelled door slid open.

"Hasten," said the Queen, from a gold bas-relief of a lion on the ceiling of the entrance hall.

This time there was not even a moment's delay in detecting the source of the voice.

"A lion?" Jeff remarked, looking up. "The Others must have brought some of Earth's animals here, too."

"Silence!" said Einkan. "Do not use that non-Izzian communication code, and keep quiet altogether if you know what's good for you." Clasping Albany's arm in a possessive grip, the Court Scientist hurried down the hall to a set of double doors that slid open at his approach.

Two more purple-clad robot guards were just inside the doors, and they lifted their arms as the Terrans approached.

"Hail to the Queen!" they shouted.

"Bow your heads," muttered Einkan, bending his own neck and moving forward slowly.

The Terrans followed, their heads bowed so that they could see only their feet.

Norby, who was in physical contact with Jeff, finally dared to attempt telepathic contact with him.

——I don't like her. She's the only Izzian I've seen with short hair and a nasty scowl.

———Have you got your hat up, Norby?

———Just a little, Jeff. Enough to see Their Miserable Majesties. They're sitting on what look like solid gold thrones.

Einkan stopped abruptly, jerking Albany to a stop, too. The three Terrans, walking abreast behind them, promptly bumped into the two ahead, and Jeff tripped over Einkan's feet. All five fell to the ground.

In the process, Jeff, not surprisingly, dropped Norby. There was, however, no resulting sound of a thump. Norby managed to get his personal antigrav into operation before he hit the ground, and as he hovered in the air, one extensible arm stretched out toward Jeff. Norby's fingers clutched his owner's ear.

"You dropped me!" Norby cried out, oblivious to all else in his indignation. "I might have been dented."

"Aha!" said a deep, female voice. "What has been masquerading as a metallic container is actually an oddly shaped undersized robot. There is not much chance of fooling *me* with such charades. Bring that object to me."

Jeff clambered to his feet and gazed at the thrones over the prone bodies of the others.

On the throne to Jeff's right was a mild-faced man with no beard, his curly red hair, unbraided, reaching to his shoulders. He wore a plain gold crown topped with little spikes and he looked tired. Jeff was sure he was King Fizzwell.

On the other throne sat a woman who was somewhat larger than the King in every direction. Her brown hair reached only to her ears, and there wasn't a braid in sight. She had prominent brown eyes, an immense array of jewels on her shimmering nightshirt, and an unpleasant expression on her regally handsome face.

As Jeff bowed to Their Majesties, he leaned slightly more to his left because he had the distinct feeling that Queen Tizz ran the show. Norby had by now settled back into Jeff's arms and was doing his best to look like an innocent barrel that had never been anything else. But, of course, he was fooling no one but himself, and not even himself very much.

"So, Einkan," said the Queen in a nasty nasal tone, "you were planning to hide these odd strangers from me; and their strange little robot, too."

"Not at all, Your Graciousness. I was merely planning to interview them before introducing them to Your Royal Majesties. Better that they should waste my insignificant time than yours that is so vitally important."

"I'll bet," said the Queen. "And I suppose you have forgotten I disapprove of garments that enclose each leg separately?"

"My humble apologies and most sincere regrets. It was an experiment that has clearly failed. I will remove them—"

"Not here, you fool! Your tunic is too short." The Queen leaned forward and frowned. "Is it true that these odd Izzians have a hyperdrive ship?"

"Quite true, Your Izziness."

"Where did they get it?"

Einkan's pointed-toe shoes seemed to curl a bit further. He turned to Albany and tugged nervously at his braided beard. "Explain the situation, Lieutenant."

Albany bowed to the King, which brought a deeper frown on the Queen's face. She said, "Your Highnesses, we come from far away—"

"I have been told where you come from," said the Queen, "and I disapprove of having any section of Izz possess so idiotic a name as Manhattan."

"Manhattan is an island, Your Highness," said Albany.

"And far, far away," added Fargo.

"Quiet!" shouted the Queen. "I am talking to your leader."

Admiral Yobo growled.

"It really doesn't matter where we are from or where we got our ship," said Albany. "We are offering our services and you dare not refuse them if you love your daughter. We can rescue Princess Rinda."

"And we are the only ones who can," said Yobo.

"Indubitably," said Fargo in a passable imitation of Einkan's voice.

Jeff grinned and at once tried to suppress it.

"Then go and do it," said the Queen. "Don't stand here and talk about it. Which reminds me—did I, or did I not, at least one hour ago, order that the small robot be brought to me? Why is it, then, that I do not have it? Guards, seize that robot *at once*. It will serve as hostage and it will be released to you *after* you return with the Princess—and not before."

As two robot guards converged on Jeff, Norby shot up to the high domed ceiling—but so did the guards. They seized him and brought him down.

"Mini-antigrav!" said Yobo. "These blasted Izzians have it, too! No wonder they were able to make an interstellar ship."

"But Admiral," whispered Fargo, "why did they only make *one* ship?"

"Stop that whispering!" commanded the Queen. "Leave at once to rescue the Princess while the Court Scientist studies the internal workings of your robot."

"No!" cried Jeff.

Albany turned back to Yobo and Fargo and spoke in Terran Basic. "I'm going to have to tell them that Norby is what makes our interstellar ship work."

"No!" said Fargo. "I'll think of something. Let me reason with this woman."

"She's not reasonable," said Jeff. "She's awful."

"Queenness," said the two robot guards simultaneously. "The new robot has disappeared from our very grip."

"Where did she go?" asked the King, speaking for the first time and looking more wide awake than before. Perhaps it was not often that he saw the Queen's wishes thwarted.

"Well, you heard the King," said the Queen to Jeff. "Tell him where the robot went."

Jeff could not help smiling. "He must have gone out the door, Your Highness. And Norby's a 'he', not a 'she'."

"Nonsense," said the Queen haughtily. "By my decree, all robots are female."

Einkan bowed. "Your Graciousness, perhaps it would be best if we leave the robot be for a while, since it is clearly only a toy of this impertinent youth. Why not keep the youth as hostage in place of the robot, and study *his* internal workings? Meanwhile, I will accompany these people on their rescue mission—"

"Don't be ridiculous," said the Queen. "You have to work on the second hyperdrive ship."

"My laboratory robots are doing that," Einkan said suavely. "If I am on the rescue mission, and it turns out that something has gone wrong with the *Challenger's* engines, only I can repair them. Besides, you wouldn't want to rely on these strangers to treat your daughter with appropriate respect. Who knows what they might do to her before they bring her back if I am not with them to prevent it."

"Well—" the Queen demurred. "There *is* something to that. Royal dignity and decorum must be preserved. Very well, go with them. But go at once."

Queen Tizz settled back on her throne and closed her eyes. In a moment she was snoring.

King Fizzwell beamed at Jeff and whispered, "Better go at once, brave youth, before she wakes and changes her mind. Please bring back my daughter unharmed, because I love her dearly. And *do* remember she is an Izzian Princess. Treat her appropriately."

"What is appropriate treatment?"

The King looked nervously at the sleeping Queen. "No doubt Einkan will tell you. Just be careful." With that, he waved a royal hand in dismissal. Einkan bowed in response, then motioned for everyone to follow him out of the throne room.

The Terrans *had* to take Einkan, for a troop of guards escorted them to the *Hopeful*, which was still watched over by Officer Luka and her police. In the control room, Einkan tried to look unimpressed, while Jeff tried to be unobtrusive about searching for Norby.

He met Fargo in the corridor.

"Still missing?" asked Fargo in a low voice.

"He's not anywhere in the ship. I'm worried."

"There's nothing to worry about, Jeff. Norby did the only sensible thing—he went into hyperspace. It's a good thing, too, because that's where he can fuel himself for a trip such as the one we're about to take."

"But Fargo," said Jeff, "nobody seems to care that we don't have the faintest idea where the Princess is. I'll bet Einkan doesn't either. That's probably why he insisted on going with us. You heard the Princess say that the coordinates to the planet Melodia must have been put into the ship's computer accidentally. That could mean no one knows what the coordinates are."

"I can't believe that. Known coordinates can be put in accidentally. Being put in accidentally is not the same thing as being put in randomly. I'm sure Einkan can tell us something about it, if he can ever get around to doing anything but goggle at my girlfriend. I may have to cure him of this tendency pretty soon by bouncing him off the wall. Well, is the airlock shut?"

"Yes, and every Izzian in the city must be outside waiting for us to leave on our mission of mercy. And even if we get the coordinates, we still can't go because Norby isn't here."

"Patience, little brother. Norby will come. Let's tackle Einkan."

They found Einkan already being grilled by the formidable Yobo and the seductive Albany.

"You had better talk," growled Yobo, flexing his arms meaningfully.

"We'll get along much better if you do," murmured Albany, lowering her eyes just as meaningfully.

"Pounding me or cajoling me won't help," said Einkan. "The hyperdrive engine is my secret on Izz, and I intend to keep it that way. As you may have noticed, the Queen is in charge of everything. You may also have noticed that she has no consideration for *anyone*. How long do you suppose I would last in one piece if it weren't for my superior intellect? That, and that alone, has enabled me to rise to my present position of penultimate importance, and it is only the fact that I alone have the secret of the hyperdrive that gives me freedom. I couldn't even wear my beloved pants otherwise."

"How is it," said Albany, "that you don't ask us about *our* hyperdrive? Are you anxious that we have secrets, too?"

"But, lovely woman, my hyperdrive is surely superior to anything your people can possess. I needn't concern myself with your clumsy engines."

"Talking about clumsy engines," said Yobo to Jeff in Terran Basic, "is Norby in good shape?"

"I hope so," Jeff said in the same language, "but he's still missing."

"You must not speak in your code," Einkan said weakly.

"On our ship," said Yobo, in his deepest bass, "we can do as we wish. Who will stop us? You?"

Einkan said, "Why are we waiting? My fellow Izzians are getting impatient. If we don't leave soon, the Queen is likely to pay your ship a visit and then we will see what you can and can't do here."

Albany said, "I think I will guard the airlock, just in case. I can handle that woman."

Einkan shuddered. "You people are strange. I can't imagine what part of Izz you come from. I have not heard that there are any undiscovered islands. And you had better not frustrate the Queen. You surely want a large reward and you can only get that if you bring back the Princess. Even then, you will be in her power again and, if she is in a bad humor, she will take the Princess and refuse a reward. I assure you that you will get an ample reward only if *I* arrange it. That's why I came with you—to make sure you get the reward. In return, I get sixty percent, of course."

"What *is* the reward?" asked Fargo.

"Two cupots of bling," said Einkan.

"And what is bling?" said Albany.

Einkan stared at her, for the first time in surprise rather than in longing. "Come now, surely you are joking—no, I see you are not. I can almost believe you don't come from any part of Izz."

"Just tell us what bling is," said Yobo, "and don't chatter."

Einkan reached into a pocket of his tunic and brought out five coins. Three were silvery and sizable, while two were orange and véry small.

Fargo picked out a small orange coin. "Bling?"

Einkan snatched it back. "One of these is my pay for a month, so don't think I can let you have it."

"Copper!" said Fargo in Terran Basic. "These people have a great deal of gold and very little copper, so they use copper for casting their most valuable coins and for prizes."

Einkan drew himself to his full height and pulled at his braided beard. He said, in a troubled voice, "Can it be that you are aliens who have adopted an Izzoid appearance? Come, I see through you. What is your true form?"

"I assure you," said Jeff, who was growing more and more anxious, "that we are as completely Izzian as you are. Come, let us talk about things other than the hyperdrive. Tell us about the robots of Izz. How intelligent are they?" Jeff thought of the unsatisfactory conversation he had had with one of them when walking to the Palace.

"Why should you be interested in our robots? They were left us by the Others—"

"Aha!" said Yobo. "The Others *were* here."

"If you aliens know about the Others, then I suppose you *are* Izzians. But have you been isolated so long that you've forgotten the legends? The Others started Izz on the road to civilization, providing us with robots to help. The robots proved so successful that they are honored by being considered female, since females, as you know, are stronger and more capable manually."

Albany grinned.

"Do the robots perform all the work on Izz?" asked Jeff.

"Of course. Don't robots do so on your island of Manhattan?"

Jeff ignored the question. "Then what do Izzians do?"

"Art, music, literature, science. I myself do science."

"Did you invent the spomes—I mean the orbital satellites and the ships that take Izzians back and forth to them?"

"Ah, no," said Einkan. "We have always had those ships and satellites, and they have always been serviced by robots."

"Do the robots teach you how to do any of that work?"

"Certainly not"—Einkan stopped, as though he felt that he might have given something away. Then he puffed out his skinny chest and said, "I have learned what I know by myself."

"Which," said Fargo in Terran Basic, "I'll bet not many Iz-zians have tried to do. You have to hand it to this guy. He's got more gumption than most of them on this planet."

"Well, he told us he had a dominating personality," said Albany.

"If people are going to talk in this code," Einkan said, "I must say that I believe you are not only impolite, but up to tricks. Perhaps you do not intend to rescue our fair Princess."

"You are right," said Jeff. "It *is* impolite to cut you out of the conversation. And we *will* rescue your Princess."

"Why do you not start, then? Why aren't we in space? Don't think I don't realize you are engaging me in conversation merely as a strategy of delay."

"You are right there, too," said Jeff. "We are waiting for my little robot, who is dear to me. And I don't want to leave without him—especially if the Queen wishes to investigate his internal workings. However, he will be here any minute. And meanwhile you can give us the coordinates of the planet Melodia."

"The coordinates?" Einkan looked flabbergasted. "I thought *you* had them. Why would you offer to rescue the Princess unless you knew where she was?"

"Well, we don't know!" Yobo said sharply. "We offered to do the rescue job because we assumed *you* had the coordinates."

"Well, *I* don't. I assumed *you* had them."

"I knew it," muttered Jeff. "I *knew* it."

All five stared at each other helplessly.

Einkan said, "Do you know what's going to happen to us now? If we don't leave, and right away, the Queen will consider it an insult and she'll send the entire army against us. This ship will be cut open like a can of zitzbar and we'll be removed and taken to the Courtyard of Guilt. Do you know what Plurf smells like—and tastes like—and what it's like to be put into it up to your chin? *That's* what will happen to us."

4

Thwarting the Queen

For a while no one said anything. Jeff shut his eyes and tried to reach Norby by telepathy. Long-distance mind contact was almost impossible unless Norby was trying hard also, and Norby couldn't have been, because Jeff felt nothing. He strained every telepathic nerve until he felt himself aching all over with tension.

——Norby!——Norby, come back!

Nothing!

Jeff thought, It *never* takes Norby this long to refuel in hyperspace. Where is he? What is he doing? Has he mixed up the coordinates for Izz and landed someplace else?

He wished that he could trust Norby not to make a mistake, but he knew very well that a mistake was precisely what Norby was most likely to make.

"Admiral!" said Albany. "Fargo—Jeff—look in the viewscreen!"

Einkan, who was already looking, said in despair, "Well, I told you. Now it begins. The Queen is coming."

Marching toward the ship, right through the flower beds, was the Queen of Izz, followed by her husband, the mild King of Izz, who skirted the flower beds and then had to run to catch up. The Queen was clearly furious.

"How muscular do you think those guards of hers are?" asked Fargo, clenching and unclenching his fists as if practicing.

Albany took off her dress-uniform jacket. "All of you stay here and be ready for a quick takeoff in case Norby shows up. I'll go outside and show this Queen a thing or two about karate."

"Lieutenant," said the Admiral, "I am in charge here as senior officer, and I—"

"I'm in charge," cried Fargo. "The *Hopeful* is mine and as its captain—"

"The *Hopeful* belongs to you and me jointly, Fargo," said Jeff, "and since Norby is my robot, I have the right to—"

"No! *No!,*" shrieked Einkan, sitting down and mopping his forehead with the sleeve of his tunic. "You have not grasped the essential point of Izz. The Queen is in charge."

"And she's charging here," said Fargo. "What do we do about it?"

"Take off, you fools," said Einkan.

The Terrans were silent. They could take off, but they couldn't get away from pursuit by Izzian spaceships without Norby. The silence was broken by a loud banging on the airlock door.

A look of hope crossed Albany's beautiful face as she raised her eyebrows at Jeff.

Jeff shook his head. "If it were Norby, the banging would be in code—TGAF."

"The Game's A-Foot," muttered Yobo, "and we'll be footing it to the Courtyard of Guilt if that miserable barrel doesn't show up."

"Take off," screamed Einkan as the pounding continued. "That's the Queen. Take off! What's all this talk about Norby? Is that your dwarfish robot?"

"I'm afraid it is," said Jeff. "My pet robot was given the—ah —key to the ship's engine. We thought that would be the best way of keeping it out of the Queen's hands. You know—who would think of searching a harmless barrel? How were we to know my robot would disappear. Now we have to wait for him to come back."

"Oh, oh," groaned Einkan, "what a stupid way to run a ship. So you all get in here and can't do a thing till an idiot barrel manages to find its way here. It never will. It never will. Oh, I can smell the plurf now."

"Open up, or we'll blast our way in!" came the Queen's loud voice.

"She's using one of her nasty loudspeakers," said Fargo. "Well, we might as well hook up one of our own."

Through the *Hopeful's* loud-speaker system, Fargo said, "If you destroy this ship, Your Foolishness, you destroy the only object that can rescue your daughter."

"Since you are not leaving," the Queen retorted, "you are not planning a rescue in any case. And Einkan will build another ship in a matter of days or he will be plunged in plurf. Or else he will repair your ship once we've forced it open and then pilot it to the rescue—or be plunged in plurf head downward till he swallows every drop."

"Please take off," pleaded Einkan weakly. "Surely there must be a duplicate key somewhere. How can you rely on a single key?"

"I'm going out," said Albany. "It's the only way."

"Look!" said Fargo, pointing to the viewscreen.

A small barrel, running on long, jointed legs, knocked into the Queen, who sat down and went "Ooff!"

Before the Queen could catch her breath, Norby knocked the code for TGAF, quite unnecessarily, and yelled, "Let me in!"

Jeff ran to the airlock, opened it, and admitted Norby. The guards did not try to interfere, for court etiquette apparently demanded that every one of the dozens of guards on the scene try to help the Queen. With the natural interference that resulted, it took ten times as long to get her upright than it would have if only one guardsman had tried, and twenty times as long than if she had been left to herself.

The Queen was finally on her feet, quite unsteady, with her crown askew. She panted hoarsely, and it seemed impossible for her to make an understandable sound.

The airlock closed before the guards could complete their bowing and their backward retreat from offended Majesty.

"Where on Earth have you been, Norby?" Jeff asked.

"Nowhere on Earth. I have been exercising my brains, which none of you are likely to have been doing. Let's leave this miserable planet immediately."

"But we have to rescue the Princess. We promised."

"A promise to that Queen is foolish. And dangerous. Let's go home to the singing contest."

"You know what I think, Norby—"

"I don't care what you think, Jeff. The Queen is having big guns and other weapons dragged up. We're going to be destroyed."

"It will take her some time," Fargo said. "I'd judge we have about fifteen minutes. Plenty of time. *Plenty* of time. What do you think, Jeff?"

"I think that what Norby means by exercising his brains is that he's spent his time finding the coordinates of Melodia, but he doesn't want to go there. He's scared."

"I'm not scared," Norby said defensively.

"If you're not scared, what's bothering you?"

"I just don't like Izz. Or Izzians. The robots here aren't anything like the ones on Jamya. These robots are slaves, and they only do what they were programmed to do long ago at the very start. Even the main computer has no mind of its own."

"Oh, there's a main computer?"

"Yes, and it read the computer on the *Challenger* so it knows—" Norby stopped and sucked in his head.

"It knows where the Princess is." Jeff pounded on Norby's hat. "That means *you* know and it means you're going to tell me."

"Oh, well, if you take that attitude, I'll tell you. But I don't like Izzians, especially that Einkan."

"I don't think he'll bother us, Norby. Come on to the control room and hear what I have to say. We've only got a few minutes before the Queen may decide to open fire."

When Jeff walked into the control room hand in hand with Norby, all but Einkan greeted them enthusiastically. Einkan's curled upper lip suggested that the very idea of being friends with a robot was shameful. Jeff ignored him.

"Positions, everybody. Norby's here with the engine key, so we can leave. I'll be the pilot this time—"

"You mean, you know where the Princess is?" asked Einkan, looking stupefied.

"Of course. You would, too, if you'd bothered to search the data banks of your own main computer. Norby thought to do that, which isn't bad for a pet robot. He found the coordinates of Melodia in information obtained from *your* ship, Einkan. Yet *you* claimed not to have that information. How do you explain that?"

The smile Einkan bestowed on Jeff was not friendly. "That is none of your business. I disapprove of your sending a *machine* to search *my* computer. I would certainly have found where the Princess is when it was necessary for me to do so."

"Oh, sure," said Fargo. He looked absently at the viewscreen, where the Queen had apparently recovered her voice and was shouting again. Albany had turned off the sound, but the contortions of the Queen's face were fearful and the banging on the ship's hull was steady.

"You know," said Fargo, "I think she's bluffing. She's making a lot of noise but doesn't dare do anything. She wouldn't mind killing us and I think she would enjoy killing Einkan, but she doesn't really want to damage the ship which may be the only way of rescuing her daughter."

"I don't know," said Norby. "Those weapons don't look friendly. Please let's go, Jeff."

"I agree," said Jeff. "I don't want to call the Queen's bluff because it might not be a bluff. I don't have Fargo's silly optimism. However, since none of us trusts Einkan, I suggest he be locked in my cabin and kept there till we get to Melodia. I'll sleep in the control room."

"I certainly do not intend to allow anything of that sort—" began Einkan.

Yobo grasped him by his shoulders and lifted him clear off the ground. "Surely you don't mean to refuse young Jeff's excellent suggestion."

Einkan gulped. "Not at all. Please lead me to the cabin."

Yobo led him out and Fargo said, "A good point, Jeff. We certainly don't want Einkan to see Norby plug himself into the ship's computer. He mustn't know that Norby doesn't *have* the key to hyperspace but *is* the key. Let's go, Norby. Hurry up, before they damage the airlock."

"Hurry, hurry," grumbled Norby. "First it's a bluff and then it's hurry, hurry." But Norby was anxious to get away, too, so it didn't take long.

As soon as the *Hopeful* began to rise on antigrav, the Izzians surrounding her fell back. Jeff took the ship beyond the atmosphere and past the orbital spomes as quickly as sub-light speed would manage. Izzian cruisers lying in wait as the *Hopeful* raced past the spome orbits, were not nearly as maneuverable as the *Hopeful*. Jeff wove in and out at accelerations that had everyone clinging desperately to the wall-straps. They could hear Einkan yelling as he crashed into the walls of Jeff's cabin.

Then, when the *Hopeful* was far enough from Izz, it moved into hyperspace. The friendly gray enclosed it protectively, and Fargo began to play softly on his tympani while Albany kissed him lightly on his right cheek.

5

The Planet, Melodia

"There it is, Court Scientist," said Albany, pointing to the viewscreen, "the planet your Princess has named Melodia."

After only a few hours of hyperspace travel, Einkan had been released from Jeff's cabin for the occasion, but he was not reacting with joy.

"I am one continuous bruise from my right ear to my left little toe," the scientist raged, totally ignoring the viewscreen. "What kind of way is that to pilot a spaceship?"

"I had to evade your fellow Izzians," Jeff said indignantly. "You shouldn't have been hurt. There's not a sharp angle or point anywhere in this ship."

"It isn't lined with sponge rubber either."

"You should have held on."

"To what? And I wasn't warned."

"Come on," Albany said. "There was bad acceleration only at first. Once we were in hyperspace, we had absolute quiet. Now there is the planet and soon we'll have your Princess. Why don't you have something to eat, Court Scientist, and let your bruises heal?"

Fargo and Yobo were not watching the viewscreen either. Their argument over a tenor-bass duet threatened to become a battle, each singing little snatches of his own part to illustrate this point or that.

Albany smiled at Jeff. "Well, that leaves you and me to enjoy the scenery, Jeff. It's wonderful that Nor—that the *Hopeful* brought us here so quickly. I love the gentleness of hyperspace travel, even though it isn't scenic."

"No," said Einkan with a shudder. "I never expected such gray nothingness."

"Oh?" said Jeff, wondering absently why the planet below was such a dull color, "you never expected it? Haven't you ever experienced hyperspace before? And you an important hyperdrive inventor."

Einkan said indignantly, "I had no chance to test my own invention. Princess Rinda has a lot of her mother in her and when she makes up her mind, well, she makes up her mind. She wanted to go, so she ordered me off my own ship to make room for herself."

"Just looking at her," said Albany loudly, and talking in Fargo's direction, "I guessed that the Princess would be that kind of person—selfish, willful, greedy, and impossible." Each adjective was louder than the one before, but Fargo apparently heard nothing but the fact that Yobo's singing was a semitone flat.

"Well, of course," said Einkan. "She's a *Crown* Princess, the next to succeed to the throne. She has to be trained for all those necessary characteristics. Anyway, she said she was taking my ship for just a short preliminary voyage circling our stellar system, but, of course, she touched a button I told her to leave strictly alone, because I suspected—or, rather, *knew* it was the button for hyperspace travel, with coordinates already prog—" Einkan stopped speaking, clearly flustered.

"Programmed, you were about to say," said Jeff, "but obviously not by you. You didn't invent the *Challenger*'s engines and computer. No way. So who did?"

Einkan's jaw clamped shut.

"Please," said Albany, bestowing a beatific smile upon the hapless Court Scientist. "Do tell us the truth while we make a nice lunch for you. We're sure you must be in trouble and we'll try to help you. *I'll* try to help you."

"Looks very muddy down there, doesn't it?" said Einkan, avoiding Albany's eyes and looking into the viewscreen for the first time.

"That's because it's mostly mud," said Norby, from the control panel. "That planet doesn't look at all appetizing. Do we have to go down there?"

"Yes," said Jeff, "but only after Court Scientist Einkan tells us the truth so we can help him."

"What truth?" asked Yobo, moving closer. And Fargo said, almost simultaneously, "What's this about truth?"

Albany said sweetly, "Oh, are you gentlemen going to stop serenading us? If you are, you might listen to the Court Scientist's troubles. Go on, dear Mr. Einkan, you were going to tell us—"

"Nothing," Einkan said stubbornly. "You are enemy aliens."

"Do I look like an enemy alien?" said Albany, pouting.

"To be truthful, my dear, you seem a perfect example of an Izzian female—" Einkan began.

"How unkind!"

"—at her best."

"That's better," said Albany, smiling brilliantly, "and I agree with you. So you see, we *are* Izzians."

"I admit it seems so, but this ship is suspiciously strange and there is that odd code of communication you use among yourselves." He stroked his beard meditatively. "Can it really be that you are Izzians that have been displaced to some other planet in our Galaxy?"

"Something like that, yes," said Jeff. "Not what's the truth about the *Challenger?*"

"You must be very powerful to have come so far on a visit," said Einkan, his long fingers laced together. "In fact, why come on a visit? Possibly you are spying us out with a mind to conquer."

"Come, come. Do we look like conquerors?" asked Albany.

"*He* does," said Einkan, pointing to Yobo. "Perhaps you plan to take our planet for its stores of bling. You," pointing to Fargo, "fondled my bling coin with obvious greed."

All four of the Terrans laughed at the thought of stealing Izz's copper when it had such stores of gold available.

But then Yobo said gravely. "I am not a conqueror, sir. Just an ordinary military leader of great skill who acts on the defensive. Not only would we not dream of taking your world, we would scorn to take your bling. We wouldn't want to upset the economy of your world. That would be against our ethical principles."

"This is all very boring," shouted Norby from the control panel. "I thought you were here to rescue the Princess. Let's do it *now* so we can leave this nasty place."

"We will, as soon as Einkan tells us the truth," said Yobo. "Where did you get your hyperdrive ship? Look, if you force us, we'll go down to the planet, pick up the Princess and your ship, leave you on the planet while we go back to Izz. You'll just have to spend the rest of your life in the mud down there—but then, you won't live long and what a comfort that will be for you."

Einkan squirmed. "You wouldn't do that. It's—it's un-Izzian."

"We say 'inhuman'," said Fargo, grinning, "but we'll do it."

"No, they won't," said Albany. "I won't let them, if you'll just tell us."

"Well," said Einkan, "I was exploring the asteroid belt in a small rented ship, the sort that goes back and forth between the satellite worlds of the Queendom—it was during my vacation time so the Queen wouldn't find out what I was doing. I found a wrecked and empty ship that had clearly never been built by Izzians, and I salvaged the engine and brought it back. I had never been able to invent hyperdrive myself, but I'd learned enough about it to see that that engine might have hyperdrive capacity.

"I brought it back to Izz and, of course, I told the Queen I had invented it myself and that it *was* hyperdrive. I was taking a risk, for it might *not* have been hyperdrive, but if it *was*, then my job was secure and I would be so famous that even the Queen wouldn't dare be rude to me. Anyway, I installed the engine in her new cruise ship, and the Princess got interested, and now I have to build a new engine with which to rescue her, and I can't —and it's the plurf pit for me."

"And that's why you insisted on coming with us," Jeff said. "If you help rescue the Princess, your deceit might be forgiven; while if you had stayed on Izz, you would have—"

Einkan shuddered. "Don't talk about it, please." He looked at Jeff sharply. "That wrecked ship wasn't one that was built by *your* people, was it? No, it couldn't be. Its controls were not suitable for Izzian hands, either mine or yours."

"Actually," Einkan went on, "what I've been thinking ever since I found that ship was that it had been abandoned by an early un-Izzian species of star-traveler long before we Izzians had been settled on Izz."

Jeff said, "You say before Izzians had been settled on Izz? Then you know that Izzians did not evolve on the planet they now live on; that they came from somewhere else."

"Of course. According to our old histories, we were especially selected for our superior genes by the Others for training in advanced civilization. We do not know our planet of origin—" He smote his forehead. "Of course! That explains everything! You people are from the planet of origin! You are descended from the Izzians, who were not selected."

Fargo said, "You know, this scientist isn't as dumb as he looks."

"Shut up, Fargo," said Jeff. "This is serious. Yes, Court Scientists, we are Terrans, from Terra, the planet of origin. Izzians are descendants of Terrans and that is why, as we keep saying, we ourselves are Izzians after a fashion."

"Where is Terra, then? Is Manhattan another name for it?"

"No. Manhattan is the name of a small portion of it; and as we've said, it's far, far away, to be reached only by hyperdrive."

"And until we learn to trust the Izzians more than we do," growled Yobo, "its location will remain a secret."

"On Terra," said Fargo, "we have done away with monarchies. I mean Queendoms."

Einkan gasped, then shouted, "Infidels! Heretics! I must loudly express my utter disapproval of such anarchy."

"Don't worry," said Fargo dryly. "The Queen isn't listening. She can't hear you."

Einkan relaxed. "In that case," he said in a low voice, "I suppose it could be wonderful having no Queen. Does it really work?"

"It really works," said Albany, "though it *does* make sense to have women in charge in an elected way."

The *Hopeful* was moving downward now toward the surface of Melodia, which continued to appear dull brown. As the ship circled the planet, the computer scanner confirmed the original impression that it was mostly mud with a few islands of vegetation.

And then Jeff remembered what had happened to the Izzian ship. "Norby," he said, "stay above the atmosphere!"

"Why?" asked Einkan. "We can't rescue the Princess long-distance. We have to get down to the surface."

"Yes, but first we have to decide what to do about the electronic field around the planet. The *Challenger* reported that it couldn't send visible images through the field, and perhaps it is the field that has grounded the *Challenger* and put it out of communication altogether."

"Ask the computer, Norby," said Fargo. "Find out what sort of field surrounds that planet."

"Unknown," said Norby promptly, after plugging in. "It detects nothing that would interfere with normal ship functioning, however."

"Then descend, descend," cried Einkan. "We can't go back without the Princess."

"And we can't get any reward without the Princess," Fargo pointed out.

Jeff's call for caution was voted down loudly, and he had no choice but to pilot the ship to a landing, while the others went back to their singing practice. Einkan, who was apparently tone-deaf, sat as far away from the kettledrums as possible—which obviously wasn't far enough for his comfort, for he held his hands over his ears and contorted his face into a mask of misery.

Jeff, still deeply disturbed, talked to Norby telepathically:

——I want you to stay in the ship, Norby. The mere fact that the field is unknown may mean it is dangerous, whatever the computer says.

——The field enters the ship, Jeff. It won't matter whether I stay in the ship or not. The field already surrounds us, in fact, and I feel fine. Besides, I *have* to go with you. Who'll protect you if I'm not there?

——Who'll protect *me?* Why, you're just afraid to—

The computer spoke: "The largest island has a metal object on it that may be a ship."

"I'll head for it," said Jeff. "It must be the *Challenger.*"

On its way, the *Hopeful* passed over smaller islands of greenery in the planetary sea of mud. Some held little wooden huts shaped like upside-down baskets. There was no sign of a technological civilization of any kind.

"Ah-ah yookh-nyem!" sang Yobo in a rolling base.

"Not that one, Admiral," said Fargo, "'Shenandoah' is much more sentimentally effective, especially with my tenor singing the melody."

"But I insist on Russian music. My African great-great grandmother was *very* good friends with a Russian."

"We are approaching the main island," said Norby. "I am checking with the ship's computer to make certain that the strange electronic field is not affecting it or the ship. Negative, so far."

"Excellent," said Yobo. "All we have to do is pick up the Princess and take her back to Izz."

"We'll have to patch up the *Challenger*, too. We can't leave its crew stranded," said the ever practical Jeff.

"Certainly. That, too."

"The air was breathable for the *Challenger* crew," said Fargo, "but let's double check. Norby, ask the computer—"

"My stars and gaskets, Fargo," said Norby, "how can you treat a computer so? You know that even the dumbest ship's computer would never allow its crew to enter an unbreathable atmosphere without the appropriate warning. If the *Hopeful* computer had emotive circuits, you would have hurt its feelings."

"Look!" said Jeff.

A small ship, newer and shinier than the Izzian ships they'd seen, was lying on the ground of the island. Next to it was a dense grove of trees and inside the grove was an open space containing a bigger hut than the others.

Norby reported again. "The scanners indicate that the *Challenger* is inactive. Its engine and electricity are off. What's more, the ship seems to be the only hunk of free metal on the planetary surface. There might be metal deep in the planet that could account for the inhibitory field but I don't know what it is."

Norby was silent for a moment. Then he said, "The scanners report there are robots in the *Challenger*."

"Of course there are," said Einkan. "Five of them, part of the crew. Where are the Izzians?"

"Not inside the ship. Only robots. And they don't move."

"Are they deactivated, Norby?" asked Fargo, his forehead creasing.

"No, but they're not moving. I don't understand it."

"If it's dangerous for robots down there, you must not leave the ship, Norby," said Yobo.

"What's the good of that?" said Norby nervously. "The *Challenger* is closed, yet the robots still don't move. What's going to happen to *me*?"

"Nothing at all," said Einkan, scornfully. "The explanation is simple. The Izzians left the ship and told the robots to wait—so they're waiting."

"Without moving? Or trying to rescue the Izzians?" asked Fargo.

"Our robots do as they're told," said Einkan. "Nothing else."

"Stupid creatures," said Norby scornfully. "Our Terran housekeeping robots might be that stupid, but not *real* robots. Now *I* am an asset, not a liability. I have frequently rescued Jeff and others. And now I'm going to rescue a Princess." The *Hopeful* was hovering over a landing spot.

"No, you're not," said Einkan. "I've been waiting for this moment. I've endured your manhandling until now, but no longer." From a hidden fold of his pants he suddenly drew out a weapon. "I am now in charge. Land this ship. Then one of you can go out, get the Princess and bring her back. The rest of you will serve as hostages."

"Ah," said Yobo, "then when the Princess comes back, you will force us out of the ship and go back with the Princess alone, stranding us and the *Challenger* crew and collecting all the credit yourself. . . . And how do you expect to pilot this ship?"

"I will not force all of you out. Dear Albany will stay, of course, and so will that robot of yours. He can pilot the ship, and if he won't cooperate, I can insert a wire in the same place that he does. After all, I know the coordinates of Izz. They, at least, are no mystery to me. Now quickly."

He waved his weapon threateningly.

6

The Slithers

"Dear Einkan," said Albany, moving closer and waggling her finger near his beard, "it is so kind of you not to want to leave me behind. And it is brave of you to face us down by yourself, but it is foolish, too. In Manhattan, we arrest people who pull guns on the police."

"Arrest?" said Einkan, stumbling over the pronunciation, for she had used the Terran word.

"Like this!" Albany flicked her finger across the base of his nose, and when he flinched backward, she seized his gun arm. In a moment he was flat on his back, and Albany was holding his gun.

"Ouch," he said. "That wasn't fair. You're just like Sergeant Luka."

"A cop is a cop," said Albany.

Norby, knowing Albany's capabilities, had paid little attention to Einkan's threats. "The scanners report life forms moving under those trees and in the mud about them," he said.

"Land the ship," said Yobo, grandly, "and we'll investigate those life forms. Perhaps we will leave Einkan to get along with *them* in the future. He obviously can't get along with us."

The *Hopeful* sank gracefully downward on its antigrav, landing on what seemed to be a hard patch of ground next to the *Challenger*.

There was a sudden metallic screech from Norby.

"What's the matter?" everyone yelled.

"Don't yell at me," said Norby, fiddling with the control board. "That just makes things worse. The stupid ship's computer amplified the sound from outside too strongly, and I was tuned into it."

"What sound?" asked Albany.

"A serenade. That's what it sounds like. Listen." Norby turned on the loudspeaker.

"That's a beautiful chorus," said Fargo. "Perfectly on key, every note. And I've heard that music before."

"It's the Izzian national anthem," said Einkan grumpily, getting up and dusting himself off. "There are too many voices for it to be just the crew of the *Challenger*, which consists of two males and a female, plus the Captain—a female, of course—and our beloved Princess."

Fargo said, "Are you speaking to us? Well, stand up and face the wall. I'm searching you for any other weapons you might have."

"The indignity!" gasped Einkan.

"If you prefer, just take your clothes off and toss them here."

At a loss for words, Einkan faced the wall. After a brief search Fargo said, "All right. You'll pull no further surprises."

Meanwhile, on the viewscreen, there was movement visible near the line of trees just in front of the two ships. Out moved a double line of orange creatures, slithering along on snail-like feet and waving what looked like old-time mops.

A closer look made it clear the mops were heads of the creatures, and the strings of the mops were tentacles. On top of each mop was an opening which moved. At the neck of each mop were two more openings, one on each side.

"They're singing through those openings," said Fargo. "Three to a creature. I wonder if it means that each Melodian sings with three voices—in parts."

"You're correct, Fargo," said Norby. "The scanners confirm it. Do you want to open the airlock?"

"Well, we came on a rescue mission, didn't we?" said Fargo, raising his black eyebrows at the sound of uncertainty in Norby's voice. "Don't tell me you think those things look dangerous."

"*I* don't think so," said Yobo. "They don't have enough technology to be dangerous, and the singing must be friendly since it is so beautiful. We will be friendly, too. I shall lead the way."

Norby grabbed Jeff's hand to speak telepathically.

——I don't like these creatures, Jeff.

——You'd be scared of a mouse, Norby, if you'd never seen one before.

——I'm not scared. I'm just being intuitive. I don't like their voices.

——You're just jealous of anyone who can sing on key.

Norby tore his hand away from Jeff and spoke aloud angrily. "Go ahead, then. You humans are too stupid to recognize danger and too cowardly to dare seem like cowards. And you're always dragging me into danger with you. Don't think I won't say 'I told you so.' Go out to those ugly *Slithers*, then, because that's what they should be called. Ugh!"

"Don't be a wet blanket, Norby," said Fargo. "Their voices are beautiful. . . . But Slithers does seem a good name for them."

As they stepped out of the airlock onto the brown soil of Melodia, Einkan's head jerked in surprise. "Listen—can you hear it? Farther away. A soprano."

"Umm," said Fargo. "It's a beautiful voice."

"It is not merely beautiful. It is a perfect Izzian voice and it's singing the *words* to our National Anthem, while these natives are not. It must be the voice of the Crown Princess." Einkan's voice shook with excitement.

Fargo said, "It does seem as if the Slithers are not singing words at all, only musical notes and chords. Maybe they have no language other than musical sounds. With my absolute pitch, I should be able to learn such a musical language easily."

"Well, go ahead and try," said Yobo, "but in the meantime, I suggest we march briskly, heads up, chins out, between the rows of Slithers to the place where the Crown Princess is. Onward, troops!"

Einkan, paying no attention—or perhaps stimulated by the nearness of his Princess—dashed ahead and disappeared into the trees.

Fargo shrugged his shoulders and said, "Let him go. If he gets into trouble, it won't bother me a bit."

Jeff marched along with Norby, worried about the little robot's anger and about his intuition of danger from the Slithers. Surely, he thought, such danger wasn't likely. The Slithers were small and fragile, had no visible weapons, no clothes to hide them in, and no sign of hostility. There were just the spherical orange bodies, the brown snail feet, and the mop-heads on top.

The Terrans came to a clearing where there was a large and solid wooden fence. They turned and walked beside the fence until they came to an opening, through which they could see another fence, made of lattice-work. Its door was *not* open.

The little Slithers chirped musically and changed their tune to something resembling a baroque symphony with emphasis on the horns. They scampered ahead and sang to the door. Instantly, an orange wave of additional Slithers poured out of the narrow passage between the two fences. The new Slithers sang to the first group, who sang back. Then they swarmed to the inner door, did something to open it, and clustered on each side of the gateway, bowing and singing to the Terrans.

"Perhaps," said Jeff, "we should peek inside and find out what's in there before we go charging forward."

"There are humans in there," said Norby. "I think five, according to my scanners."

"According to Einkan, there were five Izzians on board the *Challenger*, and if he got there, that makes *six*," said Fargo.

Yobo said, "Jeff, you and Norby go back to the ship. It was stupid of me not to leave someone on guard. I was mesmerized by the singing."

"I don't think that can be done without a bit of trouble," said Jeff. He pointed to their rear where a clot of Slithers had completely filled the path, blocking the exit through the first fence.

"I told you so," Norby said in a very low voice.

The Slithers waved their mop-heads and bowed. Then they fell silent. When none of the Terrans responded, they sang—a rising passage that sounded as though it might be a question.

"Do they want to know what we want?" asked Yobo.

"They obviously don't understand our language any more than we understand theirs," said Fargo. "Maybe we aren't fulfilling a courtesy ritual."

"That's it," said Albany. "They must want us to sing back."

"Harrumph," said Yobo, clearing his throat. His deep voice then rolled out as he sang to the tune of "The Volga Boatmen," "We-ee greet thee; we-ee come here; we come only in peace; we-ee greet thee."

The Slithers turned brighter orange and rocked back and forth on their lower extremities. As the Admiral continued, Fargo's tenor joined in harmoniously and the Slithers appeared to sway in ecstasy. When Albany and Jeff added their voices, the Slithers were clearly delirious with joy.

Jeff could hear the soprano voice in the distance, with Izzian words rising high and clear, making itself heard above all other sounds: "Don't be dumb, now; have a care, now; don't you move through the fence; stay outside, now."

Jeff stopped singing and looked at the others to see if the words had registered, but they appeared to be mesmerized by their own voices. The Slithers joined in, singing a multitude of parts and even Jeff got so caught up in the symphony of perfectly blended voices that he forgot the soprano's words.

The singing came to a natural end and, at its conclusion, Yobo, and then the others, bowed low. In response, the Slithers sang *The Volga Boatmen* softly and very simply, but without words. They then repeated it, adding trills, transposing the key, and introducing intricate modulations. Yobo continued to bow, smiling broadly.

Fargo nudged Jeff. "The Admiral will be insufferable after this. He'll insist on rowing those boatmen in the music contest."

"It's not fair," shouted Norby. "Everyone sings but me." And he launched into his own peculiar version of the Space Cadets' marching song.

The Slithers made a queer hissing noise, drew back, turned chartreuse, and waved their tentacles wildly.

"Norby, you're off key as usual," said Fargo, "and they don't like it. If we're going to be diplomatic, we mustn't offend the natives, so *shut up*."

Fargo then sang a few bars of a melting love song, hoping it would restore their good humor, and since they all promptly turned orange again, he assumed it did.

One of the little Slithers handed Fargo what looked like a blue fruit. Norby poked at it and said in a sulky voice, "If I had my way, I'd let them poison you insulting human beings, but my circuits make it necessary to protect you instead. And you can believe me when I tell you this object is safe to eat."

"It's bland but edible," pronounced Fargo, sampling the fruit. "On to dinner and to the Princess."

The Terrans were each given fruit, even Norby, but he tossed his aside. The others made various polite sounds indicating pleasure and, almost absently, stepped through the door. Norby gloomily followed.

The door shut behind them, and the soprano voice came in four angry notes, each higher in pitch than the one before, "You id-i-ots!"

It was Jeff who first realized they were in a cage. Surrounding them was the lattice-work fence, and above them was a roof of bars. The openings in the fence and ceiling were too small for any of them—even Norby—to pass through.

Off to the left was a door to a smaller cage, with solid walls and roof. At the farthest end of the main cage was a section of roof that bulged upward to accommodate a small but particularly beautiful tree with a short thick trunk and long leaves that shone silver on one side and gold on the other.

Einkan emerged from the smaller cage on the left. He was followed by four Izzians in tattered uniforms. Einkan's expression was one of misery. "The Princess tried to warn you not to come in, but you didn't listen."

"Silence!" The word was a loud whisper from the tallest Izzian, whose gold braid had a faint gleam of copper thread across one shoulder of her shimmering nightshirt-like uniform. She had long, braided black hair and she was obviously angry. "I am Captain Erig. You must either sing or whisper. Apparently the little creatures cannot hear you whisper. If you speak loudly enough to be heard—speak, that is, not sing—they will sting you until you stop."

"The *Slithers* will sting us?" said Jeff, astonished.

"Shh. Not so loud. Yes, those tentacles hurt badly, and there are millions of them."

"*I told you so!*" shouted Norby. "*I told you so.* And I don't care if they sting me. *I* won't feel it."

Several Slithers squirmed through the bars into the cage and made slowly for Norby, who retired into his barrel.

"Fascinating," whispered Fargo. "The Slithers have such perfect pitch that the random noise of speech must hurt their eardrums, or whatever they hear with."

Albany pointed at the Slithers who were swarming over Norby and flicking at the steel of his body with their tentacles. "Look," she whispered, "their brown feet are turning orange."

The Slithers soon gave up their attack on Norby and moved away, leaving oily marks on him. Jeff wiped him off carefully with his handkerchief, which he then threw away, suspecting that the oil would sting on contact with his skin. He picked up Norby and tucked him under his arm.

"Notice that their feet are covered with brown mud," whispered Fargo. "When the mud dries, it flakes off, exposing the orange beneath. You can see the flaking if you look."

"The Slithers forage in the mud of this planet," whispered Captain Erig. "I imagine that their ancestors lived in the seas that formerly covered Melodia and that they evolved to this form as the seas dried up."

"And we think they are as ugly as mud," said the other female crew member. The two males—one old, one young—nodded and groaned.

"Where is the Princess?" asked Yobo in as near a whisper as his bass voice could produce.

A ripple of silvery laughter echoed in the cage, and the Terrans spun around looking for the source. There was no one else in sight.

"Silly idiots," came the soprano voice, not bothering to whisper. "A fine rescue party you are. I recognize Einkan, but who are these others, especially that handsome one with the curly brown hair, the one carrying a barrel?"

"Me?" asked Jeff out loud and in surprise, because no woman had ever before noticed him when his handsome brother was around. "Ouch," he yelled as a Slither stung him with one of its tentacles. It *did* hurt. It hurt a lot. He rubbed his hand, then whispered, "But where is she?"

"There," whispered Captain Erig. "The tree. That's the Princess. At least, that *was* the Princess."

7

The Tree Princess

The soprano voice rang out imperiously. "Don't think for a minute that this *was* the Princess. This *is* the Princess. I am *still* Princess Rinda whatever I look like, and you will all *still* obey my orders!"

The voice was accompanied by an ominous rustling sound as it said, sharply. "You, come here at once!"

Jeff saw the leaves of the silvery-gold tree moving. "Do you mean me?" His voice quavered a bit.

"Of course she means you," Yobo said in a deep whisper. "Get over there."

Jeff walked over to the tree, but drew back a step as a branch reached out to touch his hair.

"No braids," the voice said. "In questionable, if not illegal, taste." And now Jeff saw that there were speaking apertures near the base of each major limb. "Who are you?"

"I'm Jeff Wells. I'm sorry that I must whisper, but I don't want to be stung. The dark-haired man with blue eyes is my brother, Fargo. The woman in the blue uniform is Albany Jones, a police officer, and our leader is Admiral Boris Yobo, the tallest and biggest, the one with medals on his chest."

"Ridiculous. Leaders are always female. This Albany Jones is your leader."

"Hear, hear," said Albany in a loud voice, followed immediately by "Ow!" as she rubbed the sting on her ankle.

"You speak Izzian abominably. Where are you people from?"

"The island of Manhattan, a self-governing member of the Federation."

"And where is this Federation? What part of Izz dares to set itself apart from my mother's glorious Queendom?"

"We are not part of Izz, Your Highness."

Einkan moved quickly to Jeff's side and bowed low. "Your Highness," he whispered. "I have come to rescue you. I had to commandeer the ship of these—uh—insignificant aliens because my second hyperdrive ship was not yet read—"

"All this is your fault, Einkan," said the tree. "You must have programmed the coordinates for this accursed planet into the ship's computer. You *wanted* me stranded here so that you could gain power and wealth out of my misfortune."

"But, Princess, you insisted! I begged you not to—"

"Silence, wretch!"

"He didn't invent the ship," Jeff whispered urgently, "he *found* it with the coordinates for this world already in its computer. He doesn't know how to make or use a hyperdrive engine, but we do. We will rescue you and return you to Izz."

"And just how are you going to do that, Handsome? You are trapped inside a cage and I am trapped inside this tree."

"We'll get out somehow, and get you out of the tree."

The tree began to sound as if it were crying.

Captain Erig tapped Jeff's arm. "Don't upset her," she whispered. "You can't get her out of the tree, because she *is* the tree."

"What!"

"The Slithers fed the Princess to the tree. She's part of it now."

The tree cried harder, while the Terrans looked stunned. Jeff could feel Norby, inside his barrel, bounce a little in his arms.

"Why are you carrying that barrel?" whispered Captain Erig. "Is there anything in it that can help us escape?"

"Certainly," said Norby, popping his head up. "I am an escape expert."

"Whisper," whispered Captain Erig.

"I don't want to," said Norby. "Besides, I can't."

Jeff put Norby on the ground hastily, just in time to keep a bunch of Slithers from stinging his legs as they moved toward the little robot. Norby used his antigrav to take himself to a branch of the tree, out of the reach of the Slithers.

"Get this peculiar robot off my branch," said the Princess. "I am the sacred tree of Melodia, in addition to being the Crown Princess Rinda."

Norby rose higher until he floated just under the top of the cage. The Slithers scuttled back to their guard positions along the edges of the cage, and Norby sank slowly into Jeff's arms.

Yobo strode over to Captain Erig, who was as tall as he. The high Slavic cheekbones under his dark skin made him look impressively handsome as he smiled.

She smiled, too.

He whispered, "Captain, please tell us everything you can about this planet and our position here."

"There isn't a great deal to tell. The *Challenger* brought us here on our first stop through hyperspace. We had no control over the direction the ship took. When we saw it was an inhabited planet, with a breathable atmosphere, it seemed natural to land and explore. The Princess was charmed by the musical ability of the natives, and we came to this area for a feast and a concert, during which the Princess gave an impressive recital—"

"You bet I did," sang the Tree Princess.

"The Slithers didn't sting us at first, or we'd have retreated to the *Challenger*, but after we'd eaten and sung, we found ourselves surrounded and vastly outnumbered. They began to sting us each time we'd speak instead of sing or whisper, and then they forced us into this cage. After they had fed the Princess to the tree, we tried desperately to kill them, but we couldn't. There are too many of them, and if you touch one, it stings and the rest come to sting, too. And if that isn't enough, they attack vocally."

"Vocally?" asked Yobo.

"Thousands of Slithers singing in unison at the top of their triple voices can stupefy anyone with the vibration. The Princess says there are Slithers on each of the small islands, and that they communicate from island to island through vocal vibrations. She says they are all converging on this central island in order to hear the newcomers sing. I hope you do it well, because it keeps them in a good mood and then they will continue to feed us."

"What's the food like?"

Erig grimaced. "Only their fruits and vegetables are fit to eat. The animal food they served us was worm-like creatures they find in the mud and they serve them raw since they have no fire."

"Horrible," rumbled the shocked Yobo aloud, who was promptly stung.

Norby popped out of Jeff's arms, sank to the ground, and extruded his legs. "I'm bigger than any Slither," he announced loudly, "and I will rescue all of you. They can't sting me."

Ten Slithers rushed to Norby and whipped him with their tentacles. Norby elevated at once on his antigrav, screeching metallically. "That's not fair," he yelled. "They found out they couldn't sting me the usual way, so they're using electric shocks. They could disorganize my microcircuits."

"Well, then," whispered Fargo, "stay in the air, you idiot, where they can't get at you. And if you have a plan for rescuing us, get started at once.—No," he added, with a rather uncharacteristic attack of caution, "tell us your plan first."

"It's simple," said Norby. "I will go into hyperspace and re-emerge on the outside of the cage. Then, with the *Hopeful*, I'll smash this whole building, including the cage, and we can all go back to Izz."

"And what about me," said the tree.

"Oh, yes, I forgot—I mean, I was just coming to you. We'll dig you up and get you back to Izz with us."

"And I," said Einkan, slapping his chest, "will work on the problem of restoring you to human form."

"Shut up, Einkan," said the Princess. "Listen, you're likely to kill the tree if you dig it up, and that means killing me. It will then be perpetual plurf for all of you, so think of something better at once!"

Jeff said, "Whatever we do depends on Norby being out of here and using the *Hopeful* to smash the Slithers. After that we can decide on the next step. So—go ahead, Norby."

They all waited for Norby to disappear.

He didn't.

"Oh, that thing can't help me. No one can help me," cried the Princess, rustling her branches. "If I'm going to be here all my life, you're going to have to stay here with me. Don't any of you dare be rescued without me."

Then she was silent, too, and they continued to wait for Norby to disappear. In the silence, Jeff became aware of the incessant soft humming of the Slithers. It was getting on his nerves.

The Princess spoke again. "The Slithers are getting impatient."

"How do you know?" asked Fargo.

"Because the tree tells me so. It's the sacred tree, and the Slithers don't dare touch it. That's why I can talk instead of whisper. I've got at least that much." She sniffled. "At least I can talk like an Izzian. I don't have to whisper."

"How does the tree tell you?"

"The tree understands the musical communication of the Slithers and, when it understands, somehow I do, too. I'm part of the tree. For instance, the Slithers are getting impatient because they want you new Izzoid people to give them a concert, and they want to take your nasty robot and bury him deep in the mud."

"Nasty!" Norby's eyes opened to their widest.

"Certainly, you're nasty," said the tree. "You said something about going into hyperspace and you're still here. You and your big talk about rescue. You're good for nothing."

"I'm good for more than a talking tree is," Norby said indignantly.

"No, you're not," said the tree. "Can you sing like this?" She opened several more flaps in the odd snaky bark and proceeded to sing with several voices at once, all of them a high soprano. She accompanied herself by violin-like sounds from her branches.

The Slithers joined in so loudly that further whispered conversation was impossible. Jeff reached up to take Norby's hand and they spoke telepathically.

——Norby, what's the matter? Why didn't you move into hyperspace? Do it now and take me with you. We can at least rescue the humans and then decide what to do with the Princess.

——We can't.

——Why not?

——I've failed.

——Are you out of energy? Didn't you refuel in hyperspace?

——Yes, but my supply won't last forever.

——All the more reason to get into hyperspace. Come on—

——I *can't* get into hyperspace. This inhibitory field prevents me. If you and I were in the *Hopeful,* we could go into space at sub-light speeds till we were far enough away to be outside the field, and then we could move into hyperspace. But we can't get to the *Hopeful.*

——Come on, Norby. Use your brain. Get beyond the field by your own antigrav.

——Use your own brain, Jeff. How do I get out of this cage to do that?

——Oh, my goodness!

The two looked at each other helplessly.

8

Before Melodia

The others listened to Jeff's whispered explanation of Norby's failure, and the atmosphere became unrelieved gloom. Even the arrival of a meal of assorted vegetables did not cheer them up. The vegetables did not taste terrible, to be sure, but neither did they taste good.

"Trying to digest this food while pondering imprisonment is upsetting my gastro-intestinal system," said Admiral Yobo, examining a twisted rootlike item that crunched like celery and tasted like oysters.

"Nothing upsets *your* gastro-intestinal system, Admiral," whispered Fargo.

"Talking about a gastro-intestinal system," whispered Albany, "what do you mean, Captain Erig, about the Princess having been fed to a tree. Does it eat?"

"Yes," whispered the Captain. "There is a large opening at the top of the trunk where it splits into two main branches."

The tree leaned forward as the Captain spoke and the two branches parted.

"Ugh," whispered Albany, "how terrible to be stuffed in there."

"Yes," trilled the tree. "The Slithers stunned us all with vibrations and then they lifted me up, a whole lot of them, sort of standing one on top of another, and shoved me in. I couldn't stop them."

"I'm glad it didn't kill you," whispered Yobo.

"Maybe, but now I'm part of the tree, and that's hardly any better. The tree has to eat animal protein every so often to stay healthy. Usually they feed it worms. Sometimes a Slither or two

52

jumps into it. But this time they used me to feed it."

Albany whispered, "Why you? Why not one of the other Izzians?"

There was a moment of silence and then the tree said, "Because I'm the Princess. I'm the most beautiful." She broke into shrill sobs. "I'll just *never* be rescued."

The gloom got worse. "I wish I had a pair of earplugs," whispered Yobo. "This perpetual singing by the Slithers is getting to me."

Captain Erig whispered, "It's a little better at night when they crawl into the mud. It gets quiet then, and you can sleep. I hope none of you snore, though. That would wake them and make them irritable."

"Well," whispered Yobo, dubiously, "I'll *try* not to snore."

"Uh-oh," whispered Erig. "The Slithers are approaching again. They may expect you newcomers to sing. If so, you'd better do it."

"Well," whispered Fargo, "we'll be able to run through our songs for the contest back home, and it will be a pleasure not to have to whisper for a while. After a while, whispering rasps the throat somehow."

They did sing. Albany and Fargo sang a romantic duet from an old musical; Jeff sang a short marching song of the Cadets; and Yobo pleased the natives immensely with his rendition of "Spacemen All to the Fray" in deep bass Martian Swahili.

The singing didn't stop Jeff from worrying about Norby, however, who was still tightly closed in his barrel. Was he getting weaker?

"I envy your robot," whispered the other female Izzian, during a pause in the singing, "She can close out the noise."

"She's a he," whispered Jeff morosely.

"That's impossible. All robots are 'she'."

"Not where I come from."

She sniffed, possibly in disbelief, and moved away from Jeff —and closer to Fargo. That might have been accidental, but Jeff didn't think so. The older Izzian male scowled but looked too tired to object.

The younger Izzian male whispered to Jeff, "There's a latrine in a little side cage over there. You can wash at a small pool in the corner, but don't stir up the mud too much. There's a spring of fresh water from that rock by the sacred tree. It seems to be safe to drink."

"Thanks," said Jeff. It was his turn to sing again, and he hesitated over his choice until a branch of the sacred tree reached over and tapped him on the shoulder.

"Sing a love song," demanded the Princess. "I will join in after I hear it once."

Jeff decided on "When You're Your True Love's True Love," a song hit of about five years before, which he translated into Izzian as he sang it. The Slithers seemed delighted. So was the Princess. She joined in the second time around.

"My true love," sighed Rinda, her leaves a-quiver, "perhaps he has arrived."

As the daylight began to disappear into darkness, there was general exhaustion among the group of prisoners, and they all lay down on woven-leaf mats provided for them.

Fargo, still unconcerned about their imprisonment, was sleepily enthusiastic over the musical possibilities of Melodia. "Think of it—a gigantic cantata—or perhaps I could train them to do opera—amazing how they all have perfect pitch—miracles of counterpoint—intricately perfect—"

"We'd have to get out of this predicament first," grumbled Yobo. "And dissonance has its musical value, too."

"Don't mention dissonance," whispered Erig. "It means stings."

Jeff could think only of Norby. Even after falling asleep, he dreamed that Norby was permanently closed in his barrel, and he woke in a fright. Could that be true? Norby hadn't answered his last few telepathic contacts. He had to try again. The barrel was by his side and Jeff had an arm over it.

——Norby?

——Hello, Jeff. Are the Slithers asleep?

A wave of relief swept over Jeff.

——Why didn't you answer before, Norby?

——I was pretending to be non-existent so the Slithers wouldn't bury me in the mud. I don't want to be buried, Jeff.

——You won't be. Are you all right otherwise?

——Of course, I'm not all right. I'm a failure.

——You are not. You're my friend and I have faith in you.

——You do, Jeff?

——Yes. You're very smart. You've proved that over and over.

——Thank you, Jeff. I will try to be intelligent. I will spend the rest of the night thinking hard.

———Good, wake me anytime, especially if you come up with a solution.

Jeff turned over, placed his other arm about the little barrel, and fell asleep.

Jeff woke just before dawn feeling oddly refreshed. It seemed to him that he had dreamed a solution.

Some of the Slithers were coming out of the mud, and he could hear their humming in the distance. The other Terrans and the Izzians were asleep. Suddenly he had an inspiration. He rubbed the barrel and said telepathically,

———I've got the solution, Norby. If we can't move out of space into hyperspace, we can move out of this portion of normal space by going back in time. Let's go back to a time before this cage was built. Then we can move half a mile away, come back to the present and, presto! we're outside the cage.

———I thought of that, Jeff, but suppose the planet's field stops my time travel ability as well as my hyperspace travel. I couldn't bear a second failure.

———*I'm* suggesting it, Norby, so if it fails, it's *my* failure, not yours. We'll never know unless we try. And take me with you.

Norby's half a head emerged from his barrel and, in the dim light of dawn, Jeff could see the robot's eyes open and gleaming. One arm emerged.

———Hang on tightly, Jeff, so my personal protection field keeps us both in a bubble of normal conditions.

Nothing happened. The Slithers sounded louder and nearer.

———*Think,* Norby. Think of going back into the past.

———I can't, Jeff. It won't work.

———We have to try harder. Let's *both* think.

They shut their eyes and concentrated. Suddenly there was absolute silence. Jeff opened his eyes.

———Norby, where are we?

———I'm not sure.

They seemed to be floating in a dark cloud, but Jeff couldn't tell what kind it was. At least Norby's personal protective shield gave Jeff breathable air—for as long as the supply inside the shield would last.

———Did we get above Melodia, Norby?

———Jeff, there's no planet here. We're in space and I think this is one of those clouds of dust and gas that lie between the stars.

———How did we get between the stars?

——I think it's because we went billions of years into the past, and Melodia's sun and planetary system haven't formed yet.

——*Billions* of years into the past? A few hundred would have been enough.

——I know Jeff. I just got mixed-up again. I'm sorry.

——No, no, Norby. I told you. It's my idea and anything that goes wrong is my fault. At least we're out of the cage. Am I right, or is the cloud thicker over in that direction?

——You're right, Jeff. My sensors tell me that a star is forming there. Melodia's sun, I suppose. It hasn't ignited yet.

——When will that happen?

——I can't say. Maybe a million years or so. And, Jeff, there's something strange in the direction opposite to that in which the star is forming. Whatever it is, it gives rise to the same strange electronic field that came from Melodia. There's something there.

——Maybe it *is* Melodia.

——It can't be. The planet hasn't formed yet. The object is only a few thousand miles away. I'm heading over there. Hang on, Jeff.

There was no sensation of speed, but it took only a few minutes for Norby to cross the void that separated them and the source of the field.

——Look, it's a spaceship, Jeff.

Jeff saw it straight ahead. Judging from the size of its partially dilated round door, the entire ship must have been as big as the island of Manhattan. It had no lights.

——Is it dead, Norby?

——Not if the inhibitory field is being generated by it. Shall we go in?

——Yes. Perhaps it's a ship of the Others. I won't be able to see anything in the dark, though.

——I'll use my sensors, Jeff, and describe things to you.

There was no artificial gravity in the ship, but beyond the first two compartments inside the door there was still a breathable atmosphere, according to Norby's sensors. Cautiously, Norby lowered his personal protective screen. The air seemed stale but with enough oxygen.

All the corridors were tubular, and the adjoining rooms were filled with strange, silent equipment that seemed dead. Phosphorescent paint spotted the walls in odd patterns bright enough to enable Jeff to see a little.

Jeff felt himself to be almost in a dream as he was pulled by

Norby through the long tubes whose shining patterns undulated in different colors. The patterns seemed to be giving a message that no one was left to read.

9

THE STRANGER ON THE SHIP

"It's a relief not to have to depend on your protective field, Norby," Jeff said. "I mean, it's wonderful to have it, but it's nice to have a less limited supply of air to breathe. And it's wonderful to be able to *talk* without having to worry about being stung."

"We'll need my screen again when we leave the ship, you know."

"I know. Do you think this is a ship left by the Others, Norby?"

"No, I'm pretty sure it isn't. Judging from the ship left by the Others on Jamya, it isn't built in their style. They used corridors like ours, with artificial gravity."

"Without artificial gravity, I suppose you'd want tubular corridors and spherical rooms," Jeff said. "It wouldn't matter which way is up. The aliens of this ship may have been space travelers for so long that they've evolved into creatures without the ability to live under gravity conditions."

"I've sensed no aliens, Jeff; not even anything like a robot. I don't sense any intelligence, not even devices that might be watching us and recording what we do. The ship seems unguarded and I think it's empty."

"But what happened to the occupants?"

"I don't know. Of course, we're still miles from the other end of the ship and we don't know where the control rooms are. That's where the field must come from. Maybe we'll find out more about the aliens there."

They moved on carefully as Norby propelled himself and Jeff through corridors that wound on and on like snakes that had eaten a robot and a boy without digesting them.

Suddenly Norby shot through a round door into a huge spherical chamber. Here, Jeff's eyesight failed altogether, for there were no phosphorescent patterns on the wall. "What a pity," he said. "Maybe this part is so old that the phosphoresence faded away."

Norby said, "I don't think there ever were any of those markings here. I hate to use my light, Jeff, because my energy supply is low. And as long as the inhibitory field is being generated I can't get into hyperspace. Just the same, there are no Slithers to keep us from moving outside the field whenever we need to, so I'll take the chance."

His little light gleamed and barely pierced the darkness. He and Jeff drifted through cavernous space until Norby almost jerked Jeff's arm from its socket as he pulled back.

"A force barrier!" cried Norby. "Invisible, and protecting —*that*."

What Norby was pointing to was an enormous metal ball in the exact center of the chamber. They could approach it no closer, being held off by a powerful force they could feel but not see.

"The inhibitory field sent out by the ship comes from that ball," said Norby, "and so does the force barrier. The ball seems to contain machinery to create both and—yes—" Norby paused, his sensor wire quivering as it projected out of his hat. "The ball is also shielded by tons of metal treated in some way I can't make out. And Jeff—"

Norby's hat slammed down abruptly, closing his head inside his barrel. His hand let go of Jeff's and his whole arm disappeared into the barrel, too.

Jeff thumped Norby. "What is it? What's wrong?"

Norby's hat went up part way, his eyes peeping over the edge of the barrel. He said in a tiny voice, "I just detected something else in this room. Something that's *thinking*."

Jeff looked around but could see nothing. "Is it in the ball?"

"I don't know."

Jeff was hanging by himself in the air of the circular room. He tried swimming motions to maneuver around the ball, outside the force barrier, so that he could examine the entire room. Norby followed him timorously, shining his light.

After much effort, they made it to the other side of the ball but saw nothing.

"I think it's following us, Jeff. It keeps the ball between us so we can't see it, and I can't scan it."

"It must be as afraid of us as you are of it, Norby, so let's split

up. I'll go one way and you go the other. If either one sees
anything, he yells for the other."

They parted and started in opposite directions around the ball,
watching it. As Norby and his light moved away, Jeff could see
less and less. Jeff had almost decided that his inability to see
made the whole project useless, when he heard Norby yell.

"Help, Jeff!"

Frantically, Jeff propelled himself toward Norby, although not
very rapidly, for the method of propulsion was clumsy. Norby
was jiggling up and down in midair—except that there wasn't
any true up or down in the room.

"Here I am, Norby. What's the matter?"

"There!" Norby sucked his head in and out. "Peeking around
the ball at us!"

Jeff glimpsed something—an eye? two eyes?—before whatever it was drew back behind the ball. It occurred to him that in a
gravity-free room, two hunters were not enough to trap their prey
since it could always move at right angles to the direction in
which the hunters were moving away from each other. It would
take at least three hunters to pin it down.

"Hey!" shouted Jeff, "come out, come out wherever you are!"
Nothing appeared.

"I doubt if it understands us," said Jeff.

"Maybe it's dangerous," quavered Norby. "I don't like it here,
Jeff. Let's go home."

"We can't go home! We've got to get back to Melodia, remember? And you've got to get away from this inhibitory field
and into hyperspace to refuel. How weak are you?"

"I'm still strong enough to get us out of here, past the field.
But I won't be for much longer. We can't afford to get trapped in
here."

"Just one more try," said Jeff. "I'll speak in Izzian. —Stranger, reveal yourself. We are friends."

"Friends?" said a small high voice in a form of Izzian. "I do not
know you. I have never seen creatures like you before. How is it you
speak the language of the Others?"

"We are friendly. We speak your language because we have
visited two planets where the Others, or robots left by them,
taught their language to those they found or settled there."

Then from around the giant ball a small object appeared. It
was a metal ball slightly smaller than Norby, with a bulge in one
place. On the bulge were three eyes remarkably similar to those
of the robots of Jamya, the world of the dragons. The little ball

turned and Jeff could see three more eyes on the other side of the
bulge.

As he watched, little arms similar to those of Norby emerged
from dilated openings as the small robot came closer.

"Is it true? Are you connected with the Others?"

Norby, who had suddenly gained courage as he found himself
the larger of the two, said, "My friend here has never seen the
Others. Neither have I, but some of my inner workings were
made by robots left by the Others on a planet named Jamya."

"A planet? I have never seen a planet, but I will be part of one
some day."

"What are you?" asked Jeff.

"Who are *you* is the better question," said the robot. "You
seem to be a protoplasmic creature. I have heard of such. In fact,
the Others may be protoplasmic."

"Then you have never seen the Others either?" Jeff asked.

"No. They activated me by remote control after they visited
this ship."

"Are you still in touch with the Others?" asked Jeff eagerly.

"No. They activated me in such a way that I came equipped
with memory banks full of instructions for my job, and some data
to explain how I got here. But nothing gives me any information
about the Others. Tell me, who are *you,* protoplasmic one? You
ask me for information, but you give none. That is scarcely polite."

"I'm sorry," said Jeff. "I got excited when I thought we had
finally met someone who might have seen the Others. I am indeed protoplasmic. I am Jeff Wells from a planet circling a star
far, far away. This is my robot, Norby. We are attempting to
rescue some of our friends who are in trouble." Jeff cautiously
refrained from saying that the friends were separated from him in
time rather than in space. Then he asked, "What is your name?"

"I am female in personality, and I am called Perceiver. I watch
and record and wait."

"For the return of the Others?"

"No, they will not be back. The original makers of this alien
ship will not be back, either. They are apparently a very old
species who travel from galaxy to galaxy, leaving ships like this
behind. . . . Perhaps only a very few per galaxy, for this is a very
expensive and difficult operation."

"But what and why are you observing?" asked Jeff. "And
what is the purpose of this ship?"

The little robot waved her arms. "The ship is to become the

nucleus of a planet. Soon a star will form the dust cloud in this area of space and its stellar wind will sweep away most of the gas and dust. The larger pieces remaining behind will come together about the ship, and after millions of years, will form a planet."

"But the ship will be crushed."

"The ship will, but not *that* structure," said the robot, pointing to the huge ball. "At least it's not supposed to. It is protected by treated metal and a force barrier. Its purpose is to produce an inhibitory field that will make hypertravel almost impossible."

"You mean the builders of this ship want to construct planets from which any intelligences that evolve will not easily be able to leave, except the slow way through normal space?"

"I think so, but I do not know why. Nevertheless, I have recorded much already, and I will continue to record much, much more as the new star ignites and as the planet begins to shape itself."

"But that might take as long as a million years," said Jeff, "and in the end, you'll be crushed as the planet forms. What good will that do the Others? How will they get your information?"

"This way," said the robot, opening a section of her middle. "Inside here is a small package of equipment recording all I observe. The package has a neutralizing device that permits it to enter hyperspace at once in spite of the inhibiting field. Where it goes after that, I do not know. I cannot follow. I am not equipped to enter hyperspace."

"Then you'll be crushed?"

"As soon as this package enters hyperspace and the ship is crushed, I will die and become an infinitesimal part of the planet that will form. Surely that will be a noble end."

"And the planet will be Melodia," said Jeff in a low voice, "complete with its inhibiting field."

"I do not understand," said Perceiver.

"It is not important. Will you come with us? It isn't right that you should wait here alone for so many ages, only to be crushed in the end."

"It is my job," said Perceiver. "Would you have me not do my job? That would be inconceivable. Please go."

Norby plucked at Jeff's sleeve. "Yes, let's go now. I must get out into hyperspace—"

"Yes, Norby, we're going—But, Perceiver, don't put us in your record. We do not wish to be included."

"I record only conditions of the formation of stars and planets. You will not be included. However, it has been pleasant to meet other beings and to communicate. I will be able to exercise my brain thinking about you and making songs about you."

"Songs?" asked Norby and Jeff simultaneously.

"I like to sing." Then Perceiver demonstrated. Her music was soft and sweet and sad, with a sound unlike anything they had heard on Melodia. Jeff liked it.

"Though I hate to leave you alone here, Perceiver, I know you feel you must do your job. I will remember you."

"Come on, Jeff," said Norby, pulling at his arm. "Goodbye, Perceiver. You're doing a job no one else could do. I congratulate you."

"Thank you. Your words mean much to me. Goodbye."

As he and Norby sped through the ship toward the exit, Jeff found himself brooding.

"It's wrong," he said. "Wrong of the Others to leave a robot here alone to die, especially one with emotive circuits, one who can feel as well as think."

"Still," said Norby, "they must have had a reason. The future may in some way depend upon the recordings that Perceiver is making. Therefore we couldn't have taken her away now without changing the future, perhaps much for the worse. Yet I, too, wish it were not so, for she is a robot very like me, and I don't want her to die, either."

Norby activated his personal protective shield for Jeff as they left the air-filled corridors behind. Soon they were outside the ship, speeding as fast as possible away from the field preventing Norby from entering hyperspace, the dimension that makes it possible to bypass the speed-of-light limit to travel in ordinary space.

——Past the field, Jeff. I can go into hyperspace now. Hang on!

10

OUT OF THE PAST

The grayness of hyperspace enclosed Jeff. Now there was no ship to keep him safely in a bubble of normal space. There was only Norby's protective field, which was invisible, so that Jeff felt utterly lost, surrounded by opaque gray.

Nothing was up, nothing was down, nothing was here, nothing was there—and how long would the nothingness last? Jeff didn't know how long it took Norby to refuel in hyperspace, for the robot had done it alone before. Inside this nothingness beyond nothingness, was it possible to tell how much time was passing? Or did time pass? Jeff had no answers.

A feeling of panic engulfed him when he began to wonder if the meager supply of oxygen trapped inside Norby's personal field would last. He realized that he was panting anxiously, using up the oxygen supply that much more quickly.

"I've got to use one of the meditation techniques that Fargo taught me years ago," Jeff said to himself, and felt another wave of panic when he heard no sound, not even inside his throat, and could not see his own body. Hyperspace had never frightened him so much before.

He forced himself to breathe quickly, his facial muscles shaped into a calming smile. He relaxed his feet, his legs and arms, his body and neck. Ignoring the awful feeling that he had lost the entire Universe, he said his solstice litany:

"I am part of the Universe, part of life. I am a Terran creature, from the life that evolved on Earth." He stopped and changed the rest to fit the situation. "No matter how far away I am from Earth in space and time, I will remember her. I will respect all life and know that we are all part of the Oneness. Whatever danger I am in, the Universe is One."

He felt calm, and then something squeezed his hand. He remembered he was holding onto Norby in the loneliness of hyperspace, and then the robot's telepathic thought came to him with piercing clarity.

——That was good, Jeff. It made me feel better, too.

——You're okay?"

——I'm all refueled, in perfect working order, and ready to go.

——Let's go forward in time. I've decided that I want to rescue Pera. She's part of life, too. At least she is alive to me, just as you are, Norby.

——Pera is a good name for her. Small and feminine, as she is. I also don't like to think of her being crushed, but what if rescue changes the future somehow?

——I hope it won't if we do it right. We'll go back inside the alien ship and time-travel up to the moment when the planet is forming but before the ship is being crushed. That's when Pera will send out her packet of information. She will fulfill her mission, so the future of that won't be changed. Her mass will be missing from the planet once it forms, but that's insignificant.

——Good thinking, Jeff. I'm glad we're going back. I like her.

With a sudden internal jolt, Norby took them out of hyperspace and plunged so fast toward the huge ship with Jeff in tow, that when they entered the door and got inside the first air-filled chamber, Jeff was gasping for breath.

"Whoa!" said Jeff. "Let me think. I guess this is going to be more dangerous than I thought. We've got to move forward in time to the point when the planet is forming but the ship is still intact. Do you think you can manage this, Norby?"

"I'll have to. We can't arrive too soon before Pera does her job, and we can't arrive too late. You'd better help me, Jeff. Hold my hand tightly and concentrate with me."

Jeff shut his eyes to the coruscating images on the corridor walls and concentrated, trying to link his mind with Norby's. It seemed to him that for a long time nothing at all happened, and then suddenly it felt as if he were in an earthquake.

He opened his eyes and saw that the walls were shaking so much that the iridescent patterns seemed to dance wildly. The entire ship sounded as if it were groaning aloud under the pressure of the hull.

"We're awfully close to the danger point, Norby! Hurry! We've got to get to the central chamber immediately!" Norby's response was to pull Jeff so fast that this time he wasn't sure he was breathing at all.

Pera floated serenely in the central chamber just outside the force barrier surrounding the enormous ball. "You're back!" she said. "I've had so many years of pleasant remembrance of you, making songs about you. But now you should leave again, for soon the ship will collapse and before that, I must send my package into hyperspace."

The vibration was getting louder and louder and Jeff gritted his teeth to keep from losing his ability to think clearly. "Send your package *now*. Then Norby will take us both out of the ship and into hyperspace. You don't have to die."

"Jeff!" yelled Norby, "I can't get out of the ship. None of us can. My sensors tell me the outer part of the ship is already crushed. I'm trapped here by the inhibitory field. We're all trapped."

Jeff's hands and feet turned ice cold, but he kept his voice steady. "Then take us back further into time, anywhere, to get out."

"I can't! The forces are too strong. Oh, Jeff, I've failed you! Pera, I'm sorry. This is the end for us."

Pera hovered near them. "I like your new name for me and I am sorry that you are trapped here since it makes you unhappy. Remember we will all be part of the planet in death, never separated from each other again." She paused and opened the compartment in her body that concealed the package of information. "I will send this now."

"Wait," said Jeff. "Will it go into hyperspace right from here?"

"Yes. That is the plan. It bypasses the inhibitory field."

"Then as you activate it, hold onto it and we'll hold onto you. Maybe it will take us with it into hyperspace."

"I would like to do that, but it is not as I have been instructed."

"Pera," said Jeff solemnly, "you were instructed by the Others, who did not know that Norby and I would be here. They were protoplasmic beings, and so am I, and I order you to change the arrangement. Take us with you and the package into hyperspace."

"I do not have to obey your commands," said Pera in a small voice, "but I will because I would not have either of you die."

Jeff held the hands of the two little robots, who hovered close to him. The two-way thumb of Pera's free hand stayed poised over the switch of the record package, while Norby extended his protective field to its limits, enclosing both Jeff and Pera.

All around them, the walls of the central chamber rattled and creaked ominously as the thundering noise of the collapsing outer structure of the ship came closer and closer. Just as Jeff thought he could stand the noise no longer, the chamber walls suddenly gave way and moved toward him with a great roar.

Pera pressed the switch.

Jeff was in hyperspace once more, but this time he concentrated on the sensory knowledge that his hands were holding those of Norby and Pera. He could not see the robots, but he knew the robots were there, and he did not feel alone and lost.

Norby's thought came to him. ——Jeff, we're in hyperspace but the record package that brought us here got away from Pera. I don't know where it's gone—or when.

——*When?*

——My sensors tell me it moved us through *time* as well as into hyperspace.

——How much time? And how far have we come in hyperspace?

——I don't know.

Pera spoke telepathically for the first time. ——How comforting it is to be able to hear your thoughts in this strange place. This is a new experience for me. I also do not know how far the package brought us in time, but I have discovered that I am able to sense how far we have traveled away from the alien ship.

Jeff felt a wave of hope. ——Pera, are we far enough away so that if Norby takes us out of hyperspace and back into normal space, we won't be trapped *inside* the planet?

——I think so.

——Aha! ——I'm not the only robot that isn't absolutely certain about everything (said Norby).

Jeff grinned in spite of the danger. ——Fargo says that absolute certainty is not compatible with high intelligence, so we'll have to take a chance. Take us out of here, Norby, so we can find out where—and *when*—we are.

While Jeff waited, he tried not to feel panic again at the thought that Pera might be wrong, and they might appear inside a planet, or worse, a sun. The next thing he felt was warmth on his body, and he opened his eyes to sunlight.

There was a muddy planet nearby and it seemed to be moving toward them rapidly. Jeff felt air on his face, and then it was cold wind.

"Norby!" shouted Jeff. "Antigrav! We're falling through the atmosphere!"

With an uncomfortable jerk they stopped falling as Norby turned on his antigrav.

"Is this a planet?" asked Pera. "I've never seen one. Is it one of the best?"

"It's a planet," said Jeff, "but not one of the best. It's Melodia, and since it's now mostly mud on the surface, that means we've arrived near the right time."

"What is the right time?" asked Pera.

"Shortly after Norby and I left our friends and the Izzians in the Slithers' cage. Pull us through the atmosphere, Norby, low enough to find that main island."

"I can help pull," said Pera. "I too have antigrav and the ability to travel in normal space."

"Okay," said Jeff. "I feel as if I had two motors to help me fly, but don't go too fast. It knocks the wind out of me and we won't be able to scan the surface carefully.

As they dropped closer to the mud of Melodia, Jeff told Pera all that had happened since the *Hopeful* left Manhattan on its search for the lost humans. He was particularly enthusiastic when he came to describing the Tree Princess.

"I understand that you think she is beautiful," said Pera. "I do not know anything about the beauty of protoplasmics."

"Wait till you've seen Rinda. Of course, I've only seen her in a tree, but according to her portrait, she's also one of the most beautiful human females in the Universe. I wish I could see her as she is."

"Perhaps you will," said Pera.

"There's the main island," said Norby. "And we must be at the right time. I can see the top of the big cage."

"What odd creatures the Slithers are," said Pera, looking down.

"Odd and very dangerous," said Jeff. "But why aren't they singing?"

The trio descended to the top of the central cage. Jeff let go of the robots and sat on the bars to think. "Nobody's there!"

"Look, Jeff," said Pera. "The Slithers did not come to attack you when you spoke aloud, instead of singing."

It was true. The Slithers peeped out from behind bushes and trees, maintaining a careful distance.

"I don't understand it," said Jeff. "Since nobody's in the cage, we must have arrived much too early. But then why are the

Slithers acting afraid of us?"

"Try singing, Jeff," said Norby.

Jeff cleared his throat. "Good morrow, good Slithers; good Slithers, good morrow," he sang.

The little creatures hissed and turned chartreuse.

"I didn't think my voice was that bad today," said Jeff. "Hey, come back here!"

With every word of his voice, the Slithers quivered all over and backed away, singing eerie music in a minor key that was almost a chant. Even without words, the music seemed to say, "Go away! Go away!"

"Why are they afraid of you?" asked Pera. "I thought you said you were afraid of them."

"I don't understand any of this," Jeff said. "When we first arrived on Melodia, the Slithers were friendly, and they were never afraid of us even after we became their prisoners."

"Jeff," said Norby, tugging at Jeff's shirt. "Look—there's a big hole in the side of the cage."

The hole was large, and the lattice at its edges was charred. Jeff swung down and through the hole into the cage. He saw a metal object on the ground and picked it up.

"This is one of Admiral Yobo's favorite metals," he said. "I know what's happened. Pera's package brought us so far forward in time that we've arrived after everyone left Melodia."

"They must have escaped through that hole," said Pera.

"The tree!" shouted Norby. He and Pera flew down to join Jeff inside the cage.

Jeff whirled. In the spot where the sacred tree of Melodia had grown there was only a tiny seedling with delicate gold and silver leaves. Around it were piles of decaying branches, some almost turned to dust.

"Are the Slithers afraid of you because their sacred tree is gone and it gave them courage?"

"I don't know, Pera," said Jeff. "I don't know how the Izzians and our friends escaped, because what could have made that hole? And how did they take the *Hopeful,* or the *Challenger,* away from Melodia and into hyperspace without Norby's help?"

"I'd have to be here!" said Norby, blinking all four of his eyes in agitation. "I'm necessary!"

"Of course you are, Norby," said Pera soothingly. "Perhaps you *were* here. You and Jeff."

"What do you mean?" asked Jeff.

"I don't understand time travel," said Pera, "but it seems to me that somehow you and Norby did arrive and help everyone escape. I wonder if I was with you."

"You mean it hasn't happened yet—but it did happen—and we were there—and we haven't been yet, so we don't know about it yet, and—" Norby paused, retracted his head into his barrel, and popped it up again. "I think I'm confused."

"We all are," said Jeff, "but I think Pera's got something. We must go back in time and do whatever it was that helped everyone escape."

"Whatever it was," said Norby, glaring at the quivering little Slithers, "we sure showed them who's boss. I just wish I could *remember* what it was."

"It hasn't happened yet—to you," said Jeff patiently. "We're here in the future—our future—by mistake. We've got to go back."

"Maybe we can't go back," fumed Norby. "Maybe we've messed up the past by rescuing Pera and now the future has changed. We might even be in a different universe."

"I should never have let you take me out of the alien ship," said Pera sadly. "It has endangered you."

"We *had* to rescue you, Pera," Norby said as if it had been his idea. "You see, the thing is, I'm like you—I mean, I like you—I mean, it wasn't right for you to die. . . ."

"Correct," said Jeff quickly, before Norby got any more embarrassed. "I'm sure this is the same universe, and that everything will be all right if we can go back in time." He wasn't at all sure, but he had to calm the emotive circuits of two excited robots, one of whom was absolutely necessary for traveling in that tricky thing, time. "Let's hold hands, all of us, and concentrate on going back to the time just after Norby and I left."

As Jeff reached out his hands to Norby and Pera, he discovered that he was still holding the Admiral's lost medal. He put it in his pocket without thinking anything but how pleased Yobo would be to have it back.

"Concentrate, everybody," said Norby.

"I can't," said Pera. "I'm worried. Won't you meet yourselves in the past if you don't hit it right?"

"No," said Norby. "I can't travel through time to where I already am. It's impossible to meet oneself. We'll get back to the time after we left. I hope."

"Don't just hope, Norby," said Jeff. "I want accuracy."

"I'm always accurate. Well, mostly accurate."

"Norby!" said Jeff warningly.

"I can't see that I'm getting any help from anyone." Norby jiggled up and down with his telescoping feet. "Hold hands and concentrate."

"Do it right, Norby," said Jeff.

"I'll try, but I certainly need help."

As the three vanished, the Slithers began to sing happily.

11

The Cage Again

"Ow!" said Jeff.

"You keep saying that," Norby said. "You'd think a Slither had stung you."

"Oola's welcoming embrace is inclined to be prickly," said Jeff as he disengaged the claws of his All-Purpose-Pet from his arms and tried to grasp the fact that he was not on Melodia but in his own Manhattan living room.

Zargl flapped her leathery wings and said, "Why have you returned without my beloved Fargo?" She turned off the holoTV screen she'd been studying and confronted Jeff again. "And where are the Admiral and Lieutenant Jones? And who is this strange new robot?"

"This is Pera. She's a robot left by the Others to observe and record the beginnings of a planetary system. It's a long story, Zargl."

"But Jeff," said Zargl, the tiny green scales on her forehead curving into a wrinkle of puzzlement, "all of you left in the *Hopeful* only a few hours ago. How can your adventure have been a long one?"

"Norby!" yelled Jeff. "We've messed up time again! *You've* messed it up! Why have you brought us back home?"

Norby retracted his arms until only the double-palmed hands showed, and they drooped as if to emphasize humility. "I'm only a simple little robot, Jeff, and it's you who should be intelligent. You're supposed to be my owner—I mean my partner—and the least you can be is very intelligent."

"I don't *feel* bright. I feel battered and stung and my ears hurt. I'm also hungry and scared. What am I supposed to be intelligent about?"

"Zargl, get Jeff something to eat," Norby said. "He's a growing boy, and he thinks better when his stomach is full. I want him to think about why I came here."

"I suspect, Norby, that you came here because you're afraid to go back to where you were, and because you've given up on the rescue, and because you don't care about the Princess, and because you're terrified of her domineering mother, who punishes first and talks later."

"Please explain," said Zargl, placing a bowl of peanuts and her scaly green tail upon the living room floor near Jeff.

Jeff listened to Norby's explanations, which seemed to emphasize Norby's own skill, daring, and genius. Pera's hands were clasped and she looked at Norby with what seemed to be reverent attention.

Jeff munched at the peanuts. They were a great improvement on Melodian vegetation. "No one's going to believe you're a hero, Norby," he said. "We haven't yet done what we set out to do, and you haven't explained why you brought me back to my Manhattan apartment."

"I was hoping you'd figure it out, Jeff."

Jeff had a sudden deep suspicion that Norby didn't know how or why he had come back to the apartment, but was hoping Jeff would rescue him with an idea.

Jeff said, "Were you saying something about getting help, Norby?"

Norby blinked. "That's right. We need a special kind of help."

"And you came to get me, of course," said Zargl.

"That couldn't be," said Jeff. "You're only a dragon-child and your mother wouldn't approve—"

"She doesn't know," said Zargl complacently, "and, besides, I'm very useful." She took a deep breath and blew it outward, producing a long flame from her mouth. Pera jumped back, while Oola howled like a dog and then slunk under the sofa.

"See," said Zargl, "I may be little, but I can easily burn a hole in the cage where everyone is a prisoner."

"That's it!" said Norby, "now we know how the hole came to be. Wasn't I right to come back here?" He soared upward and whirled in glee.

Zargl said, "I'm very good at flaming, actually—too good, mother says. The other day she scolded me for being so primitive when I flamed and singed the hem of the Grand Dragon's favorite cape."

"Also, Jeff," said Norby happily, "Zargl is small enough for

me to surround with my protective shield along with you and
Pera. I can't surround an elephant, you know. Furthermore, Zargl
has wings and an antigrav collar, so she can avoid being stung by
the Slithers if she doesn't sing properly. I tell you I've thought it
all out."

"What do you mean, not sing properly," demanded Zargl. "I
have an excellent voice."

"All right, Norby," said Jeff in resignation, "I admit it sounds
workable, but don't let it go to your head. Let's get back to
Melodia and try to get everyone out of the cage and into the
Hopeful—though I still don't see how we can manage the Tree
Princess."

He placed Pera under one arm, Norby under the other, and
Zargl settled herself on his shoulders.

"Ready?" asked Norby.

"Worrww?" said Oola, coming out from under the sofa.

"I forgot about Oola," said Jeff. "She'll be all alone."

"The automatic feeder is full of food and water," said Zargl.
"She'll be all right if we don't stay away too long. She strikes me
as a very self-contained and self-assured creature."

"Actually, she's not," said Jeff, "but let's be off—no, wait!
Norby, please find the earplugs in my bedroom drawer."

When Norby came back with the earplugs and was tucked
once more under Jeff's arm, Oola approached them with her back
stiff and a look of outrage in her eyes. It was obvious that she
expected to go along, and Jeff had to shove her back with his
foot.

"Meow," said Oola plaintively, looking more cat-like than
ever in an effort to please. Her whiskers twitched and the pupils
of her eyes were like slits. The All-Purpose-Pet was, at that moment, totally a cat—a cat sensing she was about to be abandoned.

"Now," said Norby.

"Wowrr!" growled Oola, her tail waving angrily. Then she
launched herself.

Just before he saw the grayness of hyperspace, Jeff felt a furry
body hit his chest, its forelegs tightly clasping his neck.

"I must say," said Captain Erig, staring up at them through the
roof of the cage, "that after being gone a week, you have come
back with a peculiar rescue party. You have a small green furry
animal, a small green scaly animal, and a small roundish robot
with six eyes. Add those to yourself and Norby, and you don't

resemble my idea of a rescue force. Furthermore I don't find your plan at all satisfactory."

"Nor do I," said Princess Rinda, rubbing her twigs together in irritation.

"I must say," said Fargo peevishly, "that I don't follow your reasoning either, Jeff. But perhaps my brain is not working in clear linear logic ever since we were forced yesterday to sing complicated fugues for five hours."

It was night time and it was therefore possible to talk openly without getting stung, but dawn was already beginning to silver the edge of the sky.

"The least you could have done was to bring non-vegetable food," said Yobo. "I suppose you ate yourself silly when you were home." The Admiral looked less imposingly massive through the middle.

"I only had a few peanuts," said Jeff, "and Oola never got her dinner. There's a limit to how much Norby can carry, you know. We didn't plan to bring Oola; she just hung on and that, as it was, stretched poor Norby to the limit."

"Yes," whimpered Norby, "but who cares about me? I'm just old workhorse Norby."

Oola was sniffing and growling softly.

"She doesn't like this planet," said Albany.

"Who does?" said Fargo. "Jeff, can you concentrate and make her turn herself into a Slither-eating sabertoothed tiger or something like that?"

Jeff said, "It's hard to make her deliberately turn into something you want. She tends to tune in on you when you're not actually thinking of her. She's not very bright, you know. And even if she ate Slithers, how many could she eat before filling herself to the ears?"

Albany stroked Oola, who had squeezed through the roof and jumped into her arms. "Nice kitty doesn't want to be a tiger, does she?"

"At least you've brought a useful dragon," said Fargo. "Hurry and burn the cage, Zargl, because my voice won't last another day and my arms are cramped from playing my tympani through the bars."

His kettledrums had been placed against the outside of the cage where Fargo could reach them—but not comfortably.

"That was my idea," said the sacred tree. "I thought if I told the Slithers to bring those drums, they would have to open the door, but they didn't. And look here, dragon, if you burn the cage, do it on the side away from my branches."

Zargl flew to the side of the cage most distant from the tree and began to breathe flame.

"It was almost amusing," said Yobo. "First the Slithers tried the drumsticks themselves, but since they don't know how to play, the noise horrified them and they turned all the colors you could imagine. Then they made poor Fargo drum for hours, demonstrating that it didn't have to be just noise."

"And in the meantime," said the tree, "I have been singing and singing, trying to keep the Slithers happy while this heroic and handsome young man was risking unimaginable horrors in the cosmos trying to find a way of rescuing us."

Jeff perked up. *Someone* appreciated him.

"I ache all over," said Einkan. "I hate this planet and having to be silent all day while the rest of you sing. It would serve all of you right if I left you stranded here."

"That," said Albany frostily, "is probably what you'd planned to do if I hadn't taken away your weapon."

"The sun's coming up," warned Yobo. "I can hear the Slithers begin to hum as they emerge from the mud. You should have arrived earlier, Norby. It's taking Zargl too much time to burn a hole. . . . Of course, if she'd come day before yesterday when it rained, she couldn't have done a thing. We all got very wet, too."

"The wood's thick and tough and still a little damp," said Zargl, pausing for breath. "It doesn't really burn, it just chars— but I'm making progress."

Oola jumped down from Albany's arms and began to pace the floor of the cage, growling fiercely, her fangs longer then usual. "It's a good thing she's a vegetarian," said Albany, "or she'd get pretty hungry. Not that the Melodian plants are particularly nourishing. I'm beginning to feel too weak to sing."

"Don't say that," said Yobo. "If you stop singing, they'll sting you into paralysis and feed you to the sacred tree."

"No!" cried the Tree Princess, waving her branches in agitation, "that must *not* happen! Her personality and mine will intermingle, and she's a commoner. Her father may be, as you say, the mayor of Manhattan, wherever that is, but mayors don't sound like royalty to me. Besides, I won't be—*me* anymore." The branches sagged listlessly until the Princess said angrily, "If you dilute my royalty, my mother will think up new punishments you won't like. Mother's good at that."

"Harumph," said Yobo. "It occurs to me, Cadet, that you might have thought to bring a weapon."

"Zargl *is* a weapon, Admiral, but I hope she doesn't have to burn the Slithers. After all, the Slithers didn't ask us to come to Melodia."

Captain Erig frowned. "We Izzians came here against our will, which you strangers did not. I suspect that when Einkan found the alien ship, the coordinates of this horrible planet were in its data banks so that its owners would know where *not* to go. It's too bad Princess Rinda pressed the wrong switch by mistake."

"It certainly is," said Fargo. "Hurry, Zargl. I want to leave Melodia as soon as possible."

"I thought it appealed to your musical instincts," said Jeff.

"Little brother, my musical instincts have totally burned out."

Zargl stepped back. "Somebody push!" She had produced a large area of thoroughly blackened wood.

Yobo, from inside, heaved at the charred wood with his broad shoulders and it gave way. One by one, the humans stepped out of the cage. Oola, emerging last, jumped into Jeff's arms.

"Wait," cried the tree. "You can't go without me! I am the Crown Princess of Izz. You can't leave me here!"

"But your Highness," said Einkan, "If we dig you up, it will kill the tree—and you."

From the tree came the sound of wild weeping. And at that point, the Slithers arrived, singing an aggressive, angry-sounding song.

"Run for the ships!" shouted Yobo, kicking out at the oncoming Slithers, "and then we'll think of some way to get the tree out without killing it."

It was too late. The sun was up and the Slithers were upon them, driving them back into the cage.

The tree, still weeping said, "Now they're going to feed you one by one to the tree. We'll become a terrible mixture."

"Why do they want to do that?" gasped Albany.

"They're angry because you aren't good zoo animals. You're trying to get away instead of staying behind bars and singing." Her branches shook and her leaves rustled mournfully.

"You didn't warn the Slithers we were leaving, did you, Princess?"

"No. Honestly! I wouldn't care if the others left, just as long as you stayed with me, Jeff."

Jeff said uneasily. "I'm sorry, Princess, I can't. I've got to get back to the Academy."

"Well, if I've got to stay here forever, kill all the Slithers and bring the Academy here. Then you can stay with me."

"We can't do that either," said Jeff, his back against the cage as the unbroken line of Slithers approached, cutting off escape. "The Slithers evolved on this planet—it's theirs. We shouldn't take it from them for our own use, even to make life better for the Crown Princess of Izz in her tree. We have to go away and leave the Slithers alone so they can develop by themselves."

"Then eventually I'll forget who I am and just be a tree and not a Princess," Rinda cried harder than ever.

"Watch out, Jeff!" Norby ascended on antigrav, dragging Jeff out of the way of a stinging Slither.

Zargl, who had been gasping on top of the cage since her task was done, now flew up in the air and dive bombed, her flame forcing the natives back.

"Good dragon," said Yobo. "Open a path to the ship."

"I can't" panted Zargl. "I don't have much flame left. I need at least several hours of rest and some good, nourishing food."

The Slithers used another weapon. Squatting down on their snail feet, they sang with such extraordinary vibrations that Jeff instantly stuffed his earplugs in. They didn't block out all the sound, but they cut down the spinning sensation in his head that was induced by the vibration. Everyone else dropped to the ground, their hands covering their ears. Terrans and Izzians were dragged into the cage.

"Take me to the *Hopeful*, Norby!"

Above the seething mass of natives, with both Jeff and Pera in tow, Norby sped on antigrave.

This failed, too, however. The Slithers blocked the airlock and there was no way of reaching the ship without being stung. While Pera remained on high, Jeff and Norby stormed the lock over and over till Jeff was in dreadful pain and Norby was staggering oddly.

Finally Norby began to run away, followed by Jeff. The Slithers opened a path for them, one that led directly into the cage.

Pera hovered above them, still on antigrav. "Ascend, Norby!"

"I can't," shrieked Norby. "The stings have upset my micro-circuits and I can't antigrav."

"I'll try to carry both of you up," said Pera.

"You're too small, Pera. Take Norby," Jeff yelled.

Pera plunged to pick up Norby just as the Slithers over-whelmed Jeff and pushed him into the cage, slamming the door after him. The escape hole was guarded by countless Slithers. Jeff tried to ignore the pain he felt. Maybe we could try again at night, he thought to himself.

Then he remembered. The Slithers would probably feed them to the tree *before* it was night.

"Meow," said Oola. She was obviously not as sensitive to the Slithers' vibrations as the humans were, but she was not happy. She meowed plaintively and clung to Jeff when he picked her up.

"Oola, couldn't you turn into something useful? Try taking the shape of a Slither. Maybe they'll think I'm special and let me go."

"Meooow!" said Oola, her fangs lengthening a little, and her tail growing shorter to compensate for the shift in mass.

"She's no help," said Norby from where he and Pera were sitting on top of the cage. They were joined by Zargl, who shook her head.

"My flame's gone out altogether. I must eat to restore my energy, but Oola ate all the vegetables while everyone was trying to escape. I'll have to go foraging."

"Better not, Zargl," said Norby. "The Slithers might capture you."

"The situation is hopeless, isn't it?" asked the sacred tree, her leaves quivering.

"No," whispered Jeff. "There must be some way out. In the future we will be all gone and the Slithers will be afraid of us."

Jeff whispered as clearly as he could, "Norby! Go into time."

"I've already tried. I can't. I've got to calm my microcircuits."

"Then, Pera, antigrav yourself and Norby into space beyond the inhibitory field, and help him into hyperspace."

"Not while my microcircuits are jangling," said Norby.

The Slithers continued to surge around the cage, plastering over the burnt-out section of the wall with their bodies.

"I've given up hope," wept the Princess. "Thank you, Jeff, for trying. I did so want to go home to Izz and be a better person. I've been selfish and willful all my life, and now I want to try to be more like you."

"Keep hoping, Princess. Maybe Norby can recover, and then he and Pera could try again to get into one of the ships. The ship's weapons could frighten away the Slithers and demolish the cage and then we'll think of some way of taking you with us."

The Slithers were easing up on their mind-boggling vibrations, and the humans were waking up. They moaned when they saw they were back inside the cage, with only Zargl and the two robots outside.

"All I want," whispered Fargo, "is a soundproof padded cell."

The tip of a branch tickled the back of Jeff's neck and snaked around to hang in front of his face. He found himself looking into a tiny blue eye that blinked at him from the end of the last twig.

"I'm sorry, Princess," whispered Jeff.

"You're still my hero, Jeff." The twig turned to look at Oola, who reached up to bat it the way cats do when they feel playful. Apparently, with a full stomach, and with the Slithers merely singing, Oola had decided Melodia wasn't such a bad place for a vegetarian cat.

The twig tickled Oola behind the ears.

"Meow," said Oola, rubbing against it.

"Oh, please help me," sighed the Princess.

"Worrwrrow!" said Oola, jumping to the place where the short main trunk of the tree divided into its heavy lower branches. She promptly vanished from sight.

It was at that fork that the tree's feeding mouth was located, Jeff realized with a sickening horror. "Oola," he called out, not caring whether he was stung or not.

She did not answer.

"Princess!"

There was silence from the tree, too.

No Slither moved to sting Jeff and, although it was broad daylight, all the Slithers stopped singing.

12

Music to the Rescue

A day later they were as trapped as ever, the cage surrounded by silent Slithers who pointed their sting tentacles at any human who walked near the lattice-work walls.

Oola had not reappeared, and the sacred tree was also silent, its leaves drooping and faded.

"Now that we're back in their blasted zoo," whispered Fargo, "Why don't they feed us when we sing to them? I'm starving."

No one answered, because no one knew.

Jeff sat on the ground inside the cage, grieving for Oola. He watched the Slithers come and go to their feeding grounds in the mud, always in relays so the cages remained guarded, its charred hole covered by the bodies of many Slithers.

I've got to try to find a way out of this mess, Jeff thought. I must have—somebody must have—because in the future of Melodia, the cage is empty and all of us have gone, even the ships.

Norby's antigrav had returned feebly, so he couldn't yet carry any human away from the cage even if the hole could be reopened. Pera was willing to try, but everyone felt she was too small to be able to lift herself and anyone else, even Norby, for as long as it might take to get to the ships. Jeff wanted Pera to take Norby above the planet's inhibitory field so he could get into hyperspace, but Norby refused, saying his hyperspatial ability wouldn't return until his antigrav was back in full force.

It is a mess, thought Jeff.

Zargl, exhausted, lay on top of the cage with Norby and Pera. She beckoned to Jeff. "I wish Norby's hyperspace ability would come back," she said. "He could go to Jamya and get my mother —her flame is bigger than mine—or bring back one of the Jamyn robots to help you escape."

"He hasn't the strength, and even if he had, the Slithers might be able to disorient the Jamyn robots too. And if you or your mother could burn another hole and frighten the Slithers, I still don't see how we could make it to the ships or get inside them."

"How about having Norby—when he's recovered—go back to our own Solar System and alert the Federation to the Admiral's danger?" whispered Albany.

"Oh, no," whispered Fargo. "Before rescuing the Admiral, those Federation scientists would take Norby apart to find out how he made it through hyperspace. We've got to keep him a secret."

Jeff groaned loudly, and the clot of Slithers nearest his section of the cage stirred ominously.

Admiral Yobo, who had been asleep, woke up and said in a hoarse whisper, "If you must groan, Cadet, do it musically. Those Slithers are so angry about the tree that with any more provocation they may kill us."

As if in confirmation of this, a long section of bark peeled from the tree, and a bushel of leaves fluttered to the ground, causing the Slithers to hiss like an army of snakes.

Captain Erig's black braids had come undone, and she didn't seem to care. She sat next to Einkan as if to protect him and whispered softly, "I wonder why the tree got indigestion from that strange pet, yet accepted the Princess without harm to itself."

"Captain," said Jeff, "how long did it take the tree to become the Princess after she was fed to it?"

"A day."

"A day!" whispered Yobo. "Will it start meowing like Oola *today?*"

"Who knows?" said Erig. "Perhaps the addition of Oola's protein was enough to cause a natural change of state in the tree—look—it's changing again!"

Jeff stared at the tree, half expecting to hear it meow but instead he saw a large crack develop at the top of the short trunk, where the mouth had been. The crack spread downward but the two halves of the trunk remained together, each swelling slightly. Above, the branches curled and withered, and all the leaves fell to the ground as if winter had come.

The Slithers began to whistle in very high notes and turned yellow. When the last leaf had fallen, they bobbed up and down like demented toadstools with fringed tops, whistling ascending and descending scales that sounded as if they had more than twelve tones.

"Nothing like this happened when our Princess was forced into it," said the older male Izzian. The others nodded in agreement.

Then, as the prisoners watched in astonishment, the tree shivered and its divided trunk fell completely apart, crashing to the ground. Each half of the trunk constricted at the top and bottom, pinching off branches and roots to leave two large smooth objects.

"The halves of the trunk look like giant pea pods," whispered Yobo, who was inclined to think in terms of food when he was hungry.

Fargo grunted. "Now, I suppose, the Slithers will plant the pods and use *us* as fertilizer. This is not the fate I had planned for myself and I don't appreciate it."

Albany gasped. "Oh, Jeff! Perhaps the seedling you saw in the future came from the pods. And we weren't in the cage because we'd already been made into . . ."

"No, no Lieutenant," whispered Yobo, patting her hand. "If that were going to happen, Jeff would have seen the ships, and they were gone. Hold on to that thought—somehow we're going to get away."

"Well, I wish that stupid animal of yours had not jumped into the tree," said Einkan sourly.

"She was just being friendly," said Norby from the top of the cage, "which is more than you've ever been."

"That's right," whispered Jeff. "The tree tickled Oola and she jumped into what she thought was the tree's lap, not its mouth."

"Oh, oh," whispered the young male Izzian. "They're coming in!"

The Slithers were sending in an extra contingent, headed for the "pods," as the humans thought of them. The prisoners backed out of their way and watched while the Slithers tried to lift the pods with their little tentacles.

"We can't let them do that," whispered Jeff, suddenly anxious. "Those pods are all that's left of—of—well, a mixture of the Princess and Oola. I don't want the Slithers to plant them here. We've got to get the pods back to Izz somehow."

"It won't matter," said Einkan testily, "because when the Queen finds out that her daughter is part of a tree that either sings or meows or both, she will revive the ancient custom of boiling in oil. There is absolutely no point in planting the pods on Izz."

"I don't agree," said Jeff. "Norby, Pera—try to break into the cage and rescue the pods."

While Norby hesitated, trying out his antigrav, Pera swooped down and pushed through the Slithers who guarded the opening. She looked like a silvery cannon ball with a bulge on one side and two sets of three eyes. She grabbed a pod and although it was unwieldy, elevated it on antigrav and pushed back through the opening to place it on the roof.

"I think I can do it!" said Norby, plunging toward the opening.

"Wait," said Zargl, "my flame's back a little. I'll frighten them so they won't sting you, Norby."

Together they managed to get the other pod onto the top of the cage, but the humans inside had no chance to escape for the Slithers immediately recovered the hole.

"Shall I try to scare them so the rest of you can get out?" asked Zargl.

"No," said Yobo, whose bulk offered many opportunities for the Slithers to practice stinging. "We've got to think of something safer."

"I don't feel at all safe here," said Fargo. "Sooner or later it's going to occur to the Slithers that all they have to do is sting us into unconsciousness, bury us in the mud, and then go after Norby and Pera and Zargl en masse, to take back their pods."

"No they won't!" shouted Norby. "My strength is reviving! My circuits have calmed down! I'm going to try to take the *Hopeful* away from the Slithers and bring it over the cage to rescue you."

"Be careful!" said Jeff. "If the Slithers sting you badly again, they'll knock out your antigrav. They might even destroy your mind!"

"Bah!" said Norby, elevating on antigrav. "I'm not afraid anymore. I'm going to show these muddy nasties what a hero can do!"

"Norby, be careful! Don't get hurt," said Pera, elevating with him.

The Slithers waved their tentacles uselessly in the direction of the two little robots, their keening song turning to an angry, loud chant.

"Yah, yah, you can't get me!" yelled Norby, zooming down as Pera remained hovering above him protectingly.

"Norby, you're making them furious," said Jeff. "Their song is probably spreading over the whole island, letting the Slithers guarding the ships know that they're supposed to sting you."

Norby paid no attention. Flapping his arms, he sailed tantaliz-

ingly close to their tentacles. He soared back and forth, driving
the Slithers to distraction. And then he began to sing, just as off
key as ever,

> "Norby to the rescue!
> Hero of the Fleet!
> I'm the Terran robot
> Nobody can beat!"

There was more to the song, but Norby's talents at composing
and singing left much to be desired. In his excitement, his voice
became ever more off key, and it cracked several times. His musical shortcomings seemed to increase his own excitement so that
he sang louder and louder, totally ignoring Jeff's shouted pleas to
stop teasing the Slithers.

But it was more than teasing. As Norby continued to sing, the
Slithers cowered. Their tentacles sank lower and contracted
tightly upon their mop-heads. They turned pale chartreuse and
their snail-like feet curled at the edges.

Jeff understood at last. "We've got another weapon!" he called
out excitedly. "We noticed it the first day and paid no attention.
They can't stand listening to music that's off key. Let's give it to
them! Norby, keep on singing."

Fargo shrugged. "It goes against my grain to sing off key,
considering my sense of absolute pitch. But if it must be done, it
must be done. All right, everybody," the light of battle gleamed
in his eyes, "sing loudly *and* off key!"

He rubbed his hands together and took up his drumsticks. He
reached through the bars of the cage and banged heavily on the
dull middle of his tympani. The Slithers shuddered and drew
back. Fargo tuned the drums at random so they'd be discordant.
He began to play and sing his tympani-tenor concerto as badly as
he could bring himself to do.

"Come on, Einkan, sing!" said Albany. "You have an even
better talent at bad singing than Norby has."

The Izzian Court Scientist burst into song. It was hard to tell,
but it might have been his own national anthem. Wincing, the
rest of the Izzians nodded to each other and bravely tore into—
and apart—their anthem, each in a different key.

Zargl flew in circles over the Slithers, singing an incredibly
speeded-up version of several Jamyn lullabies (which are difficult
to sing even slowly). From time to time she managed a short

burst of flame, which further disorganized the Slithers.

"Ah, sweet mystery of life!" screeched Albany, who was not, after all, a soprano.

Yobo's falsetto version of "The Volga Boatmen" was worst of all. He yelled it directly at the Slithers covering the hole in the side of the cage. They soon moved away in obvious retreat.

Fargo paused at the end of his concerto. He said meditatively, "This needs work. I think it should have a bass and a female voice, too."

"Fargo!" said Albany. "Don't get artistic. The Slithers at your end are barely upset. Stay off key, won't you?"

"All right, but it will ruin my gorgeous voice, my lady," said Fargo, and he began to sing in a gravelly voice:

"Onward, Outward, Fleet Patrol!
  Brave men ever so true—
  Blast off to danger; follow that stranger;
  And tell her you think she will do."

At that point Albany threw a sleeping mat at him, causing a discordant yelp that sent the Slithers scuttling. After that, Fargo switched to singing in Italian from "Pagliacci." Between his hamming and his faulty Italian, he sounded ferociously bad.

Jeff, whose voice always cracked when he tried to be a tenor, had no trouble. He chose Kilmer's "Trees," which he had never liked before. This time, his voice cracked with emotion as he sang, "I think that I shall never see, a Princess lovely as a tree—"

"Excellent, excellent," boomed the Admiral. "We've beaten them back."

"But they've still got us encircled," said Erig. "They're too far away to sting us, but how could we get through them? We can't keep on singing off key forever."

"I'll bring the *Hopeful*," shouted Norby, "now that I can scare away the guards with my powerful and heroic voice." He flew off in the direction of the ship.

"I'll go with him," said Zargl. "If I eat some of the food in the ship, my flame will get stronger." The little dragon followed Norby.

"What about *our* ship?" asked Captain Erig. "Can the small robot, Pera, carry the Court Scientist to the *Challenger*? His voice will drive away the guard and Einkan can adjust the engine to the home coordinates of Izz."

"Captain," said Einkan, his face red. "I must confess that not only is the engine an alien one, but I do not know how to run it. My air of knowledge was all a—harumph—necessary pretense. You are the Captain and I defer to you."

Captain Erig reddened in her turn. "I confess that I can't handle the *Challenger*'s engines, either. The Princess touched the panel accidentally and set it off. Afterward all that the rest of us could do was sit and wait. I'm as much a fraud as you are, Einkan, and just as helpless."

The two tall Izzians suddenly grasped each other's hands.

"Einkan, you fake!"

"Erig, you fraud!"

They embraced.

Yobo's deep bass rumbled in what sounded like the growl of a lion, "While we stop singing to watch the burgeoning of love, the Slithers are beginning to recover. I suggest we sing again until Norby comes back with the *Hopeful*."

"Wait," said Pera. "I will go to the *Challenger* and see if anything in my data bank will make it possible for me to tune into the engine and make it work. If I can, I will then bring it here. And if you tell me the coordinates of Izz, I may be able to introduce that into the ship's navigation system."

"Hurry," said Fargo. "Take a pod with you for safekeeping, and keep on screeching at the guards."

Jeff stepped through the burned hole in the fence and picked up one of Fargo's tympani. He thumped it randomly and shouted, "Wrong key, everyone. Stick to dissonance."

By the time the *Challenger* and the *Hopeful* were hovering above, the prisoners were all hoarse. Albany climbed to the top of the cage and waved at the ships.

From the *Challenger,* the Izzian robots descended on personal antigrav as impassively as if it had been Captain Erig instead of little Pera, who was giving them orders. First they carried the Izzians to their ship, and then the Terrans to the *Hopeful*. Finally they brought one pod to each ship.

Jeff shook his head at the thought of strong robots equipped with antigrav sitting placidly in their ship and not coming to the rescue of their masters—but, then, that was all Izzian robots *could* do. They had been given their orders to wait, and would wait till doomsday or till new orders were given, whichever came first.

Jeff was glad that Norby and Pera were not like them.

Jeff was the last up, and as he closed the airlock, he looked down through the slats of the main cage. He could see the sacred tree of Melodia, lying dead on the ground. It seemed to be disintegrating. There, too, was the gleam of Admiral Yobo's favorite medal lying in the dirt at the doorway to the cage.

Surely, he had the medal in his pocket! . . . He felt for it and it was gone. With a shiver, Jeff decided to let it stay where it was.

Norby was at the controls of the *Hopeful,* speaking by intercom to Pera on the *Challenger.* "Can you work the hyperdrive to take the Izzians home, Pera?"

"I think I can, Norby. You and I seem to have similar, though not identical talents. I can't get into hyperspace without a ship as you can, and you can't sing with perfect pitch as I can."

"I can *too* sing with perfect pitch," said Norby.

"Yes, Norby," said Pera diplomatically.

In a corner of the control room next to Fargo's tympani, Albany began humming a little tune.

Fargo turned on her. "Please don't sing. I love you, but at the moment I hate music."

"What about the Federation singing contest?"

"Forget it! I wouldn't enter it for a million credits, tax-free."

Yobo said, his voice booming, "What a pleasure it is to be able to speak freely. But, in any case, we're too late for the Federation singing contest. I propose that we go home at once. I don't want to face the Queen again. She reminds me of my older sister—not as dark or as good-looking, but of a similar personality."

"I would love to go home," said Albany wistfully. "I need a shower and some real food and a lot of silence. Besides father must be frantic by now."

"And one shouldn't upset the Mayer of Manhattan," said Fargo. "I've had enough of Izz, too. What's the good of a reward? If their plentiful gold destroyed Federation economy, I'd have to move out of my Manhattan apartment and into a cubicle in Luna City."

Norby said, "I think we ought to go home, too."

Yobo said, "And what says our heroic dragon?"

"I must go to Earth to continue my study of it," said Zargl.

"Well, I disagree," said Jeff. "For one thing, look at that." He pointed to an object near the control room door. It was shaped like a silvery-gold giant pea pod.

"You mean we shouldn't take it with us and plant it?" said Albany. "The sacred tree would look lovely in Central Park."

"But it may be partly Oola," said Jeff. "Do you want a tree in Central Park that meows? I can't abandon Oola to such a fate."

"For that matter," said Fargo. "The tree could be part Princess, too, and we should take *her* back to Izz. You're right, Jeff, our honor is at stake."

Norby's hat popped up and he glared at everybody with both sets of his eyes. Then he put his hands firmly on the control board. "As a matter of fact," he said, "I haven't said good-bye to Pera." He plugged his sensor wire into the computer.

"On to Izz," said Norby, taking the ship beyond Melodia's inhibitory field.

Then the ship winked into hyperspace, the is that is everything.

13

The Found Princess

The would-be rescuers of the lost Princess sat on the gold seats in the throne room of Izz, waiting for the Royal decision as to their fate. They sat in pairs.

Einkan and Captain Erig held hands and smiled shyly at each other. Pera and Norby held hands and must have been engaged in telepathic communications, for occasionally Norby's head would jiggle up and down rather emotionally. Albany and Fargo were holding hands, too, but, then, they usually did.

Admiral Yobo was holding no one's hand, but he was holding something else—a long, whispered conversation with Zargl about the dragons of Terran legends. He had gotten over his dismay at discovering that his favorite medal was missing.

Only Jeff was thinking of consequences. He stared at the two silvery-gold pods lying in front of the thrones, thought about the impossibility of bringing the Princess and Oola back to life and what it would feel like to be boiled in oil.

He also kept trying to think of a suitable way of apologizing to the Queen for the fact that her daughter was now a large seed of a tree, and probably mixed thoroughly with All-Purpose-Pet. Of course, Oola's shape-changing ability might be used to make the seed into a tree that resembled the Princess, but Oola was probably not intelligent enough to do it, and even if she did it, the Princess would be *green*.

As Jeff stared thoughtfully at the pods, it began to seem to him that they were no longer the same size. One had surely shrunk and was rounder, and greener, and—

"Fargo," said Jeff, "one of the pods is getting to look—"

Fargo was paying no attention, for the Queen swept into the room followed by the shimmering train of her long nightshirt and the King.

"So!" said the Queen, sitting heavily on her throne. "I understand that you have lost my daughter."

"Not entirely, Your Highness," said Yobo, bowing with dignity, despite the fact that his dress uniform looked much the worse for wear and that there was a vacant place in his row of medals.

"Partly is just as bad," said the Queen, while the King looked very sad and wiped away a tear as he looked at the two pods from the sacred tree of Melodia.

"The explanation you have given about the tree is highly unsatisfactory," said the Queen. "I blame you aliens for my daughter's transformation and probable demise."

"But, Your Majesty," said Fargo, still hoarse, "she was fed to the tree before we got there!"

"As a tree, according to your own tale, she was still my daughter. Now she is a vegetable pod because of the action of a creature belonging to you."

"Fargo," whispered Jeff in Terran Basic, "look at the small pod. Doesn't it resemble Oola's shell now, the one that looks like a hassock which she grows around herself when she's under stress?"

"Hmm."

"Sing the song that opens Oola's shell."

"I can't. My voice is shot."

"So what if you're hoarse. You can still hit the right notes. Try it."

The Queen rapped her knuckles on the arms of her throne. "Silence in the throne room!"

"Please, Ma'am," said Jeff, rising and bowing low. "We wish to demonstrate the power of our alien science to correct the present sad situation. My brother will now sing."

As Fargo began, the Queen interrupted. "Your voice is bad enough to deserve the dungeon, and you with it."

"At least it isn't oil, yet," whispered Albany cheerfully.

"Please," said Jeff. "It is not the voice, but the song."

Fargo cleared his throat and began again.

"Not only the dungeon," said the Queen impatiently, "but the darkest dungeon."

The King tugged at her sleeve. "My dear, let him try. Perhaps the Princess—"

"Well. Once more and that's all."

Fargo tried a third time, and this time the smaller pod—which was now distinctly hassock-shaped—began to crack. The crack widened and Jeff saw whiskers and a green paw. Oola pushed the halves of the hassock apart and bounded toward Jeff, purring like a hive of bees. He picked her up.

"That is *not* my daughter," said the Queen in a deep voice, "unless you have changed her into a repulsive green creature given to unseemly displays of affection to strangers. *Alien* strangers."

"But if we can free my pet from one pod, perhaps we can free the Princess from—" Jeff stopped as Einkan strode toward him and bent to speak softly in his ear.

"No secrets, you traitor," said the Queen, stamping her foot.

"It is part of the ritual of release that the boy has not yet learned, Your Majesty. He is not as familiar as I am with the special requirements of Crown Princesses," said Einkan smoothly.

"Umm. Hurry up about it."

Einkan whispered to Jeff. "Do you think the Princess is in the remaining pod? If another green animal comes out, the consequences will be disastrous."

"It *must* be the Princess."

"Do you know the right song?"

"No. Of course not."

"Certainly you do. It would have to be the beloved National Anthem of Izz. If it works, please let me have the credit. I know you don't think highly of me, but I've fallen in love and I have changed—I am now thoroughly honest and reliable."

Jeff's eyebrows rose quizzically.

"I *will* be," said Einkan earnestly. "I am going to be a genuine, hard-working scientist. Erig would be pleased, and I desperately want to please Erig. Please maintain that I have coached you in this singing business."

"If the National Anthem works, then you *have* coached me," said Jeff. Raising his voice, he said, "Thank you, Court Scientist. Your plan seems a wise one. Your Highness, I will now attempt to save your daughter. If I succeed, it will be due to Einkan's genius."

Jeff sang the music, but not the words, of the Izzian National Anthem, his voice cracking once. Nothing happened.

Einkan at once marched to the pod, moved it to the center of the floor next to Jeff, closed his eyes, and spread his hands over it.

"The danger is deep," he slowly intoned. "The Princess is

being held in the grip of powerful forces. She may not return to us in her former shape. We shall face the forces and no matter what the Princess has become, the total experience will teach Izzians that we must learn more. We must experiment. We must understand the forces of the Universe and go beyond the feeble knowledge our robots possess. We Izzians will advance, and we shall not allow any left-over branch of our noble species, stranded on some other planetary system far away, flaunt their technology at us. We will overcome—"

"Get on with it," shouted the Queen.

"I would like my daughter back," said the King wistfully.

"Proceed, Jeff," said Einkan, "and if the ritual does not succeed, let the fault rest with those who interrupt."

"Be quiet, my love," said the King as the Queen opened her mouth. Startled, she shut it.

Jeff sang again and this time his voice didn't crack. Oola purred. Yobo seemed to swell with held breath, and the other humans paled with tension. Norby and Pera rose slowly on antigrav, hovering near a pillar in case they had to get away from the guards and remain free to rescue the rest.

The pod didn't open slowly as Oola's hassock had. It opened with a bang, and in a blur of motion, something got out of it.

"Hello, everybody," said the Princess.

She was not green. She had curly red hair, blue eyes, and a million freckles. She was also very thin and small and was about ten years old. She was not beautiful though she might be some day.

Jeff stared with astonishment. He thought: Space and time! The tree has changed the beautiful Princess into a little girl.

He waited for the wrath of the Queen to descend upon him, along with the guards and gold handcuffs.

Jeff's astonishment was nothing compared to the emotions that swirled over Fargo's face as he stared at the little Princess. He turned to Albany with his mouth open, and she burst out into wild laughter. "She's all yours, Fargo," she said.

But the greatest excitement emanated from the thrones. "Rinda, my child!" cried the King, rushing off his throne to clasp her in his arms. She waved over his shoulder. "Hi, Mom. I made it!"

The Queen rose majestically and then burst into tears. "My darling daughter! You've come back to us!"

Jeff whispered to Einkan. "Then that is really the Princess? She doesn't look anything like her portrait."

Einkan said, "The Princess *wanted* the portrait to look grown-up and beautiful, and what the Princess wants, the Princess gets. Since you never saw the real Princess, you were misled, I suppose."

"No wonder she thought I was handsome." Jeff grinned sheepishly.

Meanwhile Admiral Yobo had advanced grandly to the throne, bowing low. "Your Majesties, having completed our task successfully, we now must consider the pressing business we have on our own planet, and we must take leave of you, taking with us, of course, any small reward you may feel we have earned."

"Or *large* reward, Your Majesties," added Fargo hastily.

"The reward will be taken care of, after the six months of celebrations, feasts—"

"Feasts? Well—" said Yobo.

"No, Admiral," said Jeff. "I've got to get back to the Academy. I'm already late."

"And I'm overdue at the police station," said Albany, "besides having to reassure my father, the Mayor, that I'm still alive."

"For myself, I feel in urgent need of a rest cure," said Fargo.

"And I'm going with them," said Norby.

The Princess looked up at Pera, hovering with Norby. "I would like one of you to stay. I suppose handsome Jeff can't stay, but perhaps I can keep Pera. Izz could use a robot like her."

"I will stay with you, Princess. We are both little and female and we can be together."

"I will grow, Pera. I won't remain little."

"I will grow, too, Princess, in mind and experience."

"We can use our hyperdrive ship if you stay with us," said the Princess, "until the Court Scientist invents a hyperdrive of our own."

"You won't use it at all," said the Queen firmly, "until you can stop it from going to that dreadful planet, which I declare off bounds to all Izzians."

"Hear, hear," said the King.

"And I declare it off bounds to all Terrans," said Yobo.

"Princess," said Jeff, "you must not treat Pera as a servant. She thinks for herself and she is therefore an *equal*."

"I know," said the Princess, her eyes downcast. "I am not the same person I was. I learned a great deal on Melodia. We shall be friends, Pera."

"Yes, we shall," said the little robot and sailed down to the little girl, "but there remains one thing. . . . Norby."

"Yes, Pera," said Norby.

"We are friends, too. Will you come and visit me now and then?"

"As often as I can. . . . But now we must leave." He sailed upward and said, "Come on, Terrans. I'll go ahead and get the *Hopeful* ready for departure." He zoomed out of the throne room.

The Queen sidled up to Fargo, "Must you go, too? You are by far the most handsome—"

"That will do, my love," said the King, taking her arm. "This alien must leave at once, or I shall be seriously annoyed."

"Annoyed?" said the Queen, her chin in the air. "With the *Queen?*"

"Annoyed!" said the King. "With my *wife!*"

"Why, Fizzy! You're jealous, you old silly," said the Queen, suddenly revealing a dimple in her cheek. They left the throne room hand in hand.

The Princess was patting Oola, who was purring loudly while Pera stood close by. Rinda said, "Could I have a few words with Jeff? . . . Alone?"

"Sure," said Fargo, grinning. "Let's all be tactful."

When they were alone, Jeff smiled down into the Princess's thin, eager little face. "I'm glad you're safe now, Your Highness."

"I want to thank you personally," she said. "You don't really think I'm beautiful, do you?"

"I think you will be some day, if—" he stopped.

"If I become a better person? Is that it?"

"I'm sure you will become a better person, day by day, as I hope we all will."

"Being a tree taught me a bit about helplessness. And I was able to watch how you were. You were very brave and you never gave up and you always thought of others. How old are you?"

"Fourteen."

"Really? Only fourteen? You must be tall for your age."

"I can't help it."

"I'm glad. You won't forget me?"

"Never, Your Highness."

"Promise that you'll visit me some time."

"Of course, Your Highness. Whenever Norby visits Pera, I will be with him to visit you." He bowed and started to walk out.

"Make it soon," said the Princess. Then she said, so softly that he wasn't sure he caught the words. "Maybe you'll wait for me to grow up before you get married."

14

RECOVERY

The control room of the *Hopeful* was once again crowded with Terrans, tympani, a small dragon, and a green All-Purpose-Pet. Norby was at the controls, with his back eyes shut. Hyperspace was as gray as ever, and they were all safely away from Izz.

Norby's back eyes opened. "It's so silent. What's going on?"

"It's dinner time," Yobo said with pleasure. "Or is it lunch? I've lost track."

Jeff said, "I'm afraid we didn't find out anything about the Others, Admiral, or about how to get hyperspatial travel without Norby."

"Well, well," said Yobo. "Another time."

"The food is good," said Zargl. "Soon I'll practice flaming."

"Not in the *Hopeful*, you won't," said Fargo.

"Speaking of practicing," said Norby, "why aren't you all singing? Don't you want to win the Federation contest?"

"It's too late," said Albany, taking the last sip of her chocolate drink. "We've missed it."

"The contest ended days ago," said Yobo.

"But I can take care of that," Norby said. "If I travel a little backward in time, we can arrive before the contest begins."

"That would be dangerous, Norby," said Jeff.

Norby waved an arm pompously. "I am an expert. While it is true that I can't hyperjump into a time and place where I already exist, I'm not going to be on Earth and on Izz at the same time. Relativistically speaking, as your Terran scientist, Einstein, would have put it, time on Izz is relatively not quite congruent with Earth time if you allow for the curvature of space and the speed of light and—"

"How sad," said Zargl. "I've been trying so hard to master

Terran Basic, but I see I still cannot understand it."

"I think what Norby means," said Jeff, "is that we can emerge from hyperspace before our Federation starts its singing contest. Is that it, Norby?"

"Exactly."

"Never," roared Yobo. "Do not fool around with time, Norby. I've travelled in time with you before, and I know you're too mixed-up to be trusted. You'll get me to Earth in the middle of the Ice Age, or when America has not yet been discovered by Europeans, or when African slaves are still being sold. I don't intend to be subjected to that." He wiped his brow and muttered something dire in Martian Swahili. Then he realized he still had part of a sandwich in his hand and returned to his dinner.

Fargo kicked the tympani. "I don't want to arrive before the singing contest, anyway. I have no desire to sing. No more music. Never again."

"But Fargo, think of it as an adventure," said Albany.

"I don't feel adventurous," said Fargo. "I may never again feel adventurous. Now that I've given up singing, I'm going to be a coward."

"Not you," said Albany, "I won't believe that."

"It's true. Not even your mellifluous contralto could move me."

Yobo sighed and nodded to Jeff. "I hate to agree to time travel or whatever is needed to get back before the contest, but I think it is necessary to get Fargo out of this mood. But be *careful,* Norby!"

Jeff touched Norby and thought:

——Not too careful, Norby. Fargo needs to know he still wants adventure.

——Okay, I'll be just a little mixed-up. Join minds with me.

The *Hopeful* shivered out of the gray of hyperspace and Norby said, proudly, "There it is—Earth! Right on target!"

"Indeed?" Admiral Yobo glared at the viewscreen. "Would you please explain why our receivers detect no radiation from our lunar colonies or from our spomes? If that's Earth, *when* are we?"

The *Hopeful* moved closer to the planet. Through rifts in the cloud cover, Jeff could see that continents were a little distorted and not in their usual positions. Norby had outdone himself.

"The *Hopeful* skimmed the surface, whistling through the atmosphere. Albany said, "I have always suspected that some dinosaurs came in shades of purple."

"Norby!" roared Yobo. "What have you done?"

Fargo sprang to his feet. "Listen! Keep the *Hopeful* hovering, and, Norby, take me down on your antigrav. There are soaring pteranodons down there, and I want to take a ride on one. With antigrav, Norby and I wouldn't be too heavy for one to carry us and—"

Albany, Yobo, and Jeff pounced on him and dragged him back to the tympani, where Oola jumped in his lap and licked his chin.

"Oh Fargo," said Zargl. "I don't think dinosaurs are *safe*."

"And I don't want to ride a pteranodon," wailed Norby.

"You won't," said Albany. "Mr. No-Adventure isn't leaving the ship. He's going to practice for the singing contest."

Fargo said, "We really need a soprano."

"Are you still hankering after that Princess?" asked Albany. "All ten years of her?"

"She'll be quite beautiful some day," said Fargo. "You'll see. Anyway, I'm not going to sing. Definitely not."

"Give me some men who are stout-hearted men," sang Albany. Yobo and Zargl joined in and Oola howled musically. Albany placed the drumsticks in Fargo's hands.

"But I hate music, I tell you," said Fargo.

Yobo thumped the various drums in turn with his fist.

Fargo winced. "They need tuning." He bent over to tune the drums, humming softly as Albany finished her song, while Norby, in a spasm of efficiency, returned to a time a few days before the contest.

"Good," said Fargo. "I need time to recover from my hoarseness."

Fargo and his group won the contest, of course, and Fargo was becomingly modest about it.

"After all," he said, "the Admiral is the best bass in the Galaxy, Albany's contralto would melt the heart of any judge, and Jeff was almost adequate. Combine all that with my musical genius, and we couldn't lose."

Norby chuckled metallically. "Of course you couldn't lose. Think of all the practicing you managed to do."

NORBY AND
THE INVADERS

TO THE HANDSOME YOUNGER GENERATION
  BRUCE
  DAVID
  ERIC
  JOHNNY
  LARRY
  RICHARD

1

Emergency!

Norby, the mixed-up robot, stood up to take his turn. His telescopic legs were fully extended and his two-palmed hands were clasped in front of his barrel-shaped body. Beneath the brim of his domed-shaped hat, the two eyes in back and the two eyes in front of his half-head were opened wide—all four of them.

Norby sang loudly and out of tune:

> "The bravest of robots I am!
> I'll get you all out of a jam!
> I fight against crime
> In space or in time,
> Although I'm as meek as a la—"

The song was interrupted because Norby had flung his hands outward in a gesture so dramatic that it unbalanced his barrel and sent him tumbling. Screeching metallically, he saved himself from completing the fall by switching on his antigrav and zooming up to the ceiling, while Fargo Wells repeated the last line of Norby's song in an altogether different way:

> "Although you're a terrible ham!"

Laughter filled the Manhattan living room of the Wells brothers: black-haired, handsome Farley Gordon "Fargo" Wells, age twenty-four, a secret agent for Federation Space Command, and Jefferson Wells, a cadet in the space academy, who had curly brown hair and too much responsibility for his fourteen years—though he never shirked any of it.

The deep bass rumble came from Fargo's boss at Space Com-

mand, Admiral Boris Yobo, who was bigger than most people
and twice as determined. Manhattan police lieutenant Albany
Jones, who was blond and beautiful, first punched her friend
Fargo for insulting Norby and then laughed in a rippling contralto.

Jeff smiled because there was no doubt that Norby *was* a ham
and because the Admiral's birthday party was clearly turning out
to be a success. He leaned over to explain to their remaining
guest what "ham" meant in this context. That guest, a small
Jamyn dragon named Zargl, clapped her claws in glee at the
explanation.

Oola, Jeff's All-Purpose-Pet, lengthened her cat-face to allow
more internal resonance, turned her nose to the ceiling, and
howled.

"Norby's singing offends Oola," said Fargo, "Though howling
isn't my favorite way of showing it. Like me, she has perfect
pitch."

Jeff frowned slightly. Norby was saying nothing, which was
strange. He should have been shouting insults in return. What's
more, Norby's head had withdrawn farther into the barrel, which
was now floating on antigrav about a meter above the floor, and
his sensor wire was sticking out of his hat.

"What's wrong, Norby?" asked Jeff.

"I don't know," said Norby. "I thought I heard something."

"The neighbors complaining, probably," said Yobo.

"No," said Norby. "You all go on with your songs. I'll just
keep listening. Zargl, sing your song now. The rest of you listen
closely, because she has a very instructive and inspiring song. Of
course, I helped her with the rhymes."

The green dragon grinned, showing all her sharp teeth in what
would have been a frightening display if the others hadn't known
how gentle and affectionate she was. She flapped her wings in
excitement and said, "The song's in Terran Basic because I
wanted to show off how much I've learned on this visit. And I
improved Norby's rhymes, too."

She sang:

"Jamya is my home—it's a planet far away,
  It was changed by unknown Others long ago.
The Others went away, but our Mentor robots stay
  To teach us everything that we should know.
My mother's aunt, her Highness, the Grand Dragon of us all
  Sent me here to be your charming visitor—

Earth is so exceptional, that there'll be affectional
Ties that bind and link our worlds forevermore."

Fargo muttered softly, "Exceptional? Affectional? Needs
work."

Everyone else clapped though, and Norby bowed in the air as
though the credit were all his.

Yobo rose majestically. "Lieutenant Jones, judging from the
ineffable fragrance emanating from the kitchen, I'm sure that my
African specialty is ready for the final basting and for the addition of my secret ingredients. Are you still interested in the rec-
ipe?"

"You bet," said Albany. Together they went to the kitchen
while the others sighed and wondered if they could supply the
room for one more course.

"Anything coming through, Norby?" asked Jeff.

The little robot sank to the floor and jiggled rhythmically on
his symmetrical feet. "I don't understand what's happening. I
keep thinking a telepathic message is trying to reach me, but that
can't be. All of you are here, but you're not touching me, so
there can't be telepathic contact with you. The only other tele-
paths I know are in Jamya, which is much too far away."

"It doesn't seem far to me," said Zargl, "because any time I
want to go home, Norby can take me there in a few minutes of
hyperspace travel, can't you, Norby? It's lucky part of your in-
sides were made by Mentor First. Otherwise you wouldn't have
the power, and I couldn't visit Earth unless your ship came for
me."

"Yes," said Jeff, "but our ship, the Hopeful, only works because Norby plugs himself into its computer."

"That limitation may not last," said Fargo. "The admiral is
certain that we Terrans will have true hyperdrive soon, thanks to
those mini-antigrav collars the Jamyn dragons gave him."

"I hope so," said Norby. "Then those Federation scientists
would leave me alone. I don't want them dissecting me!"

"In fact," said Fargo, "there's a rumor that Space Command
has one experimental ship almost ready—but who knows?"

Norby's eyes suddenly closed, and Jeff asked "What's the
matter, Norby?"

"I almost had it," said Norby.

"Had what?"

"A message." Norby's eyes opened. "Do you think maybe the
Others are trying to reach me? No, that's ridiculous. It's been

thousands of Terran years since they've been to any of the planets we know they visited. It's so annoying not to have any idea what they look like, or where they came from, or where they went."

Fargo said, "Don't let the admiral hear you say that, Norby. We don't want to inspire him to send us on another mission to find them. So far we've always failed."

"Not completely, Fargo," said Jeff, who believed in the constructive approach. "We've found out quite a bit. They were organic beings who had an advanced civilization with hyperdrive, robots, and the ability to bioengineer other creatures like the Jamyn dragons. The dragons are small and intelligent only because of the Others."

"For which I'm glad," said Zargl. "I'd hate to be as big and ugly and mean as my ancestors. Just the same, I'm glad we dragons can still breathe flame when we want to, even if my mother says it isn't civilized. You know, if the Others had not activated the Mentor robots by remote control, *they* would remember what the Others looked like."

"Pooh," said Norby. "It doesn't matter what they were like. The important thing is that they made the Mentor robots, who then made me or the part of me that an old Terran spacer put into a Terran robot."

"Resulting in extraordinary talent," said Zargl, rubbing her nose against Norby's barrel.

"*All* of me is extraordinary," said Norby smugly, "and you don't really need the Others as long as you have me." Abruptly, Norby turned to Jeff. "It *is* a message. It's coming in clearly now. It's from Mentor First!"

Everyone was shocked into a sudden silence that brought Yobo and Albany from the kitchen to see what was going on. Norby was sensing with his mind. His multi-jointed arms were still and his eyes were shut. Then his head sank into his barrel till his domed hat was tight against it. Only the sensor wire stuck out.

"Norby?" asked Jeff.

Time passed and Norby did not move. It felt to Jeff as if years were going by.

Suddenly Norby's head shot up. "I've got to leave at once!" he shouted. "Mentor First is in trouble. All of Jamya is in trouble, and I've got to go there. They've forced the message through hyperspace just to get my help."

"What kind of trouble?" asked Fargo with an excited gleam in his eye. Danger was made to be leaped into as far as he was concerned.

"I'm not sure. He didn't have time to go into detail." Norby's hands clasped each other in agitation. "But it's an emergency, a terrible emergency."

"But why didn't he explain what it was?" asked Yobo. "Why did the message end?"

"He just stopped. It was as if he'd been—I can't say it."

"Tell us what you think, Norby," said Albany gently.

Norby's voice was higher now, almost tinny. "Mentor First stopped in mid-sentence just as if he'd been—deactivated!"

"That's awful," said Jeff, taken aback.

Oola, sensing the emotional tension, began to howl again. Jeff picked her up and stroked her green fur to calm her. Whimpering like a dog, instead of the cat she usually resembled, she curled round Jeff's shoulders for security.

"Are you sure, Norby?" asked Fargo.

"That's what it felt like. I don't have emotive circuits for nothing, you know. I could sense Mentor First's strong frustration. He was powerless to stop whatever it was that attacked him, and then he was deactivated. I'm sure of it. I must leave at once."

"Certainly," said Yobo, a frown creasing the broad expanse of his black forehead. "We will start preparations at once. You and Fargo get the *Hopeful* ready, and I'll notify Space Command that I have an urgent mission to attend to, and . . ."

"You don't understand," moaned Norby. "There isn't time for all that. Mentor First said the whole planet was in danger. Just before he stopped I got just a glimpse. I think the planet is being *invaded*. I have to leave *now*."

"Not without me!" yelled Zargl, using her wings and antigrav collar to fly to Norby. She landed on his hat and clung to it. "You must take me with you. If my home is being invaded, I've got to help."

"You're too little," said Norby. "There'd be too much danger for a dragon-child—"

"No!" said Zargl, pounding Norby's hat. "Take me with you. I want to go *home!*"

"All right. Good-bye, everyone . . ."

"I'm coming, too," said Jeff in a low, determined voice. He seized one of Norby's arms tightly and pushed at Oola with his other hand. "Get off, Oola!"

But Oola dug her claws firmly into his uniform and held on.

"Now!" said Norby and he, along with Jeff, Zargl, and Oola, vanished from the Wells' apartment.

2

Jamya Under Attack

Inside the small protective field that Norby generated while he was in hyperspace, Jeff tried to relax and control his breathing. He also tried to calm Oola, who was digging her claws into his shoulder and probably growling—although, of course, none of the distance senses would work so that he could not hear her any more than he could see or smell her.

Jeff tried to reach Norby telepathically:

———Jamya's been invaded by whom? Or what?

———Mentor First didn't say.

———Is Zargl still with us?

———Here I am, Jeff, on Norby's hat. Will we be at my home soon?

———Right—this—*minute!* [said Norby.]

Jeff landed with a thump on a cold stone floor. It was dark, but not so dark that he couldn't tell where he was. They were in the Great Hall in the Mentors' castle.

"Got you here right on the bull's eye," said Norby, "as I always do."

Jeff didn't say that Norby almost never did. He had let go of Norby's hand, but Oola was still on his shoulders, snarling fiercely. Then she jumped to the ground, her green fur standing on end.

Zargl flew from Norby's hat to the opposite side of the hall.

"The Mentors are here—but they're dead!"

Jeff ran over, followed by Norby and Oola. Norby inspected the Mentors carefully, touching each one with his hand and his sensor wire.

"I don't think they're actually dead," he said. "They're paralyzed but still conscious underneath. They're just unable to function. It's as if the Mentors have been put into stasis, but there's no machine generating a stasis field." He edged a bit closer to Jeff. "I've never seen anything like this, Jeff. It's scary. What could have happened?"

Jeff looked up at the old black metal bodies of the Mentors looming above him, each with four arms hanging uselessly at the sides, their three eyes unmoving. Was it his imagination or did he detect a faint, remaining glow in those eyes, indicating they were still alive?

"Can you telepath with Mentor First?" asked Jeff.

"No," said Norby, "I've just tried. I wonder if the castle computer is out, too."

Norby went to a far wall and touched a switch. A section of wall slid back, but there was no opening, only what looked like a strange, featureless blue barrier. Norby touched it and jumped backward.

"That's a force field! Mentor First must have activated it before he was paralyzed. It protects the computer, and I don't know how to turn it off. And I don't want to turn it off either, because whatever invaded Jamya and paralyzed the Mentors would probably also want to destroy the computer."

Zargl began to sniff loudly. "I want my mother. Where is she? Maybe the Invaders have done something to her, too."

"We'll find out, Zargl," said Jeff soothingly. "You stay here, Norby. Whoever did this to the Mentors doesn't seem to like robots, so you're in danger. Zargl and I will go down to the village—"

"Not alone," Norby interjected. "With me along you can always leave Jamya in a hurry. The Mentors couldn't get away because they don't have built-in ability for hyperspace travel, but I do—so I'm coming with you."

"Who's there?" The distant shout reverberated into the Great Hall, as if it had come from far down a corridor. "Who is in the Hall of the Mentors?"

"That's the Grand Dragon's voice," said Zargl, flying across the hall into the corridor that led to the front door. Jeff picked up Oola and followed with Norby trotting along beside him.

Near the front door was the Grand Dragon, her sumptuous purple cloak trailing behind on her polished green tail as she strode toward Jeff. The diamond caps on her fangs glistened, and she looked very unhappy. Behind her was a smaller dragon who held out her arms to Zargl.

"Mother!" cried Zargl, flying into Zi's arms. "You're safe!"

While Zi comforted her daughter, the Grand Dragon clasped Jeff's hand and said in a throaty moan, "Jamya is doomed unless we can get help. It's ridiculous to think that any of us are safe as long as those revolting Invaders keep popping in and out of Jamya's space. I can't even *fly* to get away from them because they caught us by surprise and deprived us of our antigrav collars. Zi and I had to make it to the castle *on foot* to find out why the Mentors aren't doing something about the problem."

"The Mentors have been paralyzed," said Norby, "and I don't know how to free them. The computer is behind a force field and I can't get to it."

"Then we're lost," sighed the Grand Dragon, sitting on her massive tail. She was the biggest of the Jamyn dragons—as tall as Jeff.

"We'll do our best to help," said Jeff.

"I don't know if you can. Is your ship well-armed? Can you get your Federation Fleet to join you?" asked the Grand Dragon. "It will take the full Terran force, I think, to defeat the Invaders. I'm so desperate I'd even be pleased to see that large, very loud admiral of yours."

"I'm afraid we've left everything behind and have just come by ourselves," said Jeff. "Norby came so quickly—"

"You didn't bring a single ship?"

"We didn't know the conditions, your Dragonship. Mentor First gave us so little information before he was paralyzed, and we were convinced there was no time to wait. Once we find out exactly what's happening and what kind of help is needed, we'll go back and get it, never fear. Tell us about the Invaders, ma'am."

The Grand Dragon rubbed her top scales as if she were very tired. "I can't tell you much except that they look awful and act worse. They seem able to deactivate any equipment. Perhaps if you had come in the *Hopeful* they would already have grounded her, so even your ship wouldn't have helped. Oh, it's no use. Nothing's any use."

"Can the Invaders fly?" asked Norby.

"Not exactly," said Zi. "They float, and they move as if propelled by jets of air."

"They're disgusting," said the Grand Dragon. "I was flying from them, trying to evade their nasty clutching tentacles and get into position to strike back, when they plucked my antigrav collar from my neck. I have never been so ill-treated and demeaned in my life. In fact, it was all I could do to flap my wings hard enough to break my fall. Our wings are very beautiful, of course, but they aren't really big enough to let us fly efficiently without a bit of antigrav to help, especially when you are as massively majestic as I am. I feel I've let all the Jamyn people down. After all, Grand Dragons should always . . . Let's see . . . what point was I making?"

"You were being ill-treated and demeaned, ma'am," said Jeff deferentially. The Grand Dragon was an excessively royal personage.

"Precisely," she said, angrily emitting a small flame. "If you open the front door a crack and peep out, you'll probably see the Invaders hovering over our village. They appeared out of nowhere, the way you and Norby do when you come through hyperspace. They don't talk, as far as I can tell. They just float around, turning off our electricity, removing our collars, taking away our little helper robots—and now they've paralyzed our beloved Mentors! They've got horrid tentacles all around their snouts and no legs or arms. Ugh!"

Zargl peeped around the door. "Oh, Jeff, it's like the picture you showed me in the Terran encyclopedia. These Invaders look like knobby, blobby dirigibles, only much smaller I think."

Jeff looked too. The Invaders, six of them, hovered over the trees of the Jamyn village and did indeed resemble the old-fashioned airships that were used on Earth long ago—except, of course, that the airships were not lumpy and tentacled. He estimated that the Invaders were perhaps twice as long as he was tall.

"These Invaders act as if a civilized being doesn't need mechanical help," said Zi indignantly. "If we dragons have to do all the physical work that our robots do, how will we remain civilized? We may live in small villages, but our culture is sophisticated, thanks to the Mentors, and we're spreading out over all our island continent. If we don't have the means of communicating electronically, or even the ability to fly, each village will be isolated since we can't use telepathy unless we touch each other. We'll just sink back into barbarism and go about breathing fire like primitive dragons."

"Something must be done!" said the Grand Dragon grandly, lifting her claws high into the air—but she didn't say what that something might be.

At that moment, Oola ran though the opening of the door to the stone terrace outside. Jeff tried to grab her and failed. Oola jumped onto a green hassock-shaped object and meowed loudly.

The Grand Dragon sighed, "That's Mentor First's All-Purpose-

Pet, Oola's mother. One of my subjects, before fleeing the castle, reported that the pet had bravely attacked one of the Invaders. It struck her with one of its tentacles, and that hurts—I know—because it gives one an electric shock. The pet promptly grew her protective shell around herself."

Oola whimpered and raised her nose to the sky. She was evidently very upset about her mother.

"She's going to howl," said Jeff, "and that will bring the Invaders, if anything will." He dashed out, scooped her up, and stroked her frantically.

"Look out, Jeff!" called Norby from behind the door.

A shadow blocked the warmth of Jamyn's sun and Jeff, looking up, saw an Invader directly overhead, gazing down at him with yellow eyes. As a tentacle reached for him, Oola leaped at it savagely, raking it with her claws.

The Invader's tentacle shook and withdrew. The Invader moved higher overhead.

The Grand Dragon swept from around the door, her cape outspread and her claws outstretched. "See here, you bullying monster—I order you to leave our planet! You have no business interfering in the lives of other species!"

The Invader came close again. Jeff tried to maintain his hold on Oola, who was squirming away.

By this time, Oola, who was not bright enough to take deliberate advantage of her antigrav collar, had become so eager to get at the Invader that her striving brought the collar into automatic play. She pulled out of Jeff's arms and lifted to the side of the Invader's bloated body. She clawed at the Invader's side, and a distinct hissing of air was heard.

The Grand Dragon's eyes widened as she suddenly realized that Oola had an antigrav collar. "Oola," she shouted, stamping her feet and tail, "come down and give me that collar, and *I'll* let the wind out of its bag!" She bared her fangs and put her claws out to their fullest extent.

Oola, of course, paid no attention. She attacked again, but this time the Invader shoved her away with its tentacles.

The Grand Dragon flexed her muscles and took a fighting stance. "Come on down, you disgusting blob, and fight like an honest being—and while I smash you to a pulp, I will give you a large piece of my mind. Argh!"

The Grand Dragon's words were choked off as a tentacle wrapped itself around her throat. She hit out at the Invader with her claws, and her tail smashed into its gray body.

There was a crackling noise and suddenly the Invader disappeared, taking the Grand Dragon with it.

"Oh, no," said Zi. "They've taken Auntie. They've taken our beloved Grand Dragon. They'll kill her."

"I think we'd all be better off inside the castle," said Jeff. "The rest of you go there while I get Oola."

That was easy to say, but not so easy to do. Oola was looking down the hill to the village and snarling. Every time Jeff tried to seize her, she bounded away, moving further down the hill.

"Oola," shouted Jeff, "come here, blast you!"

Norby rounded the edge of the door, withdrew his legs into his barrel-body, and elevated on his own antigrav. "I'll catch her for you, Jeff."

He propelled himself toward Oola, with Jeff in close pursuit. Norby arrived first, scooped up the indignant pet and gave her to Jeff. "Now," he said, "let's go back home and see what the admiral has to say about this situation. Maybe it *will* take the whole fleet, except that if it does, the admiral will have to tell the Federation about Jamya."

"It would be about time," said Jeff, hanging onto Oola's collar and desperately thinking *down* because she was thinking *up*. The collar, obeying the thoughts of beings touching it, would follow whichever thought was stronger. If they lifted off the ground and into the air, the Invaders would certainly notice them.

Jeff, panting with the effort of mind-concentration as he moved back to the castle, said, "Maybe the Federation ought to accept Jamya as a member even if Jamyns aren't human."

But then there was a popping noise and an Invader appeared out of nowhere almost on top of Jeff. Tentacles lashed out and, as Jeff fought them off, Norby's voice made itself heard.

"Stop that, or I'll ram all the air out of you!" said Norby, who could be as brave as a lion if he were excited enough. He zoomed up in the air and directly into the Invader's hide. The Invader made a noise like "ooph," and grabbed Norby instead of Jeff.

"Worrwwrrr," said Oola, trying to hit the Invader.

"Norby," shouted Jeff, trying to reach the little robot.

Then the Invader, holding Norby in its tentacles, vanished.

"Norby!" wailed Jeff with a sudden sense of loss.

"Come back, Jeff!" shouted Zi. "Hide in the castle! The other Invaders are coming here."

Jeff scrambled up the slope, holding onto Oola, but he couldn't make it. One of the Invaders caught him just as he got to the door.

The gray rubbery tentacles wound around his waist and lifted him off his feet. The Invader soared up and up, over the spires of the castle, while Jeff held onto Oola and her antigrav collar and fought to get away.

Other Invaders joined the one that had captured Jeff, and from the gestures of their tentacles, Jeff imagined they were somehow communicating, but he could hear no speech. Was it a sign language?

His head was aching and the tentacles holding him seemed to be vibrating unpleasantly.

Oola obviously hated the sensation. She yowled horribly and then twisted around in Jeff's arms, got a good fix on the nearest tentacle, and bit hard.

The Invader who was holding them seemed to shake all over. Jeff's headache got much worse and he blacked out.

3

IN THE OCEAN

When Jeff opened his eyes and returned to a groggy awareness that the universe existed, it was nighttime. He knew at once that he was not on Jamya or on Earth or anywhere he'd ever been, for the stars covered the sky so thickly and so brightly that the effect was of a widespread moonlight.

"We must be in a globular cluster," he muttered.

The Invader was still overhead. Jeff could see it as a shadow against the bright starlight. Jeff dangled loosely from the Invader's tentacles and it occurred to him that he could easily wriggle free. Then he looked downward and gasped. No wonder Oola had her forelegs around his neck and was holding on for dear life!

They were far above what seemed to be an immense ocean, its waves shimmering in the starlight. The water extended outward to the horizon in every direction, meeting the star-filled sky cleanly. It was a clear night with few clouds and no haze. There was a slight chill in the air.

They were traveling quickly, and it seemed to Jeff that puffs of air were coming from inside two flaps of skin that opened and closed rhythmically, one on each side of the Invader's body, creating a small wind that ruffled his hair. It wasn't impossible for the Invaders to travel by jet propulsion, but surely they were too big to float without some sort of antigrav device.

Jeff put one hand on Oola's collar, the only thing that would save him from falling if the Invader released its grip.

Where were they going? A useless question, for there didn't seem to be any place to go *to*. Jeff could see nothing but restless star-reflection in all directions, and he was sure that even in daylight the ocean below would be featureless.

How long would the flight continue? Oola was beginning to

make her "I am hungry" noises, and he held her closely to console her. With the other hand, he touched the Invader's tentacle gingerly, shuddered, and wished fevently that he were holding Norby's hand. He could then wiggle free, upheld by Norby's intelligent use of antigrav and together they could move into hyperspace and back to Earth. He wished he could hear Norby's voice talking as they zoomed along in air, or understand Norby's words in his mind as they traveled through hyperspace together. As it was . . .

In his agony of futile wishing, he forgot to be careful of Oola, who found the tip of the Invader's tentacle and bit it hard.

Like a writhing snake, the tentacle uncoiled and Jeff fell—only to rise as he and Oola thought "up" simultaneously. The Invader turned around and came back for them, tentacles outstretched, its yellow eyes glittering weakly in the starlight.

"Wowrrrr!" said Oola, striking out at the tentacles.

The Invader drew back. Then, as if deciding that Oola and Jeff were not worth bothering about, it pointed itself head downward and plunged into the ocean.

Jeff looked down after it. Apparently they had arrived at their destination—or the Invader's destination, anyway—and Oola had decided to bite just a moment too soon. Now what?

"Meow?" said Oola in the tone of voice that meant, "I'm hungry and what are you going to do about it?"

Jeff was hungry, too. At Admiral Yobo's birthday party he'd had much less to eat than the others because, except for the last mysterious dish he'd never gotten to taste, he'd been the cook and had been too busy to eat much. His stomach rumbled, and there was nothing but water in sight.

Nothing but water? The starlight was rapidly dimming, the sky was growing lighter, and as a reddish sun rose above the horizon, its light hit a series of strange black objects. With difficulty, Jeff managed to get closer by manipulating Oola's collar—as often as not in opposition to her wishes.

Tall black cylinders jutted from a section of the ocean that seemed distinctly paler now that the sunlight made it easier to see. Beyond the pale zone, the water was much darker.

He had to maneuver still closer, but each time he tried he'd forget to think "up" and would sink, because Oola had apparently decided to think "down."

"What's the matter with you?" he said to her impatiently.

"Meowwwr!" she said emphatically, and licked his chin. It tickled and Jeff laughed. At once, they dropped all the way to the surface, so that Jeff found himself immersed to his waist before he thought "up" hard enough for the collar to make them rise. Even then they didn't rise far. Oola seemed set on going down.

"I don't want to get wet, Oola. I want to go home, just as Zargl did a while ago—only Norby's not here to get me there. Let's look at those cylinders."

By dint of great flapping effort, Jeff positioned himself above the nearest cylinder. It was not solid and, as he sank to the top, he found its metal rim wide enough to sit on if he were careful. The cylinder was black metal and faintly warm. He looked into the opening and could see only blackness at first, but he felt air rising through it, as if a gigantic creature were breathing through an enormous snorkel.

The hollow center of the cylinder was big enough for his body, and he was about to slip down to explore, when he caught the silvery glint of a metal grating that blocked the inside far down.

Jeff decided there was no use trying to go down to pry up the grating, and he began to work out possible alternative actions when Oola settled the matter by sniffing and jumping from his arms.

In surprise, Jeff found himself losing his balance. He gripped the rim of the cylinder hard to keep from falling into it and down upon Oola or into the water. Oola floated downward slowly, suspended on her antigrav collar, and he could see her, a barely visible spotch of green walking about the grating.

Jeff had to wait until she had satisfied herself that there was no way in. Having done that, she tried to leap up. Failing, she tried to climb. Only then did her desperation activate her collar. Up she went, spread-eagled, back to Jeff, who hugged her to him.

"That's all right, Oola. We can't get in that way, but there must be a building or something down there with air in it. We'll have to find a way of getting in."

He wasn't at all sure there was a building below the ocean surface, but the rising air in the cylinders had to be coming from somewhere, and saying it out loud made him feel better.

Oola tugged to get out of his arms, acting as if she had seen something in the water she wanted. Jeff decided it must be seaweed or something similar. Although Oola's ancestors had been bioengineered by Mentor First from particularly bloodthirsty carnivores, members of the species were now thoroughgoing vegetarians, who could eat almost anything that wasn't animal.

Almost anything, Jeff thought. Oola could eat Jamyn and Terran vegetation with equal ease, but what if the plants on this world were poisonous?

He could see the plants rising to the surface now that the air had grown warmer with the sunlight. They had small clusters of flat crescent-shaped leaves almost the same color as the greenish-blue water, and bore bunches of white flowers like tiny puff-balls bobbing above the leaves on thin, short stems. They were a little like water lilies, but not quite.

"MeOWWW!" Oola squirmed out of Jeff's arms and jumped into the ocean, right onto a floating plant. Her jaws clamped on the plant, and she elevated back to the cylinder rim, trailing a long filmy stem with leaves extending alternately in either direction; the puff-ball flowers like tiny mushrooms.

Oola maneuvered herself onto Jeff's thigh and proceeded to eat ravenously. Oola always ate ravenously.

She didn't like the flowers and discarded them after trying to eat one. The stem—after a thoughtful munch—was also rejected. The leaves, however, were chewed and swallowed in quantity. When Oola had had quite enough, she licked her chops, washed herself, and purred.

"Fine," said Jeff. "At least one of us is fed. If only I could reach Norby—" He shut his eyes and concentrated, but without success. He needed to touch Norby to communicate telepathically.

Jeff had never felt so alone in his life. Sitting above the immense expanse of an unknown ocean, without any hope of getting home, he felt himself sinking into despair. To avoid that final disaster, he took a deep breath and recited a version of his solstice litany:

> I am a Terran creature, part of the life that has evolved on Earth. I am far away from home, but I am still part of the Universe, part of its life. Everything is part of the Universe, no matter how strange or dangerous it may seem at some time. I will try to let go of my fear so that I can decide what to do.

He stroked Oola to keep from thinking about hunger and thirst and stared at the ocean. At first he wished for a ship or for something that would appear on the horizon. When nothing did, he found himself imagining sadly how nice it would be to feel at home in an ocean.

What he wanted to be was a wonderful, sleek fish with gills, or even a seal with flippers, or a beaver with a nice flat tail that would serve as a rudder. The daydream went on until his hands told him that something had happened to Oola.

He looked at her. She had changed shape. She was longer and thinner, her legs flipperlike and her tail flattened. She yawned, kissed him, and dove into the water.

"Oola! Come back!"

She paid no attention, but swam over and under floating plants. She seemed to be having a wonderful time.

Jeff knew he'd have to get wet if he wanted Oola and her collar back. Jeff dove into the water and swam to the surface, thinking that it was not as cold as he expected and that it was amazingly clear. He dove again and saw that the black cylinder went down and down to a white surface, where many plants grew. He swam over them and noted that they had the same crescent leaves as the ones that Oola had eaten. Occasionally, plants would break loose from the clump and rise to the surface.

Oola swam between his legs down to the plant garden, bit off some leaves, and returned to Jeff, champing happily. This time Jeff held tightly to her collar, for there were other creatures among the plants, crawling and scuttling and darting along, all of them unrecognizable. They looked smaller than Oola and probably weren't dangerous, but Jeff couldn't be sure.

With a queasy feeling, Jeff realized he didn't dare let go of his All-Purpose-Pet. Without Oola's collar, he'd have to float in the water forever because he couldn't climb the cylinder by himself.

Oola wanted to play, but Jeff wanted only to keep his head above water. His desperate reluctance to be deprived of air might have inspired Oola, for he felt her neck change. He tried to examine it and, as far as he could tell, there were flaps of skin on each side that opened when she sank beneath the water. Gills?

"Are you turning into a fish, Oola?" Jeff asked.

But she hadn't lost her fangs, and suddenly she bared them with a snarl that turned to bubbles when she put her head back under the water. Jeff looked down through the clear water and saw a huge gray shape approaching.

An Invader? It had the same tentacles around its snout, but twice as many as the air Invaders had had, and was twice as long. In fact the entire creature was twice as long. The body was almost tubular with a flattened portion in back that served as a tail. Only its nasty yellow eyes were the same. It was heading for Jeff.

There was no place to go but up, and Oola wouldn't go up. She wanted to face the new enemy and fight. She might be a vegetarian, but her ancestry had included something very like a saber-toothed tiger.

Using all his will and brainpower, Jeff prevailed and they rose out of the water into the air. The Invader didn't follow. It swam around and around, occasionally breaking the surface with its tentacles to grab at Jeff, who managed to stay just out of reach.

But Oola did not like *that* manner of fighting. Squirming incessantly, she managed to squeeze from between his arm and his chest and leaped into the water on top of the Invader. She was followed, of course, by Jeff, who had no antigrav collar of his own. He swam as hard as he could away from the Invader, but when he turned, the creature was almost upon him.

And then, for no reason that Jeff could see, it slowed down, its tentacles reaching back instead of forward for Jeff. Something was bothering it.

Ducking his head under the water, Jeff saw Oola clamped with long, sharp claws to one of the flaps at the side of the Invader's body. Her fangs were at saber-toothed proportions, and she was striking again and again. Bluish-gray fluid streamed from the wound, and the Invader was obviously losing its own peculiar kind of blood.

The Invader gave up quickly. It turned tail and swam quickly away from Jeff and from the line of black cylinders. It carried Oola with it, Jeff was left alone.

He swam to the nearest cylinder and tried to hug it for safety and support, but it was too wide for a good grip.

Some ocean water had gotten into Jeff's mouth, and he tasted it. There wasn't the strong taste of salt that Earth's ocean water had, but he felt it was still too salty for safe drinking. Staying away from it was difficult however, because of his thirst.

Then he noticed that water had condensed on the sides of the metal cylinder. Might that be fresh water? He made a face and licked it. He didn't taste any salt at all, but when he had licked up all the water he could reach on every side of the cylinder, he still felt thirsty, and his tongue was sore.

"Meow?" Oola's catlike head bobbed up in front of him. She had a small bump on her nose and one ear was bent, but other than that she looked very pleased with herself. Jeff put his hands on Oola's collar and decided to try to elevate to the top of the cylinder again and then to go inside and attempt to pry up that grating.

Oola had other plans. She dove, dragging Jeff with her.

Holding his breath, Jeff saw that she was swimming quickly

across the white surface below until it abruptly ended. Then she swam down over it into darker water. Jeff ran out of breath and let go, swimming to the surface as fast as possible because he needed air.

As he tried to float and take in great gulps of air, a wet furry head chucked him under the chin.

"Wowrrr!" said Oola, questioningly.

"I can't go with you," said Jeff. "I can't grow gills the way you can."

She banged at his chest with one of her flipperlike paws and meowed again, then swam away, only to turn and meow at him once more in an exasperated way.

"I *can't*," yelled Jeff, shaking his head.

She returned and he stroked her, thinking that at least one of them would survive on this watery planet. He imagined himself fully equipped for snorkling, enjoying a strange ocean—and then he felt something growing out of the back of Oola's neck even as he stroked it. He looked down startled. It was like a tube open at the free end, and it bubbled.

Jeff asked quizzically "Oola, have you invented a snorkel?"

For a second he tried to figure out how Oola could breathe through gills under water, with lungs above water, and somehow still have air to expel through an air hose. But the physiology was beyond him. Experimentally he tried breathing in the air from Oola's hose and found that it worked. There was probably more carbon dioxide in it than there would be in the open air, and it smelled of vegetation—but it was breathable.

The next time Oola dove, Jeff held on to her collar and breathed her air. She swam with undulating movements just below him, and Jeff kicked with his legs to help. They swam past the black cylinders to the edge, then down the wall of a building, large in area but only about as high as a four-story building in Manhattan. He peered into the darkness of the ocean outside the building, but could see no other intact structures, although the area seemed littered with fantastic jumbles of building stone and metal girders, all festooned with undersea plant and animal life.

Beyond the littered area, the ground seemed to slope downward to such blackness that Jeff could see nothing. When Oola wanted to go back to the building, Jeff had no quarrel with her. They had just arrived at the white wall when Oola managed to drag Jeff behind a particularly large clump of plants. When he looked back to see what she was running from, he nearly dropped the snorkel.

Invaders!

There were three of them, sleek instead of fat and blobby like the ones that he had seen on Jamya, but smaller than the one that had attacked him here. They also had the same number of tentacles as the Jamya invaders; fewer than the savage one. Perhaps these creatures came in two species.

It's the air under their skins that makes them look fat and blobby when they're out of the water, thought Jeff. He watched them swim toward the building and curve to the left, following the curve of the building itself. Then they went out of sight.

Follow them, thought Jeff as he prodded Oola. She was not telepathic and could not understand thoughts, but clearly her mind responded to the emotions and yearnings of a person touching her, so she turned her nose in that direction and started swimming with Jeff attached to her.

There was a door! It looked like an unusually large, round air lock without a handle or doorknob. The Invaders must have entered the building this way, but Jeff couldn't see how. He ran his fingers around the door and found a ridge with a dimple on each side. Holding Oola close to him, he pressed first one depression and then the other, but nothing happened.

Jeff stopped to think. The Invaders had a circular arrangement of tentacles that could stream in various directions, so perhaps both dimples had to be pressed at once. Carefully pushing Oola's lower half into his uniform so that she wouldn't swim away and take her air with her, Jeff tried pressing both dimples at once, stretching his arms out as far as they would go.

This time the door dilated open, and he swam through into total darkness, sinking down as the water inside the airlock drained away until he was standing in air. He let go of Oola's air hose and thought about a cat with four legs instead of flippers, and with no gills.

By the time the inner door opened, Oola's body was back to normal, and he walked into a dimly lighted entrance chamber.

He put Oola down. After shaking herself like a wet dog, she sat down and began to lick her fur like a cat. She was totally unafraid, and so, at the moment, was Jeff, because the room— big enough for several Invaders at once—was completely empty. It had three other doors, each round except for the very bottom, which was flattened.

Which door to try?

Jeff sighed and sat down, taking off his wet boots, which he strung together and slung over his shoulders to dry. While he sat there, he thought he felt Norby's voice.

Felt? He didn't hear it, not the way one heard a voice through air or even mind-to-mind by means of telepathy. It was a *feeling*.

He couldn't hear or understand any words, but he felt certain that Norby was trying to reach him. Norby must be here!

Now—which door?

4

In Prison

Even as Jeff wondered which door to try, the middle one dilated open and a box on wheels rolled out.

"Me-eww!" said Oola in her most beseeching voice, which was not surprising since Oola was always hungry and the box smelled good. Right now, with all her efforts to change and develop gills and snorkel (all of which took energy), she must be very hungry despite the leaves she had eaten. She trotted over to the box as it slowly rolled into the center of the chamber. She sniffed and patted it with one paw, but it paid no attention. Then it turned sharply and headed for the door to Jeff's left, followed by Oola.

"Wait for me," said Jeff, following her on bare feet. As his head cleared from the immersion in water, he became aware that there was a constant background noise, a faint hum as if the building had machinery running, which was only logical since the air was fresh and some equipment had to recirculate and refreshen it, sucking air from outside through some cylinders and giving it back through others.

The left-hand door dilated, and the box rolled through on the flat part of the doorway into a corridor beyond. Oola and Jeff followed. They were lucky, because they saw no Invaders in the corridor, and the occasional closed door along it did not open. The box moved purposefully until it came to the end, where another, larger door dilated. The box went through, and so did Jeff and his pet.

Jeff immediately picked up Oola and crouched behind a bush because, in the distance, this room seemed full of Invaders. It was hard to call it a room though, because it was more like a gigantic cavern planted with trees, bushes, and flowering vegetation. The box moved along a narrow path that turned and switch-backed down a slope. It reached a large pool of water where several Invaders seemed to be playing, tossing balls back and forth in the air above the water.

A recreation room? thought Jeff, trying to shush Oola's food noises. The box she was interested in stopped at the edge of the pool, and the top flipped back.

The Invaders clustered around the box, picking out what looked like green and brown cubes, which they took up in their tentacles and stuffed into the mouths that opened just under the snout. They seemed preoccupied by eating, so Jeff took off his uniform to dry in the warm air. He hung it and his boots on the other side of a bush and stayed out of sight behind it, peeping at the Invaders through the branches.

In the meantime, Oola had found a flowering plant to sample, which took her mind off joining the Invaders' dinner party. But Jeff was still hungry and thirsty. Thirst must sharpen the senses however, for over the background hum of machinery, he thought he heard the trickle of running water. On his hands and knees, staying lower than the bushes, he crawled toward the sound which came from the nearby wall. There was a little jet of water from a pipe in the wall, forming a tiny stream that gurgled down the slope to the pool. Jeff tasted it, found it fresh, and drank thirstily.

Instantly he felt better. When your mouth is dry with thirst, it's hard to tell that it isn't dry with anxiety. With his naked body drying off and his thirst quenched, Jeff found it a lot easier to forget he was scared and to go about figuring out what to do next.

But what *can* I do? he thought. He stared at the surroundings. The plants and trees were strange to him, of course. He followed the line of the tallest trees up to the ceiling, and his jaw dropped.

The ceiling was glass or something transparent. Beyond it there were small fishlike creatures swimming in the clear blue water. If he and Oola had traveled farther over the building's surface, they might have passed over this glass room and been seen by the Invaders!

Opposite was a wall with another door. Should he make for that door? The trouble was that the pool was in between, and the Invaders could stop swimming, inflate their bodies with air, rise above the pool, and be on his back in a moment.

As he stared at the other door, it opened and a larger box rolled in and then down another inclined path to the pool.

"I'll burn you all to a crisp for this outrage!" shouted a well-known voice in Jamyn.

This box was a cage and inside it, shaking the bars in fury, was the Grand Dragon of Jamya. Jeff managed to snatch Oola back just as she was about to run gladly toward someone she knew.

When the cage was almost at the pool's edge, it stopped just behind the food box. The Invaders picked out green cubes which they tossed into the dragon's lap as she sat on her tail in indignation.

"Monsters! Do you think you can pacify me with this nauseating stuff?" The dragon threw the cubes out of the cage and exhaled a flame that caused the closest Invader to jet backward. Another Invader dipped into the pool and up again, spouting all over the dragon and putting out her flame.

One of the green cubes had landed not far from Jeff, and his nose wrinkled at its smell. He offered it to Oola, who ate it at once with obvious relish. Jeff shook his head. She was going to have bad breath after a meal of those things.

The Grand Dragon shouted, "Now I'm not only hungry, but also wet. What sort of primitive barbarians are you creatures? Why don't you talk? You're nothing but a bunch of bloated odd-balls I'd like to puncture." She snarled and showed off the diamond points on her fangs.

The Grand Dragon of Jamya had never been noted for tact and diplomacy.

The Invaders now threw brown cubes into her cage. These she sniffed at and then tasted.

"Ugly stuff," she said, "but not too terrible. I suppose it's nourishing. Mentor First always taught me to try to stay in good health so that my mind would work better." She ate one cube and then several others, while Jeff wished he didn't have to touch the dragon in order to communicate with her telepathically.

"All right now," said the dragon, licking her chops. "You've fed me, and there's bottled water in my cage, and I suppose you think that will do. Well, it won't. I'm the Grand Dragon of Jamya and I want to go home! I demand that you take me home, do you hear?" She glared at them. "I see, you don't hear or you don't understand or you're just too stupid to talk. You couldn't possibly have built this building, so from whom did you steal it?"

Of course, there was no answer.

"Let me out!"

The biggest Invader pressed something on top of the box and

it promptly began to move back up the inclined path to the door from which it had come—with the Grand Dragon yelling all the way.

Jeff watched the cage go out and the door shut, and then he put on his damp clothes and boots. It would not do to rescue the Grand Dragon while naked.

Rescuing the Grand Dragon seemed to be impossible, at least by way of the door through which she had disappeared, for the Invaders were still bobbing around in the water and air and would certainly see him. Jeff sat down to think and to hold Oola, who promptly went to sleep in his arms. Unlike the dragon and Jeff, who fervently wanted to go home, Oola was at home whenever and wherever she was warm and fed and comfortably nestled in the arms of someone familiar.

The building seems to be circular, thought Jeff. The cage went out that way, which should bring it somewhere into the middle of the building because this recreation room is the left-hand door and next to the outer wall.

Then, thought Jeff, perhaps the dragon has been taken to the room beyond that middle door, the one the food box came out of.

Wishing he had Norby with him so he could escape into hyperspace in case of trouble, Jeff took one more drink of water and then carried Oola back through the empty corridor, through the left-hand door, and into the entrance chamber, which was still empty.

This time he headed straight for the middle door which, at his approach, opened for him automatically. There was no corridor inside, just a large room that seemed to be full of machinery and huge metal tanks. The entire front half of the room smelled like the green cubes. Jeff walked quickly through it, trying to hold his breath and hoping Oola wouldn't wake up and pretend she hadn't eaten for several centuries.

The farther half of the room contained more tanks, but at the very back were huge machines in constant motion. Standing in the middle was a robot, which turned and came toward Jeff.

It looked only vaguely like a robot, for it had a hump instead of a head. It had eight arms and a wheeled base. Jeff ducked between two tanks, but the robot passed him as if he did not exist and stopped before one of the tanks, turning switches.

A snakelike metal tube swung down from a pipe overhead into the tank. After a few minutes, the robot turned off the switches and went toward the back wall. At that moment, the wheeled food box from the recreation room entered through the outer door and joined the robot, who opened the top and let a cascade of brown cubes tumble into the box from a processing machine.

Green algaelike things were formed into green cubes, thought Jeff, and some sort of protein-plant made up the brown ones. All the Invaders' food was being made here in this factory.

The food box passed him and lined up with other food boxes at the wall in back of the tanks. They were all open, so Jeff walked over and took out a brown cube. It was reasonably good, slightly fishy and mealy, but edible. He was so hungry, as a matter of fact, that they tasted almost delicious. He ate several, while the worker robot ignored him. Perhaps it didn't even know he was there.

He stuffed his pockets with brown cubes, and, shaking his head, added some green cubes for Oola. His clothes were going to smell—his hands, too.

He wondered where the Grand Dragon was. Perhaps there was another door at the other end of this room.

Oola slept on, causing Jeff to envy her sublime confidence that she'd be able to manage in whatever strange corner of the universe she found herself, especially if she had a tame human around to help out.

There *was* another door and it opened for him, but the room beyond was much darker. After his eyes adapted to the dimness, he made out more machines, many of which looked like strange varieties of robots. And there—in a pile on the floor—was a collection of the little mindless helper robots that did the gardening and other odd jobs on Jamya. They looked deactivated.

Nothing moved in the room. Nothing spoke, yet Jeff had the feeling that something was alive. He touched this robot and that robot, but none responded. Many were quite large, but none were as big as the Jamyn Mentors, who may have been too large for the Invaders to carry off.

In the darkest corner was an immense cage stretching up to the black shadow near the ceiling. It contained many more robots, all of them encased in transparent plastic bags—no, bubbles, for they were stiff. Jeff was trying to squeeze between the various immobile robots to get to the big cage, when a crack of light at the far end of the room suddenly widened to a blaze. Another door had opened.

The room filled with Invaders in the air overhead. Jeff crawled under a curved piece of machinery and stroked Oola, who was awake and growling. After the far door closed, the room darkened and Jeff couldn't tell how many Invaders were present. They seemed to be of various sizes and were very active. They darted every which way—up, down, back and forth, right and left.

Jeff was having difficulty holding Oola down, and he was afraid that any minute she would turn into a hound and howl, a sound that might be heard even by these strangely silent creatures.

Were they looking for him? Jeff realized that to them, *he* was "the invader." But not by choice.

I wish I could go home, he thought. And then he had the added thought, but not without Norby and the Grand Dragon!

As quickly as they had come, the Invaders left. Jeff walked to the other door, the one from which they had entered, but this time he was stymied. The door did not open automatically, and there were no ridges or dimples to press.

After a while he gave up and went back to the struggle of getting near the cage of robots. He might have tried to elevate with Oola's antigrav collar, but if there were any mistake *this* time, he would land on a lot of sharp metal rather than in ocean water.

He was nearly at the cage when Oola hissed and Jeff looked up. An Invader, a little longer than Jeff was tall, was near the cage, floating up and up into the shadow.

It must have seen Jeff, but it did not come toward him. Instead, it rose higher and then floated over the cage.

Jeff held himself as still as he could, hoping the Invader would assume he was just another robot. What was the small Invader planning to do on top of the cage?

The answer came quickly. There was no top to the cage for the Invader descended *into* the cage. It seized something and rose out of the cage again, descended partway and rushed toward the door through which the other Invaders had gone.

In its tentacles was a transparent plastic bubble tightly covering an unmistakable barrel-body. The Invader was flying off with *Norby!*

5

The Vine

"Norby!" shouted Jeff, but the Invader had already gone.

Jeff ran after it, but found himself banging uselessly into the door, which did not open automatically on this side as it had on the other. It took him several precious minutes to find the ridge and press the right dimples, and when he finally entered, he found the food factory empty. The Invaders had gone, every one of them.

Disregarding Oola's insatiable hunger and wish to stay in the food factory, Jeff ran out to the entrance hall. There was no one there, and he raced back through the door to the recreation section. He didn't care how many Invaders he ran into as long as he could find Norby.

The wooded recreation room, however, was empty of Invaders, and he could find no way of opening the door through which the Grand Dragon's cage had gone. He tried pressing ridges and dimples, with and without added kicks, but nothing happened.

"It's still a circular building," he muttered to himself. "There must be another way to the rest of it."

Back in the entrance chamber, he chose the right-hand door, the only one he'd not yet passed through, and it opened for him. He walked into a dark hall with a greenish light over another door at the far end. It seemed the only other door in the room so he walked toward it. As he approached, he saw that the light appeared green only because it shone through the leaves of hanging vines that partly curtained the door. He brushed them aside and walked through.

He found himself in another vast wooded room, filled this time with animals as well as plants. He was about to move farther when he saw that the vines hanging near him were writhing. He jumped back. Snakes?

No, it was vines, perhaps all one vine, and it could move by itself. The thickest part had unpleasant round patches much like the shiny, multi-faceted compound eyes of Terran insects. Uneasily, Jeff moved back against the door which had opened automatically on the other side. It did not open for him on this side.

The vine plucked at Jeff's hair, but when Oola snarled and snapped it withdrew, and its bluish green dual leaves, like large butterflies, vibrated.

Quickly Jeff stepped out from under the vine and looked about. The room had many levels, each filled with different kinds of vegetation. The circular walls surrounding the room were covered with more of the vine that had accosted Jeff.

A bright pink creature flew by him to land on a nearby tree. It didn't look like a bird, because it had tentacles instead of feet and its head was that of a pop-eyed miniature elephant, but it acted like a bird. It sang a song, bobbed its head, then soared to another tree farther away, where its mate was in a nest. There were hundreds of different kinds of animals everywhere. In the distance was a herd of small, blue grazing creatures cropping short prickly-looking plants, and in some of the tallest trees were climbing creatures about the size of little monkeys.

None of the life-forms took any interest in him, and Jeff found himself absorbed in their strangeness. When he finally turned his gaze upward, he found the ceiling to be transparent, just as it was in the recreation room. Again he could see the swimming creatures crowding above it, only not so clearly this time, because vines had draped themselves across the ceiling.

"It's a zoo, Oola!" said Jeff in amazement. He had, of course seen many small and large aquariums where sea creatures could be seen by land creatures, but he'd never seen the reverse.

———Of course it's a zoo, you idiot!

"Who said that?" said Jeff, looking about wildly.

———I! The Dookaza! I am the ruler of this place.

Jeff could see no one, but he felt pressure upon his ankle. He looked down and saw that a part of the vine had snaked about it and was holding it tightly.

———Yes, I communicate telepathically if I touch another creature capable of doing the same. I would not have expected anything as stupid as you to be capable of telepathy, though. Your mind is a muddy muddle, so please do not try to think your

thoughts at me. Speak them in your noisy sound-form of communication because then the mental picture in your thoughts be-
comes a bit less hazy.

"You say you are the ruler of this world?"

————No, only of this zoo. How can you be so stupid? The
Hleno rule the world now that my masters have gone.

"Who are the Hleno?"

————I am placing an image in your mind. Haven't you seen
them?

"Yes, I have. I call them the Invaders, because they invaded a
planet belonging to friends of mine, and they stole a friend of
mine. For that matter, they carried me off, too."

————It is not stealing. They removed unwanted objects.

"Now see here. Whatever you may think, Norby is not an
unwanted object, and one of those Invaders has him. He's my
friend and I want him back. How do I accomplish that?"

————There is no reason for me to help you. You are a
stranger, an alien, and so backward that you cannot even use
antigrav.

"Can you?"

————I am the Dookaza. I do not need it. The Hleno need it
because that is the only way they can leave the ocean and enter
the atmosphere. Their antigrav is part of their physiology. They
are remarkable creatures.

"Maybe they are, but they're pirates and thieves and——here
they come!" Jeff tried to retreat hastily but found that the Dookaza's grip on his ankle had him pinned to the spot. "Let me go!"
he whispered hoarsely. The Invaders were pouring in at the far
end of the zoo.

The vine uncoiled so suddenly that Jeff fell, and when he
picked himself up and tried to run, he found that he had lost his
grip on Oola, and that she had promptly celebrated that fact by
running into the underbrush. Trying to follow her, he tripped over
a slow-moving creature with a double shell, something like a
highly important turtle, and crashed into a flowering bush.

Jeff crawled under the bush where Oola was crouching, her
tail lashing as though she were looking forward to tackling all the
Invaders at once. He seized her so she wouldn't.

The Invaders were spreading out everywhere, but most were
high in the room, over the trees. These would occasionally shoot
downward into the open spaces, scaring the animals. Jeff's eyes
went desperately from one to another, trying to see if any of them
were carrying Norby, but he couldn't tell through the dense fo-

liage of the bush. He wondered uneasily if the Dookaza vine
would tell the Invaders that an alien was in their zoo illegally.

"Let me out of here or I'll scorch your nasty hides!"

The familiar voice prompted Jeff to poke his head around the
bush and find out where the Grand Dragon was. Another Invader
was approaching from the far side of the room, carrying the
Grand Dragon's cage. This Invader was large and acted as if the
Grand Dragon's words were not important. Even when she
puffed smoke at the Invader, it paid no attention.

"Wings and claws!" cried the Grand Dragon in disgust. "My
fire's gone out."

Jeff knew that was not to be taken literally. The dragons of
Jamya did not actually have a fire inside, only the ability to
combine methane and oxygen by means of a catalyst in the
throat tissue. The catalyst lost its capacity with overuse (or over-
watering), and the dragons had to wait for renewal before flame
could form again.

"Why are you hanging me way up here?" she continued to
complain stridently. "I will not stand to be an exhibit in a zoo!
Don't hang my cage up here! Let me out! I am not a zoo animal!
And who's going to feed me those cubes?"

The cage remained where it was, but as if to answer her last
question, the Invader threw in an assortment of cubes.

The other Invaders were milling about to watch the cage.
They floated in circles around it, their tentacles tweaking at the
cage bars and drawing back quickly when the dragon slashed at
them with her claws.

"Nasty brutes!" she shouted. "You have no respect. I'll pay
you back for this humiliation."

With the Invaders' full attention on the cage, Jeff had time to
look carefully at each floating body and at the moving tentacles
around each snout. No one was carrying Norby.

Oola was writhing and began to rise, carrying Jeff with her.
She could obviously wait no longer to join battle.

"No!" whispered Jeff, rapidly thinking "down" and tapping
Oola lightly across the nose to give her something other than the
Invaders to think of. She sank, to Jeff's great relief. It was no
time to take on an army of Invaders. Freeing the Grand Dragon
and finding Norby were the more important tasks, and Jeff
wished the Invaders would leave so that he could at least try to
accomplish the first.

As if hearing his wish, the Invaders floated toward the door
that had locked Jeff inside. As they bobbed up and down in front

of the door, Jeff's ears and head ached momentarily, and the door opened.

"That was an open sesame," said Jeff under his breath, "only I don't see what they did to bring it about."

They were gone, and Jeff had the zoo to himself. He rose from his hiding place, clutching Oola, and thought, "up."

Slowly, quite slowly (because Oola had suddenly grown interested in something furry that ran through the underbrush) they moved upward toward the Grand Dragon's cage.

Jeff was nearly there when something fell on his back and wound about his waist, stopping him. It was the Dookaza vine.

————Where are you going?

"To rescue my friend, the Grand Dragon of Jamya." He called up at the cage, "Here I am, your Dragonship. Jeff Wells, at your service."

He could see the Grand Dragon's nose sticking out between the bars as she tried to look below the cage.

"Jeff! How did you get here? No, don't tell me. Just get me out and then we'll talk."

"I'll try to get you out if this interfering vine will let me."

"There seems to be a great deal of that vine in the zoo," said the Grand Dragon. "Is it intelligent?"

"Yes, and it talks telepathically."

————I am the Dookaza, and I do more than talk telepathically. I hear sound-communication, too. I understand Hleno and that loud animal in the cage speaks Hleno but pronounces it peculiarly.

Jeff sighed. The Grand Dragon did not speak much Terran Basic and if he spoke Hleno to her—no, Jamyn—the Dookaza would understand. Come to think of it, how could the Dookaza understand what he called Hleno? Jeff had never heard the Invaders speak at all.

The Grand Dragon was growing impatient. "Well, what's happening?"

Jeff said, "I have to negotiate with the vine. Please let go of me, Dookaza, so I can set my friend free. She is an important official—"

"*The* most important official!" said the Grand Dragon.

"—on the planet Jamya, and should not be in a cage."

The coil of vine tightened around his waist.

————You should be in a cage, too. I could inform the Hleno.

"What's *happening?*" asked the Grand Dragon louder.

"It's threatening to inform the Hleno—I mean, the Invaders."

"What is it? The zoo guardian?"

————Tell that loquacious and arrogant creature with green scales that I am no guard, but the zoo's lord.

Jeff said, "You're pretty arrogant yourself, Dookaza. You say you *could* inform the Hleno, but you don't say you will, and I don't think you will."

————Are you sure of that?

"Yes, I am. I don't think you want the Hleno to know how intelligent you are. And I think you're curious about alien intelligences who don't come from this world of yours."

————How do you know this is a planet of mine, alien? The creatures in this zoo are, like your green and insulting friend, from the many other planets visited by the Hleno.

"But I don't think you are. You've had time to grow all around the zoo, and I bet you're the only Dookaza vine here. No other voice talks to me. You've been here a long, long time, and you can only grow so successfully on this planet, in my opinion, if you are native to it."

Jeff was by no means sure of his reasoning, but he tried to be confident.

————I don't like your reasoning, alien.

"Because I am right?"

————Because it is insufficient. Perhaps I came from another planet, but one with properties highly similar to Nuhlenony.

"Is Nuhlenony the name of this planet?"

————In our language.

The Grand Dragon said loudly, "That's a silly name, and you can tell that crawling plant-snake I said so. Jeff haven't you got a knife or something useful that will cut you loose from that thing? What's the use of your being a rescuer if you don't rescue me?"

"I'm trying, your Dragonship," said Jeff, struggling to get free.

Oola, disturbed by the situation, wriggled out of his arms and soared to the top of the Grand Dragon's cage. Jeff, deprived of his pet's antigrav, began to fall.

————Why aren't you floating?

Jeff could not answer the Dookaza because the wind was knocked out of him as the section of vine holding him fell with him into a tree. The vine draped across an upper branch, and Jeff, still in the vine's grip and being held upside-down, swung like a pendulum a couple of meters from the ground.

"Jeff!" The Grand Dragon sounded imperiously irritable.

"Why did you let go of Oola? You might have been killed!"

"She let go of me, ma'am," said Jeff patiently. He grabbed part of the vine dangling him from the tree and hauled himself upright. "This vine thinks I have the same sort of built-in antigrav that the Invaders have. Can't you get Oola's collar from her?"

"What good will that do? It won't get me out of the cage."

————You seem to be a fragile species, alien. What do you call yourself?

"I'm a human being."

————Is that objectionable green creature also a human being?

"No, she's a Jamyn dragon. Now, Dookaza, let's stop fooling around. Either betray me to the Hleno, or be of some help and take me up to the cage."

"And Jeff, tell the Dookaza—"

"It can hear you, ma'am."

"Then *I* will tell it," said the Grand Dragon in her most royal tones. "Listen to me, Dookaza. You're here in this zoo pretending to be an ornamental plant, and that's just a charade. I will tell the Hleno if you don't let Jeff open my cage. And if I tell them, the Hleno will be so displeased, they will dig you up."

————Tell the offensive dragon that the Hleno will not dig me up. I am the last Dookaza.

Jeff told the Grand Dragon, who snorted. "It thinks it's a king, a ruler like me, and it's in a zoo!"

————Tell her Green Nastiness that she's in a zoo, too. But I *am* a ruler. Once each Dookaza had its own territory, its own island—

"Where was this?" demanded Jeff. "Where do you come from?"

The Dookaza was silent for a long moment, and then its mood seemed to change completely. It slid over the branches of the tree, lowering Jeff to the ground, but maintained its grip on his waist.

————You and the dragon disturb my meditation. Go.

"Aren't you lonely, last of the Dookazas?"

————I am not lonely. I have the company of my thoughts, and you have disturbed them enough. The Hleno's speech is so high and rapid that I can easily ignore it. I cannot ignore yours, and I am tired of you. Go. In return, I will not betray you.

Jeff leaped forward and grabbed the end tendril of the withdrawing vine. "Wait, Dookaza. I cannot go without the Grand

Dragon. She must be freed from her cage, and I must find my robot."

————Your robot?

"Yes. He was in a cage in the robot storage room."

————That's not a storage room. That's a prison, and I will not help anyone rescue a robot.

"Then help me get the dragon out of the cage."

————No. I have been talking to you like an equal but I see now that I was wrong. You are primitive creatures tied to technology, and I disapprove. Go away.

"You are tied to technology, too, you dumb vine!" shouted Jeff. "Technology runs this building and gives you your fresh air, your light, your water, your food. If that technology were stopped, you would die, Dookaza—so help your fellow primitive."

The vine seemed to shudder and rustled back against the wall.

6

RESCUING THE GRAND DRAGON

"Meow!" said Oola from the top of the dragon's cage.

"Ma'am," said Jeff, "can you touch Oola through the bars?"

"Yes, but she's too big to bring in, and while she's out, I can't get her collar off. You want me to throw it to you, don't you?"

"That's right. Try to stroke Oola with your claw and think about her getting thinner and thinner."

"But she's *your* pet, Jeff. Will she change shape for me?"

"I don't know. We have to try. The Dookaza is sulking and won't help. And the Invaders may come back at any moment."

The Grand Dragon looked through the bars at the top of her cage and pushed her right claw through as far as it would go. "Here, Oola, let me scratch behind your ears the way your mother likes. Nice little pet-child."

Oola flattened herself upon the top of the cage and stretched her neck so that the dragon's claw could reach the scratching place.

"Good Oola," said the dragon. "Nice, *thin* Oola—come through the bars. Thin, thin, thin, and through the bars."

While Jeff watched, the zoo around him rustled and twittered and snuffled as the animals went about their small lives, not worrying about yesterday or tomorrow. A red and black creature that resembled a lizard with antennae perched momentarily on Jeff's toes, chattered, and left. Through nearby trees flew a flock of small creatures with shimmering wings, long bills, and claws at the top of their backs—presumably for hanging from twigs, although Jeff never saw them stop moving.

Now that he studied it, he could see that the Dookaza vine had spread everywhere, but it was flattening its leaves against the walls, and none of its movable tendrils were visible. It seemed to want to be as far from Jeff as possible.

"Good Oola!" The Grand Dragon shouted it joyfully.

Jeff craned his neck and saw an elongated lizardlike Oola inside the cage, rubbing against the Grand Dragon. Her Dragonship took off the collar. "Here, Jeff—catch!"

Jeff caught the collar and thought "up." The collar obeyed and he rose to the cage. He reached into his pockets and gave a brown cube to the dragon and a green one to Oola. Clearly they deserved them.

"Now, how are you going to get me out?" asked the Grand Dragon as she munched the cube.

Jeff climbed onto the cage and was joined by Oola, who squeezed through the bars and began to go back to her ordinary shape. She nosed the collar slung on his wrist and meowed until he put it back on her. "And don't go running away from me," he said to her firmly.

He examined the bars, which proved to be of such strong metal that he had no hope of breaking or even bending them.

The Grand Dragon said, "I can't budge them, so you can be sure you can't, for I am very strong. There must be some ordinary way of opening the cage. Can't you figure it out?" She puffed out a little smoke in her irritation.

"Not just yet, your Dragonship," said Jeff. Carefully, he ran his fingers over the entire top, but could find no ridge. "Are you sure they put you in from the top?"

"How would I know? I was unconscious. Do you suppose I would have let them take me if I were conscious? They must have powerful weapons."

"I don't think they have the usual kind. The one that took me vibrated its tentacles until I got a headache and blacked out."

"I don't care what it was," said the Grand Dragon. "I just want to go home. Even if you get me out of the cage, how do I go home? How do I get back to my beloved Jamya? I don't see the Invaders taking me back." A large tear rolled out of the dragon's right eye.

"Norby could get us back," said Jeff, "and he's here. It's just that he's a prisoner and I can't find him."

"That's not very reassuring. How is it you can't find him? If you know he's here, why don't you know where he is?"

"Because one of the Invaders took him from the cage where I saw him. By the way, he's encased in a plastic bubble like all the small robots the Invaders took from Jamya."

"How I would like to sink my fangs into some of the Invaders," said the Grand Dragon, gnashing those prominent parts of her dental equipment. "Please get me out, Jeff. There must be some way, and I order you to think of one."

"I'm doing my best, ma'am."

Jeff went over the top of the cage again and ran his fingers over the sides as far as he could reach. There were no ridges, but perhaps cages didn't open the way doors did. He tried again and this time he saw something—a lighter spot on the dark metal rim of the top. When he touched it, the spot seemed slowly lower than the surface of the rim, as if a faint dimple had been made in it. Jeff tried to put his finger in the dimple, but nothing happened.

"I think you have to have a tentacle with a very small tip in order to press this little place I have found," he said.

"Try one of Oola's claws," said the Grand Dragon. "They might be the right size."

Jeff found it bothered him a little bit to have the Grand Dragon think of that first. Still, however vain and imperious she might be, there was no denying she was intelligent.

The problem now, however, was persuading Oola to put out her claws. Perversely, she was in a happy mood and presented only her velvet pads. Jeff smiled and took her paw. Gently, he put increasing pressure on it and finally out came the claws while Oola protested with rising wails.

"It's in a good cause, Oola." Jeff touched the dimple with the point of her claw. The top slid aside so quickly that it seemed to disappear so that Jeff and Oola fell into the cage and landed on the Grand Dragon. Since each of the dragon's back spines was tipped with jewels, this was uncomfortable.

"Ow!" said Jeff. "Uh—forgive me for landing on you, ma'am."

"I am strong and can withstand your weight," said the Grand Dragon calmly. "But let's not waste time. We will both hold Oola . . ."

Jeff said, "Not both, ma'am. Oola's collar is for a small animal. It works quite slowly with only my added weight."

The Grand Dragon snorted. "I am a dragon, Jeff, and have wings. They are not powerful enough to sustain my whole weight, but they can assist Oola's collar to get us safely to the ground. Shall we try?"

"Perhaps I could persuade the Dookaza vine to help," said Jeff. "Since I last saw you, you have gained—I mean you have grown more majestic."

"Nonsense. My majesty has nothing to do with it, and don't

you have anything to do with that unpleasant vegetable matter you call Dookaza." She picked up Oola and stood at her full height. "Come, Jeff."

"Wait! Look at Oola!"

The all-purpose pet was growing longer fangs, and her fur was on end, making her look twice as large. She was also growling softly.

"Invaders!" said Jeff. "A lot of them, coming into the zoo."

"Quick," said the Grand Dragon. "I'll lie down and spread my cloak out. You and Oola get under it."

"What about the open cage?"

"I'll close the lid but keep a food cube in the opening so it won't lock."

Holding Oola, she rose slightly, pulling the lid of the cage until it was almost shut and sticking a food cube in the way.

"Now get under my cloak and don't try to peep out. I'll tell you what's going on in the deepest voice I can manage. These Invaders never hear me when I give them orders, and I think it's because my voice is so majestically deep."

"Well . . ." said Jeff, not at all sure of the logic, but there was no time to argue.

He huddled under the Grand Dragon's heavy cloak and tried to keep Oola under it, too. He heard a running commentary from the dragon, spoken in an almost whispered bass that reminded him of Admiral Yobo being discreet. If the Invaders didn't hear that, then perhaps the Grand Dragon was right and they couldn't sense deep tones.

"They're all over the zoo, Jeff. Twelve of them, in assorted sizes. Now that I listen closely, I can hear them talk. Anyway, I can hear a few words now and then in very bad Jamyn, and all very high-pitched. They're just tiny squeaks and that's probably all they can hear. Uh-oh, they're coming closer!"

The Grand Dragon was silent for a moment, and then she said in a barely audible rumble, "They've come to see me. I'm the newest zoo exhibit, I suppose. How humiliating."

"Maybe they think you are grand, majestic, and mighty, and have come to stare for that reason," said Jeff in a low, husky whisper.

"I'm afraid not," said the Grand Dragon mournfully. "From the squeaking I hear, I think they are—oh, the indignity of it—Jeff, they're laughing at me."

"You don't know their sounds. The sounds you hear might be gasps of awe at your magnificence."

Jeff wanted the poor dragon to retain her self-respect, but privately he hoped they *were* laughing. Any species of intelligent creature, however unreasonable and dangerous, is bound to seem less frightening if it displays a sense of humor. Laughter can be cruel, of course, but surely for the most part, it implies tolerance.

Besides, Jeff had himself thought that the Grand Dragon's display of jewels, especially those on her spines and fangs, was much funnier than magnificent.

"They've seen the food cube I used to prop open the cage top. I think they're having an argument over who gets it."

"Don't let them close the door entirely. I'm not sure I can find that dimple again from in here," said Jeff.

"Don't worry," said the Grand Dragon. "I have my methods." The dragon seemed to be having some sort of spasm, but she was merely pushing all her cloak on him. Why had she taken it off?

"They're leaving," she said. "Good riddance. Now we can get out of here."

Jeff threw back the cloak and sneezed. It was the Grand Dragon's best cloak, but it must have been kept in a dusty closet.

"How did you keep the door from sliding shut when they took the food cube?" he asked when he saw that she had opened it fully.

"I put the tip of my precious tail into the opening. Bear witness, Jeff, how much pain the Grand Dragon of Jamya is willing to suffer in the cause of freedom."

Jeff noted the protective ruby cap that ornamented the tip of her tail and decided not to ask the dragon if her procedure for keeping the door open had caused her any pain.

Refastening her cloak, the dragon picked up Oola in her left arm and put her right arm around Jeff.

"Hang on," she said, "and think 'flying.'"

In a few seconds she rose into the air with Jeff awkwardly clutched under her arm, his long legs dragging. As soon as she had cleared the top of the cage, the Grand Dragon spread her wings and flew out across the zoo.

"My, doesn't it look pretty," she exclaimed. "From my cage I couldn't view it properly."

"Watch out, ma'am, we're losing altitude," shouted Jeff.

"I am managing just fine," said the Grand Dragon, panting a little with her unaccustomed exertions and drifting distinctly lower. "I was coming down anyway. It's just a matter of deciding *where*—"

Her left wing snagged lightly on a tree branch, just enough to throw her completely off balance. She rolled upside down and plummeted, dropping Oola and Jeff in the process.

"Meowrrr!" said Oola, floating in the air as Jeff fell past her.

"You should have tried gliding instead of flying," said Jeff, a little exasperated, for he could see where his fall would end. He fell into the pond and landed on something uncomfortable.

Jeff swam to the surface, plucking from his forehead a sticky small creature with a bill like a duck and eyes on stalks like a snail.

"Worrrww?" said Oola, suspended in the air above him. She looked as worried as an All-Purpose-Pet can look, and seemed to be wondering whether or not to turn into a fish and join him. Jeff grabbed her, and before she could protest his wet hands, thought "up" and rose.

There was a sound like a steam engine getting set to explode. Jeff looked back down and saw the Grand Dragon's head sticking out of the pond, draped in blue and yellow water plants.

"For the second time," she said slowly and with a deeply aggrieved air, "you have landed right on *me!*"

"I apologize again, ma'am," said Jeff, rubbing his bottom where it was sore. "Are you hurt?"

"My *dignity* is hurt." The dragon splashed to the edge of the pond and hauled herself out. "I did not intend to get wet. My best cloak is ruined."

"It's the second time I've taken a dip today," said Jeff. "But at least we're all out of the cage."

He and Oola descended to the Grand Dragon and sat beside her, while Oola licked Jeff's face until he put her down, saying, "I think I'll have a soggy brown cube. Would you like one, your Dragonship?" He extracted two from his pocket and held them out to her, while tossing a green one to Oola.

The Grand Dragon took one of the brown cubes. "I suppose nourishment is called for if the pond water hasn't extracted all the vitamins. Now where do you suggest we look for Norby?"

"Those Invaders that were looking at you with awe while I was under the blanket—were they carrying anything?"

"No," said the Grand Dragon bitterly. "They were just laughing."

"Then we have to find the Invader who stole Norby from the prison cage. It was a rather small Invader."

"That is certainly an insufficient description," said the Grand Dragon. "There may be any number of rather small Invaders, and if we can't find Norby, I don't see how we'll ever get off this planet. Oh, if you had only brought ships with you when you came."

"But our ship goes through hyperspace only because Norby plugs himself into it. We would still need Norby."

The Grand Dragon wrung out her cloak. "Onward, then. There's no help for it. We must find Norby."

"I wish the Dookaza vine would speak to us. I'm sure it has useful information. It did seem antagonistic to robots, however."

"I'm antagonistic to telepathic vegetation," said the Grand Dragon, looking about at the quantities of vine in every direction.

In the distance, there was a sudden yowl, and Oola, who had been prowling through the underbrush sniffing various plants, came barreling toward them and leaped into Jeff's arms.

"There's Norby," said Jeff excitedly, "and there's the thief."

The small Invader was approaching quickly; Norby's plastic bubble was dangling from two tentacles, and its other tentacles were outstretched.

7

The Small Invader

The Grand Dragon took a fighting stance and tried to breathe out flame but, thanks to her bath in the pond, only black smoke emerged. The methane simply would not oxidize completely.

"Go away!" she shouted, slashing at the Invader's tentacles with her claws, but it was no use. She was snatched up and held tightly with three tentacles.

Jeff couldn't run, because there was no place to go and because it would have been cowardly to leave the Grand Dragon. Going up in the air with Oola's collar was no use because the air was the Invader's element.

Holding Oola to himself with one hand, he leaned back against a tall, sturdy tree and waited. The Invader came closer, and Jeff kicked as hard as he could.

The Invader's pudgy side caved in for a moment as a puff of air blew against Jeff with a sound that resembled "oof."

"Help me, ma'am," gasped Jeff. "Kick it—bite it—"

"I'm trying," said the Grand Dragon, and she clamped all her teeth onto the nearest tentacle.

Jeff kicked again and the Invader backed off, then came forward again, trying to manage both the fighting dragon and the boy on the ground while at the same time carrying a heavy plastic bubble containing a closed-up barrel of a robot.

Three tentacles wound around Jeff, and suddenly he heard words in his mind; words that were a somewhat distorted version of Jamyn. The Others had taught Jamyn to the dragons; perhaps they had taught it to the Invaders as well. The Dookaza vine had been able to understand both.

————Alien! (said the voice) Why do you not answer when I speak to you?

Jeff spoke out loud, so the dragon could hear as well. "Your Hleno speech is not audible to us. It is too high-pitched."

————Then why can I hear and be heard now? You creatures are dangerous. I was going to capture you and take you back to the spiky creature's cage, and perhaps be rewarded by the zoo manager. And now you are speaking like an intelligent being, and I am hearing you, but not with my ears.

"Jeff," said the Grand Dragon, hanging motionless in the Invader's tentacles, "you don't have to repeat that because I am getting the telepathic message, too. I think my bite turned this Invader into a touch-telepath like us."

————I don't understand. How could the spiky creature's bite have made me able to hear you—and what is telepathy?

"Hearing and speaking directly from mind to mind is telepathy," said Jeff. "And the bite of a Jamyn dragon automatically confers the ability, as long as you're touching the other person. It has something to do with the hormones, I think, but I don't really know."

"This is all very well," said the Grand Dragon, "but suppose I'm poisoned from biting this awful creature? I do not feel well."

"That's because its tentacle is too tight around your waist. You have gained—grandeur, you know."

"Yes, but on brown cubes I will soon lose that grandeur. I suppose I'm not poisoned. Tell it to put us down, Jeff."

————What does 'down jeff' mean?

"Jeff is my name. I'm the one in the wet red uniform. The spiky one is the Grand Dragon of Jamyn. And the bubble you are holding contains my friend Norby."

————How can a machine in a safety bubble have a name?

"Because it does. The machine is named Norby, and he's my robot."

————Robots are bad.

"They are not! You're an idiot to think so. My robot is not bad."

The Grand Dragon said, "Don't be angry, Jeff. Jamyn dragons and Terrans like robots, but these Invaders don't seem to use them."

Jeff shook his head angrily. "But they *do* use them! The Invaders have robots manufacturing their food for them, and there's a lot of complicated equipment keeping this undersea building going."

————Invaders? Is that the name you have given us?

"Yes," said Jeff. "You and your people invaded the privacy of a planet called Jamya, where the Grand Dragon here is ruler. You paralyzed the Jamyn robots, kidnapped the Grand Dragon and put her in a zoo, dumped me and my pet Oola into your ocean and, worst of all, stole my personal robot."

"Worst of all?" said the Grand Dragon. "Stealing Norby is worse than kidnapping the Grand Dragon?"

"Please let us go," said Jeff, wishing the tentacles around him would relax. He could see Norby still closed up in his barrel. "Please take Norby out of the safety bubble and give him to me so we can go back to our own planets."

————I can't do that. It would be against regulations. I must take you to the authorities and let them decide. I will have to put Jeff and the Grand Dragon back in the zoo. And the little animal, too.

"And what will they do to you, Invader, when you report all this?" asked the Grand Dragon. "Were you allowed to remove that robot from the cage?"

The Invader didn't answer, so Jeff tried something else. "We don't understand your Hleno culture. If you disapprove of robots, why did you take Norby?"

Again the Invader did not answer.

"Why?" asked the Grand Dragon. "Tell us why or I'll bite you again. My second bite could be poisonous."

————Don't bite me or I will be forced to treat you as creatures who resist capture.

"How?" asked the Grand Dragon before Jeff could stop her.

A vibration began in the tentacles that seemed to reach inside of Jeff's skull, and he felt himself blacking out. "Stop!"

Oola wriggled until she had part of a tentacle in view. Then she clamped her teeth on it.

"Stop, Oola," said Jeff, unclamping her jaws and stroking her. "If you tell us why you took my small robot, Invader, I won't tell anyone, and I will advise you how to keep out of trouble."

There was a long hesitation, and Jeff hoped the Invader was sufficiently frightened to talk, but not so frightened as to react violently. Finally, the telepathic voice spoke.

————I've been through the factory and the zoo and the prison many times, but I've never seen anything like this robot. It doesn't even look like a robot, but it must be one or it wouldn't be inside a safety bubble. I wanted to try opening the bubble to investigate the robot. I was just curious. There's nothing wrong with being curious. You're *supposed* to be curious if you have brains. The trouble is I can't open the bubble.

Jeff frowned. There was something puzzling about that speech.

The Grand Dragon found something puzzling, too. "You mean *you* don't know how to open a safety bubble?"

———I don't. That's why I have to take it to the authorities. And if I don't keep you here in the zoo, I have to take you to the auth— (The Invader broke off and trembled violently.) Wha—at are you do—ing to me?

It writhed and jerked backward and forward.

———What is holding me?

"It's not our doing," said Jeff, squirming about so he could get a better view of the rest of the Invader. "You've just been attacked by the Dookaza."

A large section of the Dookaza must have crept through the trees from the wall. It was wrapping its coils around the Invader's bulgy body.

———But what's a Dookaza?

———I am the ruler of this zoo (said the Dookaza in all of their minds) and I have decided that you must all die. I could tolerate the presence of you aliens as long as I believed you would not be here long, but now you have made one of the Hleno telepathic and perhaps you will make them all telepathic, and that I cannot tolerate. I will choke you all and throw you into the pond. The other Hleno will assume it was a fight in which all died. Then I will be free to meditate in quiet.

As another section of the vine wrapped itself around him, Jeff struggled to keep breathing, pushing the vine down on the Invader's tentacles, which were around his waist. He felt as if he were being crushed to death by different kinds of snakes.

The Grand Dragon did not hesitate. She attacked the Dookaza as it attacked her, and then belched smoke. "Ugh! This vine tastes terrible, and it's too tough even for my fangs."

"Then get your flame back," said Jeff.

"I'm trying. I'm trying."

Oola was also attacking the vine, but her teeth made no impression on it, and Jeff tried vainly to calm her down. She was the only one of them who could escape, at least temporarily, by elevating on antigrav. But either the Dookaza would eventually find her or the Invaders would capture her. Jeff realized that his pet might be allowed to live as another animal in the zoo, but Oola was designed for pethood, and she would be unhappy without an intelligent companion. She was unhappy now, unwilling to lose Jeff.

Jeff thought: And what would happen to Norby if the Grand Dragon and I die?

"Don't kill us," he said.

———I was not going to kill you (said the Invader).

———But I will (said the Dookaza, tightening its coils).

Fighting against the vine's strength, Jeff tried his last desperate move. Was Norby within reach?

Norby's bubble was still held by the Invader, whose tentacles were beginning to droop as the Dookaza squeezed. Norby was close up, so for the first time Jeff could see that Norby's sensor wire was almost but not quite touching the inside of the bubble. He must have just had time to do that before the stasis field in the bubble held him paralyzed in the center of the small space.

Softly, Jeff began humming the Space Command anthem, hoping that the surface distraction would prevent the Dookaza vine from overhearing his thoughts. Since Norby's barrel was held in place by thin plasti-force strands it would not take much distortion to force the sensor wire into contact with the bubble!

"Invader," gasped Jeff, "you said you didn't know how to open Norby's bubble. Did you try forcing it open by squeezing it?"

———Yes, I tried, but the bubble was too strong for my tentacles. Save me! I am being squeezed to death.

Jeff felt the Dookaza vine pause in its lethal striving. It was listening.

———Why do you ask about the robot? (said the Dookaza).

Jeff said, "I just wanted to make sure that Norby would be safe even if we were killed."

———Why should that matter, alien? (said the Dookaza). What difference does it make what happens to your robot? I will simply throw it into the pond with your bodies.

"Good, because then when the rest of the Hleno find us, they will also find Norby and remove him from the bubble."

———I don't care what they do with a robot. They put robots in prison.

"But they might first be changed by Norby. Then they will not put him in prison."

———Changed? How?

"My robot is telepathic. He will be able to teach all the Hleno to be telepathic, and then your killing this Invader and the Grand Dragon and myself will all be for nothing."

———A telepathic robot? (The Dookaza sounded agitated.) I cannot permit that. I will destroy the robot.

"You cannot," Jeff said deliberately. "Even the Invader couldn't break open the bubble."

The vine's coils around Jeff and the Grand Dragon and the Invader relaxed slightly as the Dookaza turned its attention and its strength to Norby. It sent a tendril about Norby's bubble, pulling it out of the Invader's grasp, then sent another tendril about it tightly and began to squeeze.

Jeff said, "By the way, Dookaza, you want to be alone in order that you might peacefully meditate, but you will never be alone again. You will always have those you killed filling your memory, troubling you with thoughts of the lives you cut off so viciously."

The Dookaza vine ignored the statement and went on squeezing the stiff plastic bubble, paying no attention to the fact that the sensor wire would soon be touching the wall of the bubble.

————I could not possibly care (said the Dookaza) about the lives of animals and machines.

"In our philosophy, it is held to be possible to live alone and remain sane only if one feels kindly toward the universe and everything in it."

————Your philosophy is for you. I do not want it.

"Norby! Norby!" shouted Jeff, as the wall of the bubble touched the sensor wire, which bent in a very slight curve on contact.

————You needn't shout, Jeff (came Norby's well-known thought-sensation in Terran Basic). I'm not telepathically deaf.

————You're alive (said Jeff in Terran Basic. Only they two would understand it).

————Of course I am, but I can't do anything from inside this bubble unless you can persuade that lout of a balloon to hyperspace us out of here. (He switched to Jamyn.) Invader, can you hyperjump?

————I don't know how (said the Invader).

"Idiot!" said the Grand Dragon. "You Invaders do it all the time."

————Well, I never have, and I don't know how.

————Silence! (roared the Dookaza). Let me concentrate on breaking this robot in two!

"Invader!" said Jeff urgently, "join minds with my robot while he's still in contact telepathically! Let him show you how to hyperjump. You can do that, can't you, Norby?"

————Can do, Jeff! (said Norby). Hang on!

If Norby and the Invader worked together, where would they

take them? What if each had a different destination in mind? What about the Dookaza? It was in contact. Would it come, too?

Jeff's thoughts stopped as a great tearing noise filled his ears and then grayness filled his eyes.

And then he was suddenly up to his chest in mud—wet again —and alone, except for an irate All-Purpose-Pet clinging to his neck.

8

In the Mud

Jeff began to sink in the mud, its brown ooze sliding around his armpits. In a panic he pushed down with outstretched arms, trying to keep from going under and suffocating.

"Meow!" said Oola, rising gracefully from his shoulders until she hung in the air above his head, peering down at him quizzically as if to say "How can you be so stupid?"

"I forgot," said Jeff, embarrassed. "Mud is so frightening, I couldn't think straight, but now you can rescue me again."

He clasped both hands around his pet and the antigrav collar. For a few minutes nothing happened as the weak antigrav struggled to lift him out of the clinging mud. "Up," he thought, as hard as he could. "Up." With a smacking sound, he came loose and was in the air, dripping mud and feeling filthy.

He looked around but could see no one else. About twenty meters away was a small island of vegetation that consisted of grasslike plants and taller tree-forms. At the horizon were several other islands, some of them much larger. And in the air was the faint sound of singing.

Jeff was horrified. "Melodia! We've come to Melodia! Why?"

Oola tugged to go in the direction of the island, so Jeff rummaged in his pockets and fed her a mashed green cube to distract her. He suddenly noticed that the mud was moving in one area. While he watched, a shiny transparent bubble broke the glistening mud surface.

"It's Norby," Jeff cried out. "Down, Oola!" Awkwardly, Jeff waggled his body and arms until he was over the bubble and could pick it up.

"Norby?" Jeff said anxiously.

There was no answer in his mind, for the bubble had sprung

back to its normal shape, and Norby's antenna no longer touched the side.

The surface of the mud below gyrated as if a volcanic explosion were about to take place and with a mighty heave, the Grand Dragon of Jamya pushed her head and wings above the surface of the mud and panted. "Get me out of here, Jeff! I refuse to drown in mud. It's undignified."

With Norby awkwardly clutched under one arm and Oola grabbing his shoulders, Jeff held out his other hand to the dragon.

The antigrav collar had reached its capacity and could not lift the dragon all the way out of the mud.

"Try flying, ma'am," said Jeff, thinking "wings" as hard as he could. Oola got the idea and grew some leathery flaps between her front and back legs. With the extra lift of Oola's flaps and with the Grand Dragon beating her wings for all she was worth, they were able to move.

"To the island," said Jeff. "Everyone try to move there."

They sloshed their way across the mud. The Grand Dragon's hind legs and her tail were under the surface. The tail rose every now and then to slap down on the mud, though whether for propulsive force or out of anger it was impossible to tell, for the dragon muttered and fumed the whole way. Oola flapped her wings and even Jeff tried flying motions to guide the antigrav effect of the collar.

They got to the island after what seemed like hours and collapsed on its grassy shore.

"My cloak is absolutely ruined," said the dragon.

Jeff was trying to wipe the mud off himself with swatches of grass. "These islands usually have a spring of water," he said. "We should try to find it, because we'll need water to drink—and to wash, too."

"It doesn't matter," said the dragon. "I think all the indignities I have suffered have driven me mad. Here I am on a planet of mud, and I think I hear beautiful singing. Or has someone told me about a planet like this, and am I only imagining I'm here?"

"You're not imagining," said Jeff.

"Is this part of your Earth, Jeff?"

"No. I'm pretty sure this is the planet Melodia. Your grand-niece, Zargl, was here with me once, and she must have told you about it. The natives sing a lot, and it's a good thing none of them are here. I'd rather be on an uninhabited island."

"But if this is uninhabited, why do we hear singing?"

"There are islands all over Melodia's mud, and the bigger

ones are inhabited. I hope we don't have to see any of the natives again or eat their uninspired food."

"Food?" The Grand Dragon sniffed and looked about. "Where?"

"See those yellow and blue and orange things hanging from the trees and bushes? That's fruit, all edible, but not very good."

Oola had already lifted herself to a small yellow fruit, snatched it from the branch with her jaws, and was back at Jeff's muddy feet, eating it with relish.

"Oola seems to enjoy it," said the Grand Dragon.

"Oola eats almost *anything* that's vegetation and likes anything she eats." Jeff wiped the mud off Norby's bubble and said, "Where do you suppose the Invader might be?"

"I've forgotten about it," said the Grand Dragon, not at all contritely. "I hope it smothered in the mud."

"Don't hope that," said Jeff. "Unless we can get Norby out of this bubble, the Invader's ability to travel in hyperspace is the only way we can get off Melodia, and I would rather be back under the sea of Nuhlenony then stay here."

"You are not encouraging me, Jeff," said the Grand Dragon, standing up and shaking mud in all directions. "I'm going to look for the spring you mentioned, and it had better be there because I'm thirsty." Scowling horribly and showing her fangs, the dragon stamped off through the grass.

Although Jeff was thirsty too, he sat on the grass and stared out at the mud, worrying about the Invader. It had to be under the mud, since only the Invader could have brought them away from Nuhlenony, although only Norby could have forced upon it the coordinates of Melodia.

Oola raised her head from the fruit she was eating, a piece of it dripping from her jaws. "Worry," she said, placing the piece carefully on Jeff's shoe and stepping back as if she were a Terran cat who had just brought her master a juicy mouse.

Jeff picked up the fruit and munched on it, satisfying some of his thirst, and went on staring at the mud. Was the Invader under the mud surface and, if so, how long could he survive there?

As if in answer, the mud seemed to convulse and spray upward like a geyser. Hastily Jeff picked up Oola. Soothing her with soft cluckings as she began to protest, he removed her collar and fastened it tightly about his upper arm.

It was hard getting back to the section of mud where he'd originally landed, but that was where it was heaving. He hovered

over the area, got spattered by more wet mud, and finally saw a
gray shape pushing up.

"Invader!" he called. Then he remembered that it couldn't
hear his low-pitched sounds. He would have to touch it and
transfer the message telepathically. When he tried to reach down
to make contact, the Invader shot skyward, knocking him out of
the way.

Around the Invader's body was what looked like an enormous
snake whose tail disappeared into the mud. The Dookaza vine
had also come along, and a branch of it swung out, aiming at
Jeff, who twisted and turned in an attempt to avoid it.

Something else wound around his arm. It was a tentacle from
the Invader, hanging on tightly. At once Jeff could make out the
Invader's thoughts.

————The Dookaza is squeezing me, trying to pull me under
the mud again. I will die if I go under once more, because there
is no air to breathe and not enough water for my other breathing
organs. Help me.

"Keep trying to rise, Invader. Perhaps only part of the Dookaza vine had come along. Perhaps it has no roots and will
die—"

Jeff stopped speaking, for the utterly alien voice of the Da-
zooka spoke in his mind.

————I will not die, for my roots are here, even if most of
my body is dying in the zoo back on Nuhlenony. I am getting
stronger on this wonderful planet with its rich nourishing mud, its
clean air, real sunlight, and good vibrations. You and the Hleno
will serve to fertilize the mud about my roots, after they are
well-planted in a place of my choice.

"Dookaza," shouted Jeff, knowing it would sense him since
both it and he were in physical contact with the Invader, "do not
murder us. The mud of Melodia is rich enough for your growth as
it is."

————It is not your fertilizing power alone. You are telepathic, and I cannot endure the minds of your kind, or of the
Hleno who has come with you. Nor need I be further disturbed by
your robot's telepathic powers. He is still imprisoned in the bubble, and there will be no Hleno to release him. If I leave him to
himself, it will be to me as he were dead.

Oola was standing at the mud-shore of the island, snarling and
hissing. The sounds of the angry All-Purpose-Pet brought the
Grand Dragon on the run. She had evidently found water for she

looked free of mud and her cloak was dripping wet.

"Jeff!" she cried out. "You're in danger."

Jeff said, "I'm trying to save the Invader from the Dookaza vine. The Dookaza wants to kill us all."

————Help me (said the Invader). I cannot fight the pull of the vine much longer.

Desperately, Jeff tried to pull the vine away from the Invader's body, but it was too firm in its hold. His attempt only immobilized him long enough to allow the Dookaza to throw a branch about him.

As the coils wound around his waist, Jeff quickly removed Oola's collar from his arm.

"Ma'am, try gliding out across the mud so that I can throw the collar to you. You are the strongest of us and might be able to handle the Dookaza."

"Coming, Jeff." The Grand Dragon might have been vain and self-absorbed, but no one could doubt her bravery. Casting aside her cloak, the dragon ran back into the grass of the island and then ran forward at full speed. At the edge of the island she opened her wings fully and leaped far out over the mud.

She was too heavy. The glide lasted only a few seconds, and then she was down in the mud. "Jeff! Part of the vine has my left leg."

"Never mind. Keep moving those wings! Keep on the surface!" Jeff was finding it more and more difficult to breathe as the Dookaza squeezed. He managed, however, and then the dragon was directly below.

"Ma'am, take the collar!" He managed to drop it directly onto her claw, which curved shut, holding the collar fast. Now she had the antigrav of the collar plus the assistance of her own wings. Together a greater upward force could be exerted on the vine than Jeff could have managed.

The Grand Dragon lifted from the mud, dragging her section of the vine with her.

"I am going to teach this bully a lesson," said the dragon, clearing her throat and licking her lips, "a lesson it won't forget."

The Grand Dragon was not referring to her lifting power, as Jeff was assuming she was. She was dry enough and rested enough to do something more spectacular. She opened her mouth with all her fangs glistening. A tremendous roar vibrated the air and blasted Jeff's eardrums as the Grand Dragon's mouth shot out a hot blast of flame that struck the main stem of the vine.

The Dookaza crackled and blackened, and then the vine broke

apart, the lower section falling back into the mud.

The Invader shook itself free of the dead remnant of the vine, and the dragon flew triumphantly away from the part that had been trying to hold her.

Jeff, in the meantime, had neither the collar nor the upthrusting vine to hold him up. He fell into the mud again, head-down this time.

Something dragged him out. When he wiped his eyes, he saw that he was suspended from a tentacle of the Invader, who was slowly moving over to the island, accompanied by the Grand Dragon, who was dipping and soaring as only a Jamya dragon with large wings and an antigrav device in addition could do.

"The spring is over there," said the dragon solicitously, "with a small pool."

Wearily, Jeff picked himself up from the grass where the Invader had deposited him and went to wash. Overhead, brushing against the trees, came the Invader, while on the ground, brushing against Jeff's legs, was Oola, anxious to see he did not get into trouble again.

Jeff got clean—and wet, since there was nothing to dry himself with. He removed his boots and socks, hoping they might dry in the sun. It felt pleasant to wriggle his bare toes in the grass.

The Invader touched him with a tentacle.

————We Hleno need water to live in. I cannot live in this muddy world. I can stay in the air for a long time, but not forever. I want very much to go home. Please take me home.

"Only you can do that," said Jeff. "You have the power to travel through hyperspace, not I."

————But I've never learned how! Your robot did it through me and directed us to this awful planet. We must leave, for the Dookaza vine's roots are not dead and it will grow again.

"If that's so," said Jeff, "then there's all the more reason to get Norby out of his bubble."

————I don't know how to do that. And the bubble can't be forced merely by muscular strength. Even the Dookaza vine could only bend the bubble, not break it.

"Do you suppose a bit of dragon flame could melt a section of the bubble?" Jeff asked.

————I don't think so. The bubbles are highly resistant to heat. If that green animal could produce enough heat to break through the bubble, there would be enough heat to damage the robot inside.

"Comet tails!" said Jeff in discouragement.

He listened to the faraway music of Melodia as Oola went to sleep on the grass. The Invader swayed against the trees as if it were tired, too.

"What's your name?" asked Jeff suddenly, stroking the tentacle that was touching him.

————I am Hleno. You call us Invaders.

"Yes, but I mean your own name. Don't each of you have a personal name that belongs only to you? My name is Jeff and that's Oola, my pet."

————My name is Uhfy. I am sorry I have caused you so much trouble. You and your friend, whom you call ma'am, saved my life and I thank you for it.

"We haven't saved your life yet. We have to get you away from this terrible world and take you home."

————You will do that? You don't hate me for the trouble I've caused you?

"One fits the universe best," said Jeff, "if one does not hate. I try not to." He felt in his pockets once more and found two brown cubes in terrible shape. "Are you hungry? Would you like these?" He held out his hand, and another tentacle whipped down to take them.

The food cubes disappeared into the creature's odd mouth and through the tentacle touching Jeff, Uhfy spoke.

————Thank you. I was growing faint with hunger.

Jeff was sleepy, but he felt that he must stay awake in case a living remnant of the Dookaza might still be capable of attacking them.

"Uhfy," he said. "Can you reach that orange fruit up there with one of your tentacles? I'm sure it will be sour, but I'm hungry enough not to mind."

While Jeff was eating, he decided that he and the Invader were now friendly enough for him to ask a question that still bothered him.

"Uhfy," he said. "Why did you really take Norby? I'm sure your doing so will get you into trouble, so why did you? It can't be just that you're curious."

————But it is. I was just curious. It is such an odd robot. I've never seen one like it. And I *will* get into trouble. My father will be furious.

"Your *father?*"

————He's a high official of the Hleno. And I'm his favorite son. Or I was. Now he won't like me as much.

"Uhfy, how old are you?" Rather overcome, Jeff was thinking of Uhfy's small size for an invader, of his curious way of speaking, the fact that he had not learned yet to indulge in hyperspace travel, and so on.

———I don't know how you measure these things in your world, Jeff, but I am only half as old as I must be to be considered an adult.

Younger than I am, thought Jeff, and here I'm treating him as though he were a grown-up villain.

"Uhfy," he said, "I can hear the Grand Dragon snoring, and Oola's been asleep for quite a while now. You sleep, too, while I watch for the Dookaza or the Melodians. When I wake you, you can watch and I'll sleep."

———Very well, Jeff, but I don't like being unable to communicate with you. You and your friends have been a comfort to me.

"I'll be right here when you wake up, Uhfy. I can't go anywhere. I'm certainly not going into the mud."

———Thank you, Jeff. I know you'll think of a way of saving us.

The young Hleno withdrew his tentacle and floated over to the big patch of grass. With a sound like air whistling out of a balloon, he sank to the grass and lay there quietly.

"I wish I *could* think of a way of saving us," Jeff muttered to himself.

9

The Mind of the Vine

Tired as he was, Jeff felt terribly restless. He walked back to the Grand Dragon, who was snoring loudly. He gazed out over the sea of mud but could see no break in the surface.

Norby's bubble still lay on its side at the edge of the island. Jeff carried it to a tree where the grass was shorter and softer and sat down with his arm around the bubble. Nothing was going to try to steal Norby without Jeff being made aware of it.

Just touching the bubble and knowing that Norby was alive and nearby soothed Jeff to the point where his eyelids kept closing. He forced them open time and again.

The sun of Melodia sank behind the horizon of mud and islands, and gradually the faraway singing of the natives died away as they went back into the mud for the night. There was only deep silence under the great bowl of the sky that was now filling with stars, not as numerous as in Uhfy's world, but not quite so sparse as the Earth's sky.

————Alien. Please listen to me.

"Whuuh?" Jeff had fallen asleep after all, and now, with a feeling of shame, he came to with a start.

————I will not harm you. Listen.

Jeff looked about wildly, but there was no one visible. Then he became aware of something wet on his bare right foot. He looked down and could just make out, in the star-broken darkness, that a thin tendril of vine, trailing from the mud, was delicately pressed against his foot, but not encircling it. The leaves of the vine were muddy and drooping.

Jeff said, "Now, look, Dakooza. If you try to drag me back into the mud, I will awaken the Grand Dragon, and she will finish burning you. She'll destroy every part of you, and you'll be dead forever."

Jeff was not sure how long it would be before the Grand Dragon would be able to flame again after her attack on the Dakooza, but the vine wouldn't know that. And, in fact, the thought processes of the Dakooza were mild and humble.

———I do not wish to oppose you again. I want only permission to rise above the mud and experience sunlight. I must have the sunlight for photosynthesis and energy. Please let me survive.

"You weren't going to let *us* survive."

———I crave your pardon for that. I was frightened, and perhaps I have not been entirely sane for many years.

Jeff said suspiciously, "I can't believe you think that. Are you going to tell me you've suddenly become sane?"

———I may have. At least I may have become a little less insane. The artificial light of the Nuhlenony zoo and the poor nutrition of the soil must have done me harm. The rich soil here seems to have cleared my mind already, and the good sunlight when it comes should help me even more. I think I will be different from now on—if you telepathic creatures will leave this planet.

"We plan to do that, but we'll need your help."

———How can I help?

"By squeezing Norby's prison bubble so I can communicate with him, and so he can join minds with the Hleno to hyperjump us away from here and away from you."

———I will try. I am weaker now, there is so little left of me. Still, when the sun rises I will spread my leaves out to dry on the surface, and after I have absorbed enough sunlight, my remaining vine may be strong enough to squeeze the bubble. Meanwhile I will absorb nourishment from the soil through my roots.

Jeff relaxed against the tree. The Dookaza's thoughts seemed sincere. Surely it would be harder to lie in the mind than in words. The uneasy mind will give itself away, in a way that words would not. It might be wise to test the matter though.

"While you are nourishing yourself, Dookaza," said Jeff, "tell me more about yourself. You didn't want to before. You were friendly enough till I asked you where you came from, and you've been hostile ever since."

———I know. I didn't want to remember. It filled me with hostility.

"Please tell me of your past now."

————I will, but first I must warn you. I think you have made friends with the young Hleno who brought me to this wonderful planet, but when you go back to Nuhlenony you will not find it so easy to win the friendship of older Hlenos. And unless you can find someone else strong enough to help you make contact with your robot, you will be forced to stay there on Nuhlenony—and in the zoo, as I was.

"I know. I will think about getting away from Melodia, but it is important to think about the right things at the right times, my brother always says. It is time now for you to tell me your life story. It will help keep me awake."

————You may sleep. I will give you a story while you sleep.

Give me a story? What an odd way of putting it. He could feel his mind whirling, and at once he tried to snap awake. How could he be *that* sure he could trust the Dookaza?

Perhaps the Dookaza understood that.

————I will not try to harm you—Jeff.

The humility in the mind. The use of his name. Jeff thought: I must trust it. If I turn away from it now, it may lose its last chance at sanity.

"I will trust you, Dookaza."

————And will it be all right if you give me your knowledge?

"Knowledge?" Jeff yawned and found he could barely think, "I'm just a school kid. My older brother knows much more."

————But you have been to many places, and if I make your knowledge part of me, I will have been to those places, too. Open your mind to me, and I will give you my story as you give me yours.

Jeff yawned again, his eyes shut. "Okay, Dookaza. Give me—a story—"

Dry land . . . good . . . roots in soil . . . rain . . . sunlight . . . good!

Jeff . . . Dookaza . . . Jeff . . . both!

Memories . . . back . . . beginning in ocean . . . long years . . . Nuhlenony turning around sun . . . sea filling with life . . . land rising above sea . . .

Dry land good . . . roots in soil . . . rain, sunlight . . . good! Stay here, no change now . . .

Other creatures changing . . . one animal grows intelligent, walks upright . . . cities . . . volcanoes destroy . . . They build again . . . They change some creatures . . . change—me! Me . . .

I am myself. I am I! They have bioengineered only me, no

other Dookaza vine. I, the only intelligent Dookaza on Nuhlen-ony, put part of my root system into a house They built for me. What do They want of me?

. . . I can communicate with Them now through touch, and I have learned They want nothing of me except that I exist and enjoy the universe in my own way. They have done this with other creatures on Nuhlenony and on other planets they visit. They are kind, and leave me alone to meditate, but I am not lonely. I am part of the cosmos and that is enough. . . .

The environment is changing and They are worried because their technology is to blame. The machines burn fuel and produce carbon dioxide which heats the atmosphere. The ice caps at the poles of Nuhlenony are melting, and the ocean is rising . . . rising . . .

Into the volcanoes! Danger! I have moved entirely into the building They said was mine, but it is mine no longer for They are bringing in specimens of all the animals, building more rooms and stronger walls to shut out the sea that creeps up over the land. . . .

While the ocean rose They went away for a long time, and now They are back, sad because the planet did not grow cooler and the sea level did not sink. The islands are forever gone under the ocean. Only our submerged building has land life, and in it I rule the zoo and remember sunlight and sky and freedom. I am unhappy. I do not like to be reminded of what I have lost. . . .

Primitive sea swimmers called Hleno live in the ocean, but They have bioengineered some Hleno to be intelligent, with abili-ties greater than mine; the planet now belongs to Hleno who swim in water, float in air, and eat food made in factory vats where only one-celled animals and plants must die to feed others. . . .

They have destroyed all of their artifacts except this building, and They are leaving Nuhlenony forever. I want to go, but there is no place for me in the starships. The Hleno call Them "the ancient ones" and say the ships will never return because the dry land will never come back. The Hleno say technology is danger-ous and must be stopped everywhere. . . .

So much time has passed. I miss Them, the ancient ones, with their three eyes and six limbs, walking upright as the Hleno are not able to do.

. . . The Hleno have learned to leave the planet without ships. They bring back specimens for my zoo and also intelligent ma-chines the Hleno fear and imprison. Is it true that intelligent

machines will destroy any civilization?

. . . More and more captive machines arrive for the prison. The soil in the zoo grows weak and I feel strange. I do not think clearly. I cannot communicate with the Hleno to get their help. I understand what they say, but they do not hear me when I touch them and try to talk mind to mind. . . .

There is a new creature in the zoo! It walks upright like Them *but has only two eyes, thin tendrils growing from the top of its head, and only four limbs—a weakling compared to* Them. *. . .*

It can talk through the mind! It is intelligent! It even has a name—Jeff. It wants to find a robot, but there must be no more robots, no more technology. It asks about my past, and I do not want to remember. I am sick—I am unhappy—I want to be left alone—I must destroy the new creatures, this Jeff and the two others, green . . . I am sick. . . .

Why is there no one to give me freedom and a home?

What is freedom? I have forgotten. Is it dangerous?

Should I kill these creatures or do they know about freedom?

"Jeff! Jeff, wake up! It's morning and the Dookaza vine is around your foot!"

Jeff opened his eyes to sunlight and put his finger to his lips. "Shh, your Dragonship. I'm in communication with the Dookaza. The vine is friendly now."

"Don't trust it!" The dragon snorted and belched some dark smoke. "I'm not in firebreathing shape yet, and it's our only weapon."

"Wait. I have to communicate some more."

"Do you mean talk? Why are you using a big word?"

"Because it hasn't exactly been talking. I mean, we haven't really exchanged words, even telepathically. I was inside the Dookaza's mind, feeling its emotions, and thinking its thoughts through a series of memories that go back so far my mind boggles at it. Please let me close my eyes and concentrate once more, and please go get Oola—I can hear her meowing. She may be up a tree after some more fruit and unable to get down. You still have her collar."

"I am taking good care of it, and I will return it in time," said the Grand Dragon stiffly. "And I will go where I am wanted. Dear Oola, at least, appreciates me."

Jeff smiled at her scaly back as she walked away. He knew that the Grand Dragon knew he liked her a great deal, but her dignity wouldn't let her admit it.

He settled back against the tree, holding the vine's tendril in one hand and placing his other over Norby's bubble. He closed his eyes.

————Dookaza (said Jeff in his mind, not talking out loud), I have lived your life with you. Have you experienced my memories?

————I have, young Terran. You come from an interesting planet with interesting creatures, but do not tell them about Melodia because I would prefer not to have visitors. (The Dookaza stopped for a moment and then continued.) Only you, Jeff. And I suppose you'll have to come with your robot if he ever gets out of that bubble.

————That's the only way I can travel through hyperspace. It is Norby who makes it possible.

————I will enjoy seeing you once in a while. Not often.

————I understand, Dookaza, you like being alone and, as long as you are on Melodia, I will like leaving you alone.

The Dookaza vibrated and it seemed to Jeff it was laughing.

————You are sadly lacking enough eyes and limbs, but you have goodness. I am glad now I did not kill you. In this beautiful place you and your robot found for me, I feel better than I have for many long years, as if a sick excess of myself has been burned away. I have freedom and good soil here. I will not bother the natives I can hear in the distance, and they will not bother me. I am grateful to you, young Terran, because you trust me even though I tried to kill you. It has taught me the importance of trust and love, and the evil of hate. Perhaps some day my old masters, *They* of Nuhlenony, will visit this planet. And perhaps the young Terran will visit, and we will tell each other what we have learned since our parting.

"Thank you, Dookaza," said Jeff aloud. "I will remember. My life is short, and as long as you have a safe planet, you are immortal. Yet I think I will live in your memory long after my body returns to the basic structure of the universe. Cling to your faith in the value of love over hate."

————I will remember you. But get the Hleno ready for traveling, because I now feel strong enough to try to compress your robot's bubble, so that you can communicate with him.

Even as the Dookaza thought this, Uhfy sailed overhead and sank close beside Jeff, one tentacle reaching out to touch his arm.

————Greetings, Jeff (said Uhfy). The Grand Dragon woke

me. She fears the Dookaza might harm you and she says you are too stubborn to accept protection. Is everything all right?

"Yes, Uhfy. I'm going to take you someplace where my friends might be able to get Norby free."

———Do you understand, Norby? (Jeff added in Terran Basic).

The Dookaza, with many turns of the tendrils that still existed, had compressed the plastic, and Norby's sensor antenna was now touching it.

———I understand (said Norby, also in Terran basic). I gather you have made friends with this peculiar vine that's making it possible for us to talk, and now you want me to take the Hleno to Earth.

———Let's go to our apartment. Uhfy—that's his name— will fit into it.

———No, he won't. He'll knock things over. How about the roof? Anyone passing in an air taxi will just think we've got a gray balloon up there.

———Hurry (said the Dookaza in its Nuhlenonian version of Jamyn). I cannot maintain this pressure for long.

"Your Dragonship," shouted Jeff in Jamyn. "Bring Oola and hang on to Uhfy's tentacles. We're leaving."

Uhfy grasped the Grand Dragon, who was holding Oola (who didn't want to leave because she was in the middle of eating another fruit). He also wrapped a tentacle around Jeff, who held Norby; the bubble bent by the strength of the Dookaza.

———Dookaza (said Jeff), one more thing. The ancient ones who developed civilization on your planet, Nuhlenony, must have had a name for themselves. What was it?

———I cannot pronounce it. Neither can the Hleno.

———Think the name and perhaps I will sense it.

The Dookaza thought, recapturing the name as *They* spoke it.

I'll never be able to pronounce it either, thought Jeff.

The Grand Dragon, also receiving, said, "I've heard it before."

———So have I (said Norby) but it's time we left. Open your mind, Uhfy, because I've got to direct your hyperdrive to the right place.

———If we go to my home (said Uhfy) my father and the others might not agree to let you go free.

———That's why we're not going there (said Norby). Come on, Jeff, concentrate on those coordinates! I need your help! Let's go!

————Good-bye, Dookaza (said Jeff).

————Good-bye, young Terran (said the Dookaza).

The vine slipped out of his hand and off the bubble and withdrew to the surface mud just as Melodia disappeared.

Jeff found himself in hyperspace.

10

In Manhattan

Jeff had the natural impulse to scold Norby for the mixed-up way in which he had brought them home but, of course, he couldn't. As soon as the Dookaza had let go, Norby's sensor wire no longer touched the bubble so communication was lost. Besides, Norby *had* brought them back to Earth. He had even brought them back to Manhattan.

The trouble was that he had brought them back to the middle of Fifth Avenue and the skycars were gathering to see what was causing a commotion on an important thoroughfare of the sovereign state of Manhattan, North American sector of the Terran Federation.

"But, oficer," said Jeff as softly and politely as he could, "I didn't mean to make trouble—"

"Listen, kid," barked the policeman, "you and your friend here in the dragon suit had better use an air taxi when you go to a party. Do you have a license for this balloon with which you knocked over a citizen."

"But, officer, the lady attacked the balloon with her umbrella and let out some of his air. It was only self-defense—I mean she just bounced off the balloon and sat down. If you'll just call Police-Lieutenant Albany Jones, I can explain everything to her."

"Lieutenant Jones? Are you a friend of hers?"

"I'm Jefferson Wells. My brother is Fargo Wells."

"*That* troublemaker?"

"Please call Lieutenant Jones. I really need help with my—uh—computerized balloon. I've got to take it to the roof of my apartment, and I don't know if it can rise now."

———Jeff (said the Grand Dragon, holding Jeff's arm and trying to control a squirming Oola), I can't understand a word you are saying. Don't your Earthpeople understand simple Jamyn?

————No, they don't (said Jeff), and Uhfy, please try rising. I'm sorry one of our citizens let out some of your air.

————I am not really hurt (said Uhfy). Is this creature in blue dangerous? Shall I fall on him and knock the breath out of him?

————No!

"Listen, Wells," said the policeman, "don't give me that empty stare. Are you listening to voices or what? You're a little young to be drunk, aren't you?"

Jeff swallowed. "I'm not drunk, officer. Please call Lieutenant Jones."

Jeff explained to an indignant Grand Dragon, mind to mind, that she was to pretend to be a human being dressed up in masquerade, and to a totally puzzled Uhfy that he was to sway like a balloon.

The crowd around them was as solemnly curious as a crowd could be, and it was growing larger.

"Mister," said a boy to the Grand Dragon, "why did you paint your cat green, and where did you get that dragon suit? It looks nifty."

Jeff said, "My friend can't talk while he's in the suit, and the cat is green because it's part of the story—"

"Ah," said the policeman, returning. "I get it. This is a holoTV show, isn't it? You're all going to be in some movie. Do you have a permit to shoot here in Manhattan?"

"Well—" said Jeff, hesitating.

The boy shouted, "It's a movie, everybody. Look, Mom—actors. They've even got a plastic bubble with a big cookie barrel in it. Are those cookies for giving out? Can I have one?"

The boy crowded up to Norby's bubble, and Jeff snatched it away.

"Don't fool around with the movie props, kid," said Jeff.

Another skycar zoomed over the trees of Central Park from the park precinct station house. Albany ran out of the car as soon as it stopped.

"Hi, Jeff? What's the matter?" she called out.

"See," said a young man in the crowd. "It's like I tell you. The movies have no sense of realism. Real cops aren't that beautiful."

"Lieutenant Jones," said the first policeman, trying to keep order. "These actors are using this balloon, and I don't think it's safe—"

"Of course it is, Officer. If Jeff says it is, it is. I'll show you. Jeff, can the—uh—balloon rise with me? Where do you want me to take it?"

"To the roof of our apartment house," Jeff said as casually as he could. "We actors will just walk up the stairs. Just grab one of these ropes." He held out one of Uhfy's tentacles to her. "And tell it to move according to your directions."

"Certainly," said Albany, who was never afraid of anything. She let Uhfy's tentacle wind about her waist, and then her eyes widened so that Jeff knew she was receiving a telepathic message from him.

There were numerous policemen present now, busily dispersing the crowd.

Albany said, "Well done, officers. I will take over. I know something about this enterprise."

She and Uhfy rose gently into the air and soared toward the apartment house where Jeff and Fargo lived.

Norby's barrel, especially inside the thick plastic bubble, was heavy when the robot's antigrav wasn't lightening the load. Jeff shifted it from one arm to the other, sighed, and started walking toward the apartment, followed by the Grand Dragon, who cradled Oola and reached out to touch Jeff.

"All those two-legged monsters—no offense, Jeff—were so surprised to see me. Don't they know about Jamyn dragons?"

"Not very much," said Jeff. "Perhaps they were awed by your dignity and regal bearing."

"Ah!" said the Grand Dragon, lifting her head higher.

It was not until they were back in the apartment that Jeff could let himself relax. The two days they had spent away from home seemed like two years, and he wanted to take a shower.

Once out of the shower and in fresh clothes, Jeff felt almost normal as he took the elevator to the roof where the *Hopeful* was docked and where, he hoped, Uhfy and Albany Jones were safely ensconced.

They were, and Fargo was on the ship, too, staring at Norby's plastic bubble. With the Grand Dragon, Oola, Uhfy, and Albany all present, Jeff had a little trouble getting in.

Fargo looked up at Jeff and said, "Well, little brother, you've really managed to mess up this time. What do we do with this thing? Acid won't touch it, hammering just makes noise; the drill slips off without leaving a mark. Nothing seems to work."

Uhfy squeezed himself into a corner and let out a good deal of air in order to take up less room. The Grand Dragon, on the other hand, sat proudly on her haunches taking up all the room she could. Oola, who was at home everywhere, chased her tail in happy circles. Albany, who sat at the control board, said sweetly, "How about something simple? Have you tried a can opener?"

Fargo glared at her. "We'll have to throw a chain around it, stick a rod through the links, and twist, Jeff, get to the nearest hardware store and buy a length of chain and an iron rod if they have one. Heavy-duty. I'll pay you back later."

When Jeff got back, Fargo grunted his thanks and threw the chain around the bubble. He twisted the rod while Jeff and the Grand Dragon held the chain steady at either end.

Fargo grunted, "I hope this thing doesn't crack suddenly and kill us all."

Jeff said, "You're just doing what the Dookaza vine did, and it didn't crack then."

Nor did it now. It compressed in the middle till Norby's sensor touched the plastic and, at once, Norby's indignant thoughts filled the minds of those who touched the bubble.

————How inept can you be! I thought once you got me back to Earth you could figure out some way of getting me out of this thing. What about that air-filled child there? This is a product of his people. Can't he open it?

————No (said Jeff), he doesn't know how. He's only a child. We have to do it ourselves.

————Have you tried a laser knife?

"Have you still got your laser knife, Fargo?"

Fargo hesitated. He had bought one during his sculptor-phase when he was working in steel. "That's a dangerous tool, Jeff."

"But we've got a desperate problem."

Fargo took the instrument out of its locked container, after taking some time to find the key. "At least it's charged up."

He worked away at one end of the bubble, since he didn't want to bore through the plastic and melt away part of Norby before he could stop. He didn't have to fear. The laser had *some* effect on the plastic, at least it left an opaque spot, but it didn't cut through.

"It's not powerful enough," Fargo said. He was sweating a little, and he hated to sweat. He thought everything should be simple and easy, even when it was exciting and adventurous.

"What about the water knife?" asked Jeff, rubbing the opaque spot on the bubble absently.

"How can that work when the laser doesn't?" said Fargo sarcastically.

"It just seems to me that the plastic bubble was made on a water world, and the Invaders must make use of water-based technology more than we do." He seemed to wither under Fargo's scornful glance. "Well, it was just a suggestion."

————Try it, you nincompoop (yelled Norby).

The water knife, which Fargo had also bought during his sculptor-phase when he was working in rock-salt, used a very narrow stream of water under enormous pressure. It was in its way as dangerous as the laser knife.

As Fargo hooked it up, Jeff said, "By the way, how long have Norby and I been gone?"

"Two days our time," said Albany.

"Two days our time, too," said Jeff, relieved.

"We were getting quite worried," said Albany, "and Fargo tried to get Admiral Yobo to let him have the experimental hyperdrive ship to go after you."

"The ship's not finished," said Fargo gloomily. "I suspect it never will be."

"Well, let's hope the water knife works," said Albany.

"No chance," said Fargo. "It won't."

But he was wrong. He directed the thin, nearly invisible stream of water toward one end of the bubble, and it promptly sliced it off—like uncapping the end of an egg with a knife. Indeed, once the plastic bubble was punctured, the whole structure was instantly interlaced with fine cracks. These widened so that the entire bubble came apart in shreds.

"It took you long enough," said Norby, his head popping up under his hat. He pointed at Uhfy, touching him so he'd understand, "And it's all your fault."

————I beg your pardon (said Uhfy).

"It's not his fault," said Jeff, outraged, "and don't start blaming everybody. Uhfy had nothing to do with the bubble. In fact, he rescued you. If it hadn't been for him, you'd still be in the robot prison."

"Well, it was his people. And nobody seemed to use any brains about getting me out."

Fargo said, "We did our best, and we *did* get you out. And it was Jeff's suggestion that did it. You had no ideas yourself, except to yell."

"What's happening?" demanded the Grand Dragon. "Talk Jamyn!"

Jeff explained in Jamyn, and the Grand Dragon said, "The question of who put Norby into the bubble or who took him out is totally unimportant. What *is* important is that he must take me home at once. The Jamyn will be lost without my strength and wisdom, and the Mentors must be released from paralysis."

"That's true," said Jeff, "but it won't do any good to release the Mentors, even if we knew how. The Invaders—I mean, the Hleno—might just return and do it all over again. They have this horror of technology—and, in a way, I can't blame them considering what it did to their planet—so they want to stop it everywhere. We've got to go back to Nuhlenony and figure out some way of getting them over their technology-phobia, before we can do anything else."

The point was clear and beyond argument. Nuhlenony it was.

Norby went to the control board and plugged in. Anyone looking at the roof of the Wells' apartment house might have noticed, at that moment, that a ship suddenly disappeared.

11

On Nuhlenony Again

The planet, Nuhlenony, seen from orbit, was beautiful. The blue-green ocean stretched from pole to pole, lighter in areas where the sunken land was closer to the surface.

"You've done well, Norby," said Fargo, taking over the controls. "We didn't know the coordinates of this world."

"I didn't either," said Norby, "but I got enough information out of this Invader child to be able to work them out. I'm very good at hyperspatial mathematics."

"Obviously," said Fargo, "but I trust that in addition to bringing us to the right place, you've also brought us to the right time."

"I *always*—" began Norby, and then seemed to think better of it. "Well, anyway, I brought you to the right time *this* time." He waved his two-way hand at the viewscreen. "Take us down, Fargo. I have a bone to pick with the Hleno."

———Oh, my (said Uhfy, who had been timidly touching Norby, since the robot had demanded all the astronomical information from him that he had learned at school). You seem very annoyed. Are you armed? Will you hurt my people?

———We mean no harm, Uhfy (said Jeff, who had been stroking him), unless we are forced to defend ourselves. And even then we'll try not to. We come in friendship to all intelligent beings and to all life.

Five minutes later, Jeff was a little less certain about how far this attitude of universal benevolence ought to go. A platoon of Hleno surrounded the *Hopeful* as soon as it had entered the lower atmosphere. Their tentacles grabbed any part of the ship that was grabbable. They hung on while Fargo tried to shake them off but, with numerous buoyant "balloons" attached to the *Hopeful*, maneuvering of any kind was sluggish and difficult.

"What do we do?" asked Fargo. "They don't respond to any attempts at communication. Do you suppose your Hleno friend can try?"

————Can you talk to your fellow-beings, Uhfy? (asked Jeff).

The young Hleno waggled his tentacles in despair.

————My method of speech does not work with your devices. Can you let me out of the air lock?

Unfortunately, before Jeff could respond, everyone in the control room, including Uhfy, was moaning with pain. The Hleno outside the hull were causing vibrations that made Jeff feel as if his brains were frying.

Fargo said, "We can't stand this," and sent the ship shooting upward. The Hleno were forced to drop off.

"Let's leave," said Norby, and the ship winked out of normal space.

"No, Norby," said Jeff, "we can't leave Nuhlenony. We've got to reason with them."

"They are not reasonable," said Norby. "They are dangerous, and I don't want to go back there."

"I thought you had a bone to pick with them," said Fargo slyly.

"And I'll pick it as soon as I come back with Admiral Yobo and a fleet of ships," said Norby.

"Are we leaving Nuhlenony?" asked the Grand Dragon, who couldn't understand the Terran Basic that was being spoken. "How do we get Uhfy to find out how to release the Mentors?"

"You are right, my dear Majesty," said Fargo in Jamyn. "We must go back, Norby. I'll try reasoning with them."

It was true, thought Jeff, that Fargo could outtalk almost anyone, but he had the feeling that the Hleno would not stop to listen even if he were telepathic, which they were not.

"I think we ought to go back," said Albany, "but stay in the upper reaches of the atmosphere where the Hleno can't reach us. Perhaps we'll find some way of communicating with them, or some way of going down just far enough to let Uhfy out to plead our case."

"And Uhfy will probably get spanked by his father," grumbled Norby, "and be sent to bed without supper because no one will listen to a kid. Still, I'll try it even though I'm still dizzy from the vibration. Here goes."

The grayness disappeared and was again replaced by a view of a beautiful planet.

It was not the same view.

"Norby, you're mixed-up," said Fargo. "That's not Nuhlen-ony."

"It is so. It's the same coordinates."

Jeff stared at the strangely-shaped islands dotting the shining blue-green ocean. "It's Nuhlenony, I think, but in the past, before the ice caps melted and the sea level rose above the land."

"It's not my fault," said Norby promptly. "I told you I was still dizzy, but no—you had to make me do it."

"How do you know we're in the past?" asked Fargo, ignoring Norby.

"I learned it from the Dookaza vine that I told you of. The dream I had was like living the Dookaza's life, so I know the history of Nuhlenony." He held Uhfy's tentacle as he repeated that history as briefly as he could.

————Some of this I know (said Uhfy) but I never heard that the Dookaza was bioengineered by the ancient ones. We were taught in school that only the civilized Hleno were bioengineered and that's why the planet belongs to us. I hope my father doesn't mind when he finds out about the Dookaza. He is a very proud Hleno.

Below them the planet gleamed in the sunlight, and no troops of Hleno rose this time to confront the *Hopeful*.

"Maybe the ancient ones are still there," said Albany. "Wouldn't it be wonderful if we could see them?"

Fargo said, "They might come to see *us*. They might be no more friendly than the Hleno are, and they might be even more dangerous."

Jeff stirred uneasily. He had not told anyone what the ancient ones looked like, and he wasn't sure he wanted to meet them.

"However," Albany said firmly, "let's go down and see."

And Fargo, who would do anything that seemed risky, said, "Sure thing," and down they went.

"I wish the Dookaza were with us," said the Grand Dragon. "I detest intelligent vegetables and that one was most unpleasant, but it could tell us whether or not the islands are the same as they were when the ancient ones lived on Nuhlenony."

Jeff studied the viewscreen. "Fargo, take us on a different orbit, over the poles."

"Good idea," said Fargo, who saw the point.

After a while, Jeff said, "See the polar ice caps frozen thickly onto dozens of islands? We *are* back in Nuhlenony's distant past, before the ice caps melted at all. The ancient ones must be down on the islands in the warmer parts."

————Please (said Uhfy suddenly) let us land on an island right now, and make it near the shore. I must have water. I've had no water since we left Melodia—well, I had the mud there and it was wet—and my skin is beginning to feel funny. We're water-creatures, you know, and can't stay away from water too long.

"Uhfy's right," said Albany in concern. "His skin is blotchy."

Jeff sighed. They would have to go down since they couldn't risk Uhfy's health. He decided to make the best of it.

"It would be exciting to take a look at the civilization of the ancient ones. According to the Dookaza, it was wonderfully advanced, with magnificent cities—"

"No cities," said Norby, as they dropped lower toward the surface of the planet. "There are no lights on the dark side. No electricity. As far as I'm concerned, no civilization."

"I want to go home," said the Grand Dragon. "I'm not interested in strange civilizations, even if they're *not* there. We've got to find the method of freeing the Mentors so that I can return to Jamya with it."

Uhfy began to whimper.

————I want to go home, too. I want my father. And I want water to swim in.

"You'll have water," said Jeff, "just as soon as we land."

They landed on the edge of a small island, and Jeff and Fargo helped maneuver Uhfy out of the air lock and onto the shore.

Uhfy rolled on the wet sand back and forth, then made a complete sideways somersault, and circled into the water. Farther and farther out he went, then rose to the surface, his tentacles waving.

"I can't hear what's he's saying, but I guess he's okay," said Jeff.

Fargo frowned. "He speaks ultrasonically, doesn't he?"

"Just barely," said Jeff. "Sometimes you can hear him squeak when he is speaking as low as he can."

"You know, I think there's a way to fix up the computer to shift the pitch of sound waves. If it can receive ours and send it out at the Hleno range, and receive theirs and send it out at our range, we'll be able to talk Jamyn to Uhfy. More important, we can speak to the adult Hleno and maybe get somewhere with them."

"That would be great," said Jeff. "How long would it take you to do that, Fargo?"

"Half an hour, perhaps, if my idea is correct. Otherwise, I

might not be able to do it at all." He sat down excitedly at the computer.

Albany whispered, "If Fargo's going to get all computerized, I'd better consult with Norby about getting back to our own time. He's a little cranky after being imprisoned for two days, and I suspect he doesn't enjoy your spending all your concern on Uhfy."

"But I've *got* to be friendly with Uhfy. He might be the key to the Hleno."

"Yes, but you know Norby," Albany's whisper was even lower. "If I don't smooth him down, he might *never* manage to hit the right time." She disappeared down the corridor.

Jeff waited at the air lock, feeling miserable and swinging his feet as he sat at the rim, watching Uhfy cavort in the water.

"What's the matter, Jeff?" asked the Grand Dragon, coming out of the air lock and blinking in the sunlight. Oola was at her feet, stretching and yawning.

"Well, if you want me to give it by the numbers, your Dragonship, then: one, I hate being lost in time because I'm always afraid we'll be stuck there; two, I wish I were home; and three, I'm hungry. This is my third day without a decent meal."

"There's nothing to be done at the moment about getting you to your right time and place, Jeff," said the Grand Dragon, "but at least you can eat. I will make a snack with my own claws."

"That will make it taste all the better, ma'am," said Jeff politely. "Could you make something for Uhfy, too? Something like those green or brown cubes the Hleno eat?"

"Ugh," said the dragon. She went off quickly and returned quite soon with a peanut butter and jelly sandwich on protein bread for Jeff and a large hunk of protein bread for Uhfy.

"Hey, Uhfy," she yelled in the highest note she could reach.

The young Hleno, who had just popped to the surface again, looked up, and she threw the bread. He caught it easily, ate it quickly and, waved at her.

"I guess he likes it," she said.

Jeff chewed away hungrily at his sandwich. It wasn't the most sophisticated food in the world, but it tasted like heaven to him. He was astonished to find that putting just a little of it in his stomach eased his longing for home perceptibly.

Oola, with a thoughtful meow, was watching Uhfy cavorting in the water. Bunching her feet, she jumped into the air, was carried over the water by her collar, and dropped into the ocean. She came up dog—or rather cat-paddling.

"I didn't know Oola could swim," said the Grand Dragon.

"She can do more than that," said Jeff proudly. "She turned into a fish when we first got to this planet and saved my life that way."

It was warm in the sunlight and, with his stomach crammed with bread, peanut butter, and jelly, Jeff felt himself beginning to drop off. Maybe they were so far back in time that the ancient ones had not yet had a chance to develop a civilization. He slept with his head on the Grand Dragon's shoulder. She slept, too, and was snoring.

Jeff dreamed he was the Dookaza vine, watching the early efforts of those who became the ancient ones. *They* were primitive, but *They* built little huts and cooked their food and made boats for fishing. *They* had not yet trained the Hleno to do their fishing for them—

He thought he felt someone brush past him, but he resisted waking and kept seeing *them* in his mind, tall and slim and strange—

"Jeff! Help!"

He woke with a start and looked down at the water. Fargo's head was there, and around him underwater were Hleno but so near the surface that their shapes were visible. They were very small, much smaller even than Uhfy, and as sleek as sharks!

"They're circling me," Fargo called out, "and they're not friendly. They are primitive Hleno, and there's no intelligence here to speak of." He threshed and kicked at the small Hleno.

The Grand Dragon was awake. "I'll tell Norby to bring the ship closer so we can get him up. What's he doing in the water anyway? And where's Uhfy? And Oola?" Then, with astonishment, she called out, "—Look, Jeff!"

In the distance, but coming rapidly closer, was a fleet of boats shaped something like long canoes, with tiny outrigger floats lashed to boards that crossed the center of each boat. Tall, slender creatures that vaguely resembled human beings were paddling the canoes toward the *Hopeful*.

Albany came running with a stun-gun in her hand. "Fargo! If you can get a little distance away from them, I'll stun every last one of them."

"Wait," said Jeff, "they may not be dangerous. Let's not use any weapons unless we have to." He put his hands to his mouth, "Fargo! Oola's out there. Find her and come back using her collar."

"I can't find her anywhere and I'm getting tired of fighting off these creatures."

The canoes were still far away, and Jeff didn't know whether they were full of additional enemies or of possible friends. He stood up, ready to dive to his brother, when the *Hopeful* lurched and began to move. Jeff caught the side of the air lock as the ship drew so close to the surface that each small wave wet his shoes.

Fargo swam toward Jeff's outstretched hand, but the small Hleno were also reaching for him, and he suddenly yelled and went under.

"They've got him trapped under water," said Jeff. "Get Norby! The ship has to get to him. Meanwhile—"

"Don't jump," said Albany, getting a firm grip on his pants. "You'll be caught, too. I'll fire at them."

"But you might stun Fargo and then he would drown for sure."

Fargo's head broke the surface again, and he took a deep breath. "One of them has his tentacles around my legs, but I gave him a karate chop and he's not pulling me under at the moment. They haven't got the kind of mouths they can bite with, fortunately, but if they keep pulling me under the water—Well, isn't anyone going to help me? Where is Norby, the rescuer?"

"I'm trying!" called out Norby's voice through the ship's speaker system. "The Hleno keep moving you just as I am about to maneuver the ship over you. Can't you keep still?"

Fargo's head went under, and he came up again sputtering. "No, I can't. Now another one's got hold of me."

"Well, look at that," shouted the Grand Dragon.

Beside the lead canoe was a gray shape racing through the water. It pulled ahead of the canoe, plunged so deep that Jeff couldn't see it anymore, and then the water around Fargo began to froth.

"Hot dog!" yelled Fargo, swimming free just as Norby brought the *Hopeful* directly over him again. Jeff leaned down and pulled his brother back to the air lock. Except for a few marks on his legs, Fargo was intact.

Waves heaved up to splash everyone at the air lock, and the Uhfy rose from the water, shaking assorted primitive Hleno who dropped to speed away through the water.

"What were you doing in the ocean, Fargo?" demanded Jeff.

"I wasn't there to fool around," said Fargo. "I went to give Uhfy my new gadget."

Uhfy floated to the air lock and held on to the edge with a tentacle, while another touched Fargo.

————If I'd known you were planning to go swimming, Fargo, I'd have warned you about the primitives.

Jeff reached down to touch Uhfy and said, "Where's Oola?"

————I can't find her, Jeff. She was swimming with me in the water when the Hleno arrived and then she disappeared. I thought she went back to the ship.

"She didn't," said Jeff, feeling heartsick.

At that point, the canoes arrived, and the lead paddler raised his paddle in what must have been a greeting.

"Here, Uhfy," said Fargo. He unclipped a small metal box from his belt and pulled out two cords. He fastened the box to Uhfy's throat, tying it around with the cords. "Try this."

"Greetings, stranger," said the creature in the canoe. His reddish-purple skin was smooth, and it bulged with muscles. He had three eyes, a short neck that flowed down from a bulbous head, and two sets of arms that were not joined the way human arms are.

"I can hear them!" shouted Uhfy. His voice, through the speech box, was high and tinny, but it could be easily heard by human ears.

"Can you hear us?" asked Fargo, not touching Uhfy.

"Yes! Yes!"

"I can hear you, too," said the being in the canoe. "Your language is understandable, but your accent is vile. I do not understand why you do not return my greeting. Why are you involved with this large Hleno?"

"We do not mean to be impolite to you, sir. You catch us, however, in what is part of a long, complicated story," said the talkative Fargo, drawing a deep breath.

"Which we won't bore you with," said Jeff, kicking Fargo. "This Hleno is from another place, where the Hleno are civilized and can fly." It was impossible to say more than that. They were in the past, and Jeff knew that any knowledge they imparted now might result in changes in the future—their own present. Fargo would think of that in a moment, Jeff was sure.

"Excellent," said the native. "He seems to be a variety we can hear easily. The others we cannot."

"This one has a hearing aid," said Albany. "A hearing and speaking aid."

"Interesting," said the native. "You seem to be intelligent, so it is puzzling that you cannot speak the language any better than you do. It grates on the ear as you pronounce it. Nevertheless, if you would like to visit our village, we will make you welcome."

"No," said Norby's voice. "We don't want to."

"What we mean to say," said Jeff politely, "is that we would dearly wish to, but we have important work that must be done first. We regret this very much."

"Yes," said Fargo, switching to a whisper in Terran Basic. "We'd better return to our own time before we louse up all of history."

"We still can't go," said Jeff out of the corner of his mouth. "Oola is missing."

"Jeff," said Norby's voice, "I have been scanning the canoes with our sensors. I suggest you ask the chief or whoever that is to give you back your property. I think it's in the last canoe. I saw them pick up something from the water on the way over here."

"What property?" asked the chief suspiciously.

Uhfy let go of the *Hopeful* and sailed out over the last canoe, whose occupants cowered in fear. Uhfy descended, plucked something out of the canoe with his tentacles, and sped back to the ship.

"Is this what Norby means?" asked Uhfy, handing it to Jeff.

It was a short, broad, leathery green cylinder, rather like a hassock, except that it had prickly spines upon it.

Jeff said with delight. "That's Oola. That's the form she takes when she's in danger. She must have grown spines to make sure the primitive Hleno didn't eat her." He would have hugged her but for the spines.

"Odd," said the chief. "You refer to that object as 'she.' Is it a stage in the life-cycle of your people? That is possible, I suppose. Anything is possible, since there are no people like you on the world. We know that, for we have explored every island. Unless you come from under the ice."

Jeff said, "We come from—elsewhere."

The chief thought about that. Then he said, "I think perhaps I see what you mean. This is a world and we call it Nuhlenony, and it is ours. There is the large light in the sky that we call our sun, and at night there are many small lights. Why should not the small lights be suns, far away, with other worlds around them? We have reasoned this out, and I think you must come from another such world and, if so, that proves our reasoning is correct."

Jeff listened to the other's musical, elaborate version of Jamyn with admiration but he said in a low voice. "I think he's already learned a dangerous amount from us. We must leave."

"Good," said the Grand Dragon. "Let's go to our own time."

"Yes," said Fargo, "since Oola's back."

They all stepped back into the ship and helped Uhfy struggle aboard.

"Farewell," Jeff shouted to the chief, still standing proudly in his canoe. "What is your name?"

The name rolled out of the chief's mouth, many-syllabled, musical, unpronounceable by any human.

"Thank you," said Jeff. "I am Jeff."

"Will you return to visit our village, strange Jeff?"

"Perhaps not. But I think some day you will visit other worlds. I wish you well."

The air lock closed and the ship took off.

"Thanks for saving Fargo's life, Uhfy," said Jeff.

"I was glad to do so, Jeff. You and the Grand Dragon recently saved mine. If you have forgotten, I have not."

Once again, Norby threw the *Hopeful* into hyperspace.

12

The Hleno

Nuhlenoy was, once again, an all-water planet. The *Hopeful* had to orbit it a number of times before Jeff, watching the viewscreen intently, could locate the lighter patch of ocean where the underwater building sent its black air vents up from the water.

Once more the Hleno rose from the water with their tentacles ready to meet the ship as it sank downward, but this time the *Hopeful* was ready—and so was Uhfy.

With the speaker apparatus around his neck and the *Hopeful's* communication system adjusted, Uhfy spoke to his kindred.

"Hello, father," said Uhfy in a rather diffident tone. "This is your son, Uhfy. I was rescued by these kind and civilized creatures who have gone through a great many perils and dangers to bring me safely home. Please don't attack the ship because the creatures here don't deserve it, and because the vibrations injure me, too."

His own speech was broadcast outside by the ship's communication system and was, at the same time, deepened in pitch inside for the rest of the *Hopeful's* occupants to hear.

"Uhfy! My son! Your mother and I thought you were dead when we found you gone and the Dookaza vine ripped from the soil of the zoo."

Uhfy's father's voice was picked up by the ship's adjusted sensors and given to the control room at two pitches of sound, one for Uhfy and one for the others. Uhfy's father spoke in rolling tones like high thunder.

"I will explain everything, father, if you let us join you in the recreation room. These creatures cannot breathe under water so we must meet them there, where everyone can be comfortable."

"We will accede to your request, my son, but request these

creatures to bring no mechanical devices with them. We cannot permit technology upon this planet."

"Tell your father," said Fargo grimly, "that we can't possibly swim to the air lock of your building without our scuba equipment."

"And I cannot go without Norby," said Jeff.

While Uhfy attempted to explain this to his father, Fargo said, "Listen, Albany dear, you stay aboard the *Hopeful*. You can navigate her reasonably well, and if we have to run—uh, swim for it, you can pick us up."

Albany frowned. "Am I being left behind because I'm a woman? You'll need me down there."

"Let's not argue, Lieutenant. I outrank you. This is an order."

"Who outranks whom? I'm higher up in the Manhattan police force than you are in Yobo's secret service."

"Please, Albany," interposed Jeff. "If you don't stay, Fargo will have to, because we have to get Norby into that building, and Norby won't come without me. And if Fargo stays behind, he'll sulk, and you know him—if he sulks, he will probably decide not to pick us up if we try to leave in a hurry."

Albany smiled. "Your argument is a good one, young Jeff. In view of Fargo's childish personality, we'd better let him have his way."

"Childish personality?" began Fargo indignantly, but Uhfy interrupted.

"I'm not getting very far with my father," said Uhfy. "He's a *very* proud Hleno."

Uhfy's father's voice sounded at this moment, "You may bring your equipment that will keep you alive, aliens, and you may bring your pet robot, but you will have to stand trial for your earlier invasion of the zoo."

"No trial," said Fargo, "or we stay here and keep your son."

Uhfy began to cry at this, great tears gushing out of his yellow eyes. "My father is so proud," he whimpered.

"Don't cry, Uhfy," said the Grand Dragon, rubbing him gently with the scales of one arm. "*I* will talk to your father. I can't stand people who are proud without reason. It isn't as though *he* is Grand Dragon of Jamya. You there, Hleno. Are you the chief? What's your name?"

"I am Sector Chief of this portion of Nuhlenony, alien, and my name is Buhlric. Release my son."

"Do not take the liberty of giving me orders, miserable Sector Chief of a minor planet. You are speaking to the Grand Dragon of

Jamya, the world you raided without warning and deprived of its Mentor robots in a barbaric manner. I will puncture your wind-bags and scorch your hides if you don't learn some manners. The ancient ones were far better mannered than you are."

Fargo had been making violent gestures at the Grand Dragon to speak more gently, but he might as well have waved at a thunderstorm.

Buhlric, however, in markedly softer tones said, "The ancient ones? Have you indeed seen them?"

Fargo took advantage of the change in attitude at once. He said, "We have indeed seen the ancient ones, and they have treated us well—as they should, since we are related."

There was a great stir among the Hleno at this. They withdrew some meters and clustered together, vibrating as though engaged in a great and solemn discussion.

Jeff whispered to Fargo, "How can you say that, Fargo? There's no relation at all among us."

"The Hleno don't know that. So far all they've seen is the Grand Dragon. No Hleno but the one who brought you here—and Uhfy, of course—ever saw you. Your kidnapper was probably only a common soldier who knew nothing about the ancient ones, and Uhfy's only a kid. Now we're dealing with at least one important official, maybe others."

"Yes, but—"

"Never mind the 'buts.' We stand upright and have a head and arms and eyes in the right place. We're short an eye each and two arms, but they won't notice that. They'll just see a resemblance to the ancient ones. I'm going to open the air lock and let them see us. Jeff, you get the scuba equipment for yourself and me and the Grand Dragon."

"There are only two sets," said Jeff. "The Grand Dragon will have to stay here."

"Not at all," said Norby. "I can protect Jeff in my personal field as we go through the water. The two sets can be for Fargo and her Dragonship. The only thing is—is it safe for me? Even if those horrible beings think you're some version of the ancient ones, they have this barbaric dislike for robots and they may put me in prison again."

"I don't think Uhfy would allow that," said Jeff uneasily.

"Buhlric himself won't allow that," said Fargo, with an air of perfect confidence. "Not after he gets a good look at us. They have looked up to the ancient ones as the beings who made them intelligent and gave them civilization. Even though they destroyed the planet with their technology in the end, the Hleno still venerate them. Look at how they reacted when they thought we only *saw* the ancient ones."

"Well," said Jeff, still uncertain, "let's show ourselves to the Hleno and see how they react. And Albany, please take care of Oola while we're gone. I don't know how long she'll stay in her hassock form."

Fargo had opened the air lock and stepped out to its rim. He hunched up his shoulders to make it look as if he had no neck, and he held his arms diagonally upward to emphasize their presence, even though he was two short. "Stand behind and to my right, Jeff," he said, and Jeff did so.

The Hleno reacted as Fargo had predicted. Their tentacles splayed out stiffly on all sides from their heads, and slowly, tail first, they sank downward till they almost touched the water.

"That's probably their gesture of abasement," said Fargo, grinning.

"I hope so," said Jeff.

There was no question about it once Buhlric spoke. His voice no longer sounded like high-pitched thunder. It was mild and slow. He said, "Aliens, we give you all respect and ask your pardon for any threats we may have made. You are representations of the ancient ones, and you will all be safe with us. We will take no exception to the machines you need for life or even —even the small robot you bring, if you will do us the great courtesy of holding it tightly at all times and taking it with you when you go."

"That we will guarantee," said Fargo and, adjusting the scuba apparatus, he dropped into the water.

Jeff helped the Grand Dragon with her scuba gear and said, "Your most graceful jump, your Dragonship."

She jumped, and Jeff, holding Norby tightly, jumped without any apparatus at all.

When they were all in the recreation room of the underground building, the Grand Dragon, Fargo, and Jeff (holding Norby tightly) were standing near the pool. Uhfy floated very near them, protectively, while his father Buhlric faced them all head on, with several other Hleno in respectful positions to his rear.

Uhfy had finished telling his story, and there was silence—as far as human ears could tell—while the Hleno talked among themselves. Then Uhfy handed his communicator to his father and helped him put it on.

Buhlric said, "We never realized the Dookaza was either intel-

ligent or dangerous. We are glad that it is gone and that my son
has been rescued from it. We will not forget that you are the
agents of that rescue. How is it, though, that my son has become
able to understand speech that is not said aloud—what you call
telepathic?"

"Telepathic only when touching another who is telepathic,"
said Jeff. "We human beings are telepathic only because we are
friends with the dragons. If you let the Grand Dragon take a small
bite of you, then you will become telepathic also."

Buhlric looked at the Grand Dragon and didn't move.

Uhfy took back the communicator and said, "It won't hurt,
father. The Grand Dragon is very friendly. She stroked me when I
was unhappy. Isn't that so, your Dragonship?"

"That is so," said the Grand Dragon solemnly. But, of course,
Buhlric, without the communicator, could not hear her.

Nevertheless, he held out a tentacle toward the Grand Dragon.

Delicately taking it in her claws, the Grand Dragon poked at it
with one front fang, just enough to penetrate slightly. Then she
tilted her head at the Hleno, turned away, and said, "It didn't
work, Fargo. I thought at him and he didn't respond."

For a moment, the brothers were silent, and then Jeff said,
"Don't dragon teeth have a tiny core in them with fluid that seeps
into the bloodstream of anyone bitten?"

"That's quite true," said the Grand Dragon.

"Well then, the diamond caps on your queenly fangs, ma'am,
may prevent the fluid from entering Buhlric."

"I think Jeff is right," said Fargo. "Try again with one of your
back teeth, Stately Monarch."

"I love the way you talk," said the Grand Dragon. Taking up
Buhlric's tentacle again, she punctured it again with her back
teeth.

Buhlric's response was noiseless, but the blast of thought entering the Grand Dragon made it plain that he was now telepathically gifted—and also outraged.

———Sorry (said the Grand Dragon), I didn't know my own
strength.

She turned to Fargo and Jeff. "I did it that time, but I think
he's just a little annoyed."

Jeff walked up to Buhlric and put his hand on the Hleno's
broad back.

———Can you hear me, Buhlric? I speak to you with my
mind alone.

————I hear you, human being! What a marvelous thing! We must all have it.

"He wants the Grand Dragon to bite the other Hleno present. I think we had better, Fargo."

"Hmm," Fargo hesitated. "I'm willing, but will he expect the Grand Dragon to come back every once in a while for further inoculations till the entire world is telepathized? And will he expect to have the Grand Dragon come back and bite any new babies that are born?"

"I think that's a problem we'll have to take up only when it arises. Perhaps the Hleno won't like telepathy after a while and want no more. Perhaps their children will inherit it automatically, as is true in the case of the Jamyn dragons. And, if not, they have hyperspatial travel, and they can bring their children in for biting. The dragons can do it in return for peace with the Nuhlenonians, who will be Invaders never again."

The Grand Dragon was tired by the time she finished, but the Hleno who had accompanied Buhlric experienced their new gift with excitement and delight.

"After this gift to us," said Buhlric, "we grant you freedom forever."

"Thank you, but I'm afraid we need more than that," said Fargo, with his most charming smile. "You have taken the work robots from Jamya and imprisoned them here. You have also paralyzed the Mentor robots who are still on Jamya, perhaps because they were too heavy to carry easily. We must have the work robots back and the Mentors restored to activity."

Buhlric gazed at Norby and shuddered. "Robots! Yes, the ancient ones thought they were essential, too. They thought all of technology was essential and allowed it to destroy their own civilization on Nuhlenony. After the ancient ones left, we Hleno made a vow never to use technology again except to keep this museum and food factory going. What is more, we have solemnly vowed to save other planets that we come across in our search for the ancient ones. We destroy their wicked and harmful technology for their own good."

"But that is wrong," said Jeff. "Technology cannot be totally abandoned. You are civilized because you do not hunt the ocean for food the way our primitive relatives do. You depend on the food factory, which is run by robots. That is technology, and it is that which gives you spare time for thought and culture, without which intelligent life is not worth living. It is not technology itself that is harmful, but the unwise use of it. You cannot correct this by wiping out technology and destroying civilization. Correction comes when you learn to use technology moderately and with wisdom."

"Father," said Uhfy. "This human creature is being logical. We need technology to stay civilized."

"But we are trying to keep faith with the ancient ones," said Buhlric angrily. "Someday they will return, and we must show them we have learned the lesson: that we have not ravaged the planet the way they did; that we have preserved it so that they may correct the past mistakes and live upon it again in better fashion."

"Think about what you have just said," said Fargo. "They can't restore the planet without using machines and, as *we* know, they have never actually abandoned technology."

"How would you know that? Uhfy tells me your visit to them was in the distant past. How do you know what happened to them after they left Nuhlenony?"

"In our own exploration of the universe we have come across their traces. They went to other planets, but never stayed. They sometimes didn't change anything, but merely took specimens of animal life. That is what they did on my planet, Earth. On Jamya, they bioengineered the dragons, just as they did you Hleno here on Nuhlenony. They also left Mentor robots to teach the dragons—the same Mentor robots you paralyzed. Do you call that keeping faith with the ancient ones—destroying what they have made?"

"How do you know it was the ancient ones who made the Mentor robots?"

"Because the Mentors *look* like the ancient ones," said Fargo gravely. "We saw the ancient ones, and we could not help but note the resemblance. You see, sir, the Mentors have not abandoned technology, but labor to use it wisely as the ancient ones taught them to do."

The Grand Dragon turned to Fargo. "I was struck by the resemblance, too, Fargo. When I saw the six limbs and three eyes, I thought of the Mentors at once. The ancient ones are the Others, aren't they?"

"I think that must be so."

"How curious," said Jeff. "We've gone searching for the Others several times and ended with nothing. This time, when we weren't searching for them at all, we came across them."

Buhlric frowned in deep thought and finally said, "Can you

tell whether the ancient ones, or the Others as you call them, are still alive today? Can you tell whether they still use technology?"

"We can't say," said Fargo. "Like you, however, we search for them, and we think we will find them someday. Meanwhile, give us back the robots you have taken from Jamya. Reactivate both them and the Mentors that are still on Jamya."

Buhlric hesitated. "I feel myself experiencing the impulse to do as you say and let you have your robots, but we do not know how to undo what we have done. When we vibrate our tentacles in a certain way to produce intense ultrasonic sound, we can damage or even destroy both organic and mechanical organisms. However, we do not know how to undo the effects once they go so far as to produce paralysis or deactivation."

Jeff said quickly, "That is why I have brought Norby. I ask that he be allowed to study the robots and make use of your computer. He is, in some ways, cleverer than we are, and he may be able to find ways of restoring the robots."

"Is that absolutely necessary?" asked Buhlric, pained. "Despite everything you say, it is hard for us to let a robot move about freely on this world."

Fargo said, "Wait, Albany is trying to reach us from the ship —Albany, I'm receiving you. What's wrong?"

Albany's voice sounded. "Fargo and Jeff, there's a kind of crisis here. Oola's hassock, or whatever you call it, was thinning, cracking, and beginning to be absorbed."

Jeff said, "Oh, that's all right. Usually it takes a certain melody to stimulate the opening of Oola's security form, but it can happen by itself."

"That's not the crisis," said Albany, "I was watching the process with interest, and then Oola emerged and, before I could do a thing to stop her, she leaped through the open air lock into the ocean. She's gone."

13

The Egg

The intercom was silent and Jeff said, his voice cracking, "Can you see where Oola is, Albany? Can you see her swimming?"

"No, I don't see a thing. Shall I jump in—"

"No!" shouted Fargo. "Stay in the ship. *Someone* has to."

"I'll go, Jeff," said Norby, making choking gestures with his hands. "I'll find that insufferable, unintelligent pet that you obviously think more of than you do of me."

"When you find her, be gentle," said Jeff. "I do *not* think more of her than I do of you."

"Hah," sulked Norby. "I'm going out into the ocean."

He didn't have to. There was a commotion at the far end of the recreation hall, and a couple of Hleno came in through the door that Oola and Jeff had once used. They conferred with Buhlric, who spoke through the communicator so that all could hear.

"An animal has come into the air lock, one that had gills upon entering and now does not."

Jeff sighed with relief. Obviously, Oola had merely wanted to join them. "It's my pet, Oola," he said. "Please bring her to me."

She was brought in, held carefully in a Hleno's tentacles. She looked quite lively and well, though she was wet, of course, and seemed considerably thinner. She was carrying something that would ordinarily be too large for her jaws, but she had enlarged those jaws somewhat to allow them to do the job.

"That animal!" said Norby with disdain. "Next time we'll leave her in Manhattan. She's incredibly disobedient."

Oola paid no attention to Norby nor, after she was released, did she do more than glance at Jeff. She went from one low-hovering Hleno to another, sniffing, until she found Uhfy, and then she dropped her burden at his tentacles.

It was a miniature hassock, green and leathery.

"How do you like that?" said Fargo. "She's produced an egg."

"But what is it?" asked Uhfy plaintively. "What am I supposed to do with it?"

"It's something out of which another All-Purpose-Pet will come. It's Oola's child, and I think she wants you to have it, Uhfy."

"Is the child inside this object?"

"Yes," said Fargo, clearing his throat. "I will now sing you the All-Purpose-Pet's hassock-opening song, in perfect pitch." He proceeded to sing the whole thing through without a mistake.

Yet nothing happened. Oola's egg stayed shut.

"Perhaps it's not ready yet," said Fargo, a little disconcerted. "Don't hens sit on eggs for days before they're ready to hatch?"

"Oola isn't a hen," said Jeff. "I don't know what's wrong." He added in Terran Basic, "Norby, think of something. The Hleno are getting restless."

"I don't trust them," said Norby. "They said we were free and that they were grateful to us for the telepathy, but I don't like the way they look at me. I think they hate me. I want to go home."

"It is impolite to speak in another language that we do not understand," said Buhlric, "and it is a poor return for our willingness to tolerate you. What are you plotting against us?"

"Absolutely nothing," said Jeff quickly. "We're only conferring on how to open Oola's egg."

"I don't see why it's important to do so," said Uhfy's mother haughtily. "I think my husband is too ready to treat you aliens as friends. We have no use for a green, air-breathing animal, except as an exhibit in the zoo, and I, for one, have no use for any of you and especially not the robot."

"But they're all my friends," said Uhfy and began to cry. His mother swatted him with a tentacle.

"I dislike these Hleno more and more," said Norby.

Jeff squatted down to pet Oola, whose fur was still wet. She seemed awfully pleased with herself, rolling onto her back to have the underside of her chin scratched. He kneaded the soft fur and whispered, "Oola, shall we take the egg with us to the *Hopeful* or leave it here?"

Jeff knew that an All-Purpose-Pet understands no language, not even Terran Basic, but Oola was made to be very responsive to the wishes of her owner. However, she gave no sign—but merely purred as if Jeff's anxiety was of no consequence.

Buhlric said, "You see, then, that there is a limit to what we can do for you creatures who resemble the ancient ones only slightly. We will not return to Jamya, or destroy the technology on any planet. We promise you that much. However, we cannot help you with the Jamya robots we have removed or deactivated. That is done and cannot be undone, so you might as well leave this planet now. We give you permission to do so."

Fargo said, "We can't very well leave till our robot, Norby, determines how to undo what you call done."

"If I explore this building," said Norby, "I'll find a computer. It doesn't make sense for a building like this not to have one."

"You'll do no exploring without me," said Jeff.

"He will do no exploring at all," said Buhlric, more angrily than before. "Leave at once."

"Father," cried Uhfy with a wary eye on his short-tempered mother, "don't do this. These are my friends. They helped me, even when they thought I was an enemy. They were very kind to me, and I promised them that we Hleno would restore their robots to them in working order."

Buhlric shook all his tentacles at Uhfy. "My son, you should not make promises to aliens you can't keep. It is because they were kind to you that we have set them at liberty and given them permission to return to their own planets. We can do no more."

Jeff shook his head and murmured to Oola, whom he was still stroking. "See what you've done, Oola. If you hadn't delayed us and complicated things by bringing that egg . . ."

"Meow?" said Oola, getting to her feet and lashing her tail. She picked up her egg in her jaws, walked to the Hleno swimming pool, stuck her head out over the water, opened her jaws, and dropped the egg into the pool.

"Hey!" shouted Jeff. "I didn't mean for you to *destroy* it."

And at that moment, a very wet Albany Jones burst into the recreation room with scuba equipment slung around her neck and brandishing two stun devices.

"What are you doing here?" asked Fargo. "Why aren't you in the ship?"

"I've put the ship on automatic pilot," Albany said, "I just couldn't stand not knowing what was going on."

"But how did you get in?" asked Jeff.

"I remembered your telling us how you did. I found the two dimples in the door and pressed them both at the same time. Are you in trouble? I don't think these dirigibles look friendly."

Buhlric burst out, "You continue to speak an incomprehensible language. That cannot be endured. Nor has this new creature been given permission to enter. Seize her."

Two of the nearest Hleno extended their tentacles toward her, but the gun Albany held in her hand fired. The Hleno were hurled backward and, after a pause, drifted upward, rubbing their heads with their tentacles.

Jeff shouted in Jamyn, "Don't do that anymore, Albany." Turning to Buhlric, he said, "That was a very mild stroke. We have dangerous weapons designed by our ancestors who used technology unwisely at times. We have tried to deal with you kindly and not threaten you with such weapons. You see that if we had done so, you would be in great danger, but we do not wish to put you in danger. Can't you treat us with similar generosity?"

At that moment, Oola stopped the proceedings by yowling in a high pitch so that reverberation filled the room.

"She's safely here," Albany said joyfully as she noticed the All-Purpose-Pet for the first time. "Well, that's a relief. But why is she screaming like that?"

Jeff pointed to the pool where the hassock was floating on the water and slowly splitting open. Something came out and Oola stopped yowling at once. She sat down to wash herself as if absolutely nothing had happened.

"What is polluting our pool?" demanded Uhfy's mother.

The head of the creature from the hassock could be seen clearly above the surface of the pool. It looked exactly like Oola in one of her thinner cat phases, only miniature.

"Ooff!" said the creature.

"Wowrr," said Oola, getting up, bending over the pool, and hauling up her offspring by the scruff of its neck.

Oola's baby had a full set of gills, powerful back flippers, and little front flippers. It sat on the hind ones and looked up at the Hleno, making tiny little yowls almost too high to hear.

"It must have lungs, too," said Fargo in an awestruck voice. "It's breathing air."

"Just like me," said Uhfy. "I can breathe in air or water. I've always wanted a pet like this."

"She's yours," said Jeff. "Oola must have wanted you to have her, because she brought her to you. Except that the other Hleno may be wanting her as well."

The Hleno crowded around, reaching out tentacles toward the little thing. Even Uhfy's mother seemed interested.

Uhfy charged in, squeezing between the various bodies, pushing tentacles aside and lifting the little creature in his own. "She is mine. She is a gift from the strangers. If you want to touch her, you'll have to be kind to the strangers."

Buhlric said, "My son is right. We cannot take without giving." He pointed to Jeff with a tentacle. "You and the robot may explore the building, but I do hope you will not take long."

The only way down from the recreation room was by way of a narrow stone staircase that wound downward into such darkness that Norby had to turn on the light in his hat. Their footsteps echoed, and the air smelled damp.

At the very bottom was a series of rooms, filled with machinery, some of which was still working.

"The stuff in this room is for air circulation," said Norby, "and there's no computer. We'll have to go on."

Norby led the way. Jeff was glad because he felt more than uncomfortable. He wished he'd asked Fargo—or better yet, Albany and her gun—to come along. He was ashamed of himself, but he didn't like the feeling that he was walking through the distant past of Nuhlenony, a past forgotten and now perhaps dying out completely.

They entered another room which seemed larger than the first. It did not have much equipment in it, and one wall looked as if pieces of stone and rubbish had been piled against it.

"Jeff! I feel something! There's a machine back there. We'll have to remove all this junk to get at it."

Jeff and Norby worked to take away what had been piled against the wall. Norby had it the easier because, with antigrav, he simply took hold of an object and sailed over to another corner with it. When they were finished, Norby shone his light on the bared wall.

"It looks like the front of a strange computer," said Jeff.

"Not so strange," said Norby. "It's like a much more primitive version of the computer on Jamya in the Mentor's castle. The Others—I mean the Nuhlenony ancient ones—must have made the one on Jamya much later than this one."

"Of course," said Jeff. "Nuhlenony was where they started, after all. Just think, Norby, this may have been the one computer they left running when they abandoned the planet to the Hleno. Is it dead now?"

"Not completely, but it seems to be partly turned off. I hope the data banks are intact." Norby moved slowly through the air, passing over the entire surface of the computer wall, studying the ridges, dents, and other aspects of the surface that were part of any Terran computer.

"Norby!" said Jeff. "I hear something. Listen!"

After a moment, Norby said, "It's just water dripping."

"But that might be bad for the computer."

"It's not here, Jeff. It must be in the far room. Go and look."

"How? I can't see anything in the dark."

"Just a minute. I think I can fix that." Norby played his hands over the surface of the computer, and suddenly the room lit up. It was appallingly dirty with fungus growing over everything.

The next room seemed to be lighted also, so Jeff clamped down on his nervousness and walked into it. It was a vast room of many levels, some below the one on which he was standing. There was water everywhere, almost up to Jeff's feet, and he could see it dripping slowly from side beams in the wall. He ran back to Norby.

"The building is leaking! And I bet the Hleno don't know how to repair it."

"Of course they don't. They can't repair anything," said Norby contemptuously. "They've destroyed or paralyzed all the robots who could have kept this place going."

"Like the many I saw in that prison behind the zoo," said Jeff. "I wonder if any of them still work?"

"Why not? I did, when you got me out of the bubble," said Norby. He began jiggling on his two-faced feet. "I've got it! I've found out how to turn on the computer fully! Keep quiet, Jeff, while I see if there's a data bank and anything useful in it."

While Jeff waited, the dripping water sounded loud and ominous. Unless the building were repaired, the sea would eventually possess it completely; the last building of the Others would be lost, and with it all the land plants and creatures preserved in the zoo.

Just when the wait began to seem interminable, Norby said, "I've finished, Jeff. Let's go." Norby took Jeff's hand, elevated, and pulled Jeff through the air, all the way up the winding stairs to where the rest of them were waiting.

Norby insisted on doing the talking. "That bag of wind has to learn how to be polite to me," he said. Just the same, when he spoke to Buhlric, he was careful to be tremendously polite himself.

Norby said, "It is clear, sir, that the building must be repaired or it will be destroyed. The walls have deteriorated to the point where there are numerous leaks, and eventually the machinery will be brought to a total halt. My suggestion is that several of you journey to Jamya and bring back a few reactivated Mentor robots. They will help you fix it. Meanwhile, you can reprogram the worker robots locked up in your prison. They will also help so that repairs can be made quickly, and all of the robots can be returned to Jamya with, I hope, your thanks and gratitude."

Buhlric's tentacles hung down despondently. "I see you are correct in saying intelligent species must keep their technology or become primitive once more. We no longer know how to reactivate the robots, so we can't carry out the repairs. And who knows what will become of us? The last building of the ancient ones is doomed."

"Not at all," said Norby. "I found the instructions for reactivation in the data banks of the computer in the base of the building. After all, the robots were manufactured by the ancient ones, you know. And so was part of me."

"Will the robots punish us?" asked Buhlric a bit timorously.

"Certainly not," said the Grand Dragon, "but I hope they will teach you a few things about tolerance and open-mindedness." She sniffed, breathed out a tiny flame just to emphasize her remarks, and stalked toward the air lock exit.

14

BACK HOME AT LAST

Some Mentor robots had already gone to Nuhlenony, stolidly suffering themselves to be carried in the tentacles of the visiting Hleno, who had apologized over and over to the Jamyn dragons. The lights were on in the Mentors' castle, and everyone was celebrating the liberation of Jamya.

"I wish Uhfy's mother had let him come to Jamya with us," said Jeff.

"I think that the All-Purpose-Pet baby will console him," said Norby. "You can be friends with me instead."

"I'm always friends with you, Norby," said Jeff. "There's no one else like you."

"I am very glad to be freed from paralysis," said Mentor First. "It was a most unpleasant experience. And as soon as all the robots come back, Jamya will return to normal."

Fargo stretched and said, "I feel as if I've been exerting myself excessively. I think I'll just relax and make up a few new songs in praise of the Grand Dragon. What's more, I do not plan to go swimming for a long, long time."

"*You* don't?" said Jeff indignantly. "I was dropped into the ocean on Nuhlenony twice and into the mud on Melodia twice. Which reminds me, Norby, what possessed you to take us to Melodia anyway? I should think you'd never want to see that dreadful place."

"It wasn't my fault," said Norby. "I was in the bubble, and I only had contact with you for a few seconds. And, in the hurry and excitement, the only coordinates I could remember were Melodia's. It's *your* fault for letting me be trapped."

"I wouldn't mind relaxing for awhile," said Albany, stroking Oola. "When we get back to Earth, though, let's go to the water carnival in Hawaii that you were talking about, Fargo."

"I've changed my mind," said Fargo, shuddering. "No water."

"Well, I've got to get back to the space academy!" said Jeff. "For the last few days everyone has been wanting to go home. First Zargl, then the Grand Dragon, then Uhfy, then Norby. Everyone is home now except us, and it's my turn. I want to go home."

"We'll all go home," Fargo reassured him. "Let's just have some rest and relaxation first."

Zargl flew into the Great Hall, landed in front of her great-aunt, and said in excitement, "Ma'am, there's a ship outside."

Everyone rushed out and gazed upward—and then downward, because the very small ship wobbled in the air and slowly fell partway down the hill in front of the castle. It dented its nose only slightly.

"What are those strange markings on its side?" asked the Grand Dragon.

"What do you know!" said Fargo in amazement.

"Is that what it says?"

"No," said Jeff. "It says 'Property of the Terran Federation.' I think my species has just reinvented the hyperdrive."

The air lock of the ship opened, and a familiar bald, black head appeared. He craned his neck to get a good view of everybody, said "Huh!" loudly, and the rest of him emerged, resplendent in his best uniform.

"None of you looks in any danger whatsoever," said Admiral Yobo. "I needn't have taken the trouble to come here to rescue you."

"No, sir," said Jeff, "but welcome back to Jamya anyway. We're having another banquet tomorrow and . . ."

The admiral groaned. "Nothing I'd like better. I love Jamyn food, but I can't stay. We can't stay. You, young Wells, are overdue at the academy, and you, Lieutenant, have used up your vacation time, and you, Farley Gordon Wells, have been given a new assignment. Come along, all of you. Get into your ship and we'll go home."

Fargo scowled. "You realize, Admiral, that you're spoiling a very good time. How were you going to rescue us in that ship anyway? It's obviously big enough only for you and no one else. Were you going to do it all by yourself?"

"This ship," said Yobo, "has plenty of room for two people——three, if they're skinny. As it is, I am alone, but I can run the ship myself, and I am all that is required for any rescue. And now, with my regrets to you, ma'am,"—he bowed to the Grand Dragon—"we must go *home!*"

It was not that easy, however. The admiral's little ship refused to budge. Not even Norby could do anything with it.

"It's not my fault," said Norby. "I don't even know how it works. The admiral knows, and he should fix it."

Yobo scratched his head. "It worked perfectly coming here."

"Well, we'll have to attach it to the *Hopeful,*" said Norby, "and I'll tow it home."

"What!" said Yobo in an indignant roar. "No ship I have ever commanded has had to be towed."

"There's always a first time, Admiral," said Albany cheerfully.

Jeff put his hand on Norby's hat and spoke telepathically.

————Norby, are you sure the Admiral's ship will come along when you take the *Hopeful* home?

————Absolutely, positively sure, Jeff. Almost.

Jeff shook his head and said gently, "Maybe we should leave your ship here, Admiral, and you can board the *Hopeful* with us."

"Impossible!" said Yobo. "I can't come back without the ship. Have you any idea what the *Hyperspace-1* has cost? I shouldn't have risked the ship just because you've all been missing for a month—"

"A *month?*" they all yelled.

"Certainly. You didn't think traveling with Norby was safe, timewise, did you?" Yobo shook his head. "Let's go."

They attached the *Hyperspace 1* to the *Hopeful* with a thick cable, and Yobo, surveying it, muttered, "It'd better work or you'll all have to come back and rescue me, and we can't keep on rescuing each other forever."

Slowly the *Hopeful* rose on its antigravity, and slowly the *Hyperspace-1* rose with it.

The Grand Dragon followed the ships up into the atmosphere, shouting, "Good-bye, and thanks for rescuing me."

"Thanks for all *your* help and your unfailing, heartening courage, your Dragonship," said Jeff through the communicator.

Norby said, "If everybody's through saying good-bye, we're leaving. I *hope* we're leaving. I've got wires running along the cable attachment from our computer to the admiral's computer, and I hope that that serves to reactivate his stupid hyperdrive. That will make it easier than towing, I hope. Now, we're going *home.*"

Jeff looked at the viewscreen to make sure the admiral was well. He insisted on sitting in the tiny control-room of the *Hyperspace-1*. "A Yobo," he had said, "never abandons ship."

Then suddenly, they were in hyperspace, judging from the familiar gray in the viewscreen.

————Norby (said Jeff), is the admiral with us?

————The computer says his stupid ship is here as well as ours, so I think he's all right.

————I hope so.

And then they came out of hyperspace, and it was possible to see something on the viewscreen besides gray. The admiral was there, large and formidable, and Jeff heaved a sigh of relief.

"There," said Norby grandly. "We're *home!*"

"Cadet," said Yobo ominously, "look at *my* viewscreen!"

Over the admiral's shoulder was his viewscreen and in it was a fish.

"Are we in the Pacific Ocean? Are we on Earth at all?" shouted Yobo.

"Norby," asked Albany with a frown, "where are we?"

Norby said, "We're right here on Earth. We're right here in Manhattan. We just happen to be on a rock in the boating lake in Central Park, and the *Hyperspace-1* is behind us, under water. And it's not my fault. The computer got a little mixed-up trying to handle both ships at once and it missed the top of our apartment house by a few blocks. I'll readjust the computer, but if you don't want to wait, just get out and walk home. It's only a little lake and it's raining, anyway. You'd have gotten wet even if I had landed on the roof."

"Wet," said Fargo. "Not soaking."

Yobo rose, removing the jacket of his uniform. "I, for one, will not wait. If I do, who knows where Norby will take us next? Now I'll have to get wet, and I *hate* getting wet."

"But, Admiral," said Jeff, "you don't have to get wet at all. Albany can call police headquarters and have them send out a tow-flitter. It would handle us just like a broken-down air taxi."

"No!" said Yobo. "My ship is not to be treated like a broken-down air taxi."

"I was just making an analogy. Your ship would be treated with the utmost respect, I'm sure."

"No, Jeff, the truth is that I would prefer not to call attention to the *Hyperspace-1*. I took it in a rather irregular fashion in my eagerness to rescue you."

"He means he stole it," whispered Fargo, opening the *Hope-*

ful's air lock, which was just above the water's surface.

Just then a rowboat charged toward them from under Bow Bridge. One man rowed, three others huddled in the stern with evil-looking devices, and a fifth sat in the prow, looking angry.

"Get that thing out of here!" shouted the man in the prow.

"What's he saying?" asked Yobo, tuning in through the *Hopeful*'s computer.

"It's English," said Fargo. "It's a kind of cousin to Terran Basic."

"I'll speak to him," said Albany, smoothing her golden hair. "I speak perfect English, being a native Manhattanite."

"I'm a native Manhattanite, too," said Jeff.

"Albany has more than linguistic power," said Fargo. "Let her."

"We've had a little accident," said Albany, beaming at the rowboat from the open air lock. "We'll leave as soon as possible."

"I don't want you to leave soon, I want you to leave *now*. I've got to get on with the shooting while the rain has stopped. Look, lady, I rented every boat in the boathouse so that no one else will use the lake, and my permit for shooting in the park expires tomorrow—"

"Shooting?" asked Jeff in a low voice.

Albany fingered the stun-gun she had at her waist. "See here, buddy, no one is allowed to shoot anything in Central Park."

"Oh, yeah? I've got a permit. I'm shooting a guy and a gal in a love scene with rain threatening, and you've got to get out or I'm going to sue."

Fargo said, "I get it. They're shooting for holoTV."

"We're not shooting for holy TV. We're shooting legitimate *film*, and the money involved is plenty holy. One last time—get out of here."

At that moment, it began to rain hard again, just as Jeff was staring at the Fifth Avenue skyline, looking toward his own apartment building.

The man in the prow cursed, shook his fist at the sky, and ordered himself rowed back to the boathouse at the other side of the lake.

"Reprieved for a moment," said Albany and called out, "Norby, are you finished? We're in a hurry to get home."

"Wait," shouted Jeff. "The apartment house *isn't there*. The whole skyline is wrong. We're not home at all. We're in the past. No wonder the lake is so dirty and the park is so littered."

"In that case," said Fargo, "I guess part of the litter is what used to be called a newspaper." He dashed across the rocks through the rain and picked up a soggy paper. He glanced at it and came back groaning. "We're in the twentieth century!"

"The *late* twentieth century," said Norby plaintively. "I found that out from the computer, and that's what's taking me so long. It's not my fault if I have to drag along two ships instead of one."

"I want to go home," said Albany, her usual cheerfulness dimmed. "I prefer a century that knows how to keep the air and water clean, and where people take care of their environment."

"I don't mind Jamya," said Fargo morosely, "but I certainly mind the twentieth century. I want to go home, too."

"Well, I'm *trying*," said Norby, "and you just make it worse by getting me upset. And besides that stupid Oola just jumped out of the air lock and is chasing seagulls. You shouldn't have left it open."

By the time Jeff came back with Oola, he was soaking wet, but Norby only said, "Jeff, I think you'll have to link minds with me. I can't do it myself."

"Go ahead, link minds," rumbled Yobo, "and if you fail this time, don't think I'm just going to smash you into scrap. I'll also take away your honorary cadethood."

"Yes, sir," said Norby. "I mean no, sir. I won't fail, I hope."

Jeff sat at the control board and touched Norby.

————You've been trying, Norby, I know that. And I know you do your best, even if you do get mixed-up now and then. Just the same let's try specially hard now, because I *really want to go home*.

They concentrated.

"All right, then, we're *here*," said Norby. "I got everything to where all I needed was another mind. We're in our own time *exactly*."

"Good," said Yobo from the viewscreen. "I'll just run down to your apartment and notify the lab that the *Hyperspace-1* worked fine on the trial run and that they can pick it up on your roof—"

"Well, Admiral, that's the only thing," said Norby. "We're still in the water in Central Park. *Cleaner* water."

"That does it," roared the admiral, "Norby, I'm going to—"

"Now, Admiral," coaxed Albany, "it could be worse. We could be in a twentieth century jail trying to explain what we're doing here, without giving away anything that would change history. Thanks to the rain, I'm sure our exit was unnoticed."

"There's one other little problem," said Jeff, looking into the *Hopeful*'s viewscreen.

"What?" demanded Yobo, glowering in the viewscreen when Jeff turned it back to the interior of the *Hyperspace-1*.

"The pond, having been dredged and cleaned many times since the twentieth century, is much deeper. *Both* ships are completely under water so we'll have to lift off—"

"We can't," said Norby. "I fixed part of the computer so we got here through time, but ordinary travel is out. It'll just take a day or two to fix. . . ."

"What! I'm due at an important meeting at Space Command!"

"I'll take you, Admiral," said Norby. "I'll whisk you through hyperspace. . . ."

"Never!"

"Admiral," said Jeff, "if we both swim to shore and go to my apartment, you can call for an air taxi to take you to the nearest transmitter. Albany and Fargo and Oola can stay in the ship while Norby repairs it."

"Good," said Fargo. "Albany and I need a little time together. We'll plan which waterless desert to visit on our next vacation."

Jeff swam out of the *Hopeful*'s air lock and met Yobo plowing through the water like an angry whale.

"I'm sorry you had to get wet, Admiral," said Jeff.

The admiral slapped him on the back so hard he thought he'd drown. "Cheer up, cadet. I should have known that adventures with Norby are like this."

"Wet?"

"No. In spite of everything, we always get back *home*."